GLYN

JENNIFER R. POVEY

AITUNE

1

SKYT

SHOUTS AND RATTLING pursued Skyt as they fled the building. They were only too glad to make their escape.

Outside, rare raindrops fell from the slightly yellow-hued sky, plinking slightly off their carapace but doing nothing to cool the air. If anything, the rain was warmer. It almost sizzled as it fell.

It was hot even for Vakra City. Hot enough that Skyt scurried as quickly as their limbs would carry them to the nearest juice bar. They ducked inside and got halfway to the counter when the world blew apart.

Shrapnel from the window jabbed against them as they ducked under a table. Their entire body rang like a bell from the force of the shockwave. They could smell a faint, acrid, stench, as if something metal had burned.

This was bad.

This was very bad.

They didn't know who was responsible, but they knew what this was. Something the citizens of Vakra had never worried about in the past. Something that nobody had worried about since the world had formed.

This had always been a peaceful city, where people from all over

Glyn came together to learn and to work. Even people who might have political and ethical differences set them aside when there was a good project involved. Vakra had *always* been peaceful. Even more than other cities on a world that had never used war to solve its problems.

Now it wasn't.

Skyt blamed the offworlders.

No, that wasn't fair.

It was the way people reacted to the offworlders. They stayed still, very still, until they were sure there would not be another explosion. Tucking feet and wings under their natural armor. It was all they could do.

Then they got up, counted their limbs, and scuttled back outside to see what they could do to help. The rain fell harder across a scene of carnage. Glen and pieces of glen had been flung across the courtyard. The burning smell was thankfully not glen flesh, but a burned out groundcar that might, or might not, have been the explosion's source.

Their body still ached, but they saw others far worse off. Worst of all, the body of a child, their exoskeleton still juvenile-soft, flung against the wall. Their care-parent was keening loud and high, although Skyt could only feel it from their distance, through their antennae rather than their ears.

The air oppressed, the rain falling through it, the heat enough for even glen to suffer.

It didn't matter anymore.

They were going to...but it was not their job to find out who did this and why. It was their job to study and learn.

And, for now, to help patch people up and wonder what was becoming of a world which had never been known for violent solutions to its problems.

It was hard not to blame the offworlders.

2

GRAEME

Graeme was not a scientist. He still knew that the solar system they were approaching was...wrong.

It made no sense even to somebody who had just slid through layers of space, tugged by a tame black hole in the ship's back pocket.

That didn't make a huge amount of sense either. He was not a stupid man, but he also had not put in the effort needed to deeply understand the physics.

He'd leave that for people who *enjoyed* that kind of thing. Who thrived on it like Charles thrived on engineering, although his husband was also a surprisingly good analyst when he put his mind to it.

He almost wished Charles could have come along, could have met these aliens that weren't quite insects and weren't quite *not* insects either. He even more wished that Charles could see this solar system, for perhaps the mind of an engineer would see something the mind of a diplomat and spy missed.

But bringing along his family right now, while it might seem like a gesture of trust to the glen, felt far too risky.

Once they had an established embassy...but right now, he wasn't bringing a six year old here, not his lovely daughter who came from their combined DNA and his sister's willing donation of her eggs and womb.

He could never repay *that* debt. So he didn't try. He just loved Marion, and his husband *and* his sister and her two boys.

But no, this system was wrong. Two stars and a single planet that spun idly in a Lagrange point, stuck there rather than orbiting. Stable, but not stable forever.

Nothing else but debris.

Nothing but the planet and a ship or two and the station that orbited the planet. This was the home world of the species which had somehow caused more disruption to the human psyche than even the predatory ky'iin (the tyrar were cuddly, and it was acceptable for aliens to be cuddly).

They were beautiful bugs, the glen. Angelic and terrible and alien enough that they had thought they might be silicon based for a moment.

They weren't, it was all forms of carbon not used by Earth life. Spun out diamond-like to form a carapace and limbs, but not as hard as diamond, no.

All forms of carbon and beauty and evolution, but looking through the observation dome at this planet he wondered if it was evolution at all.

Or if something else was going on here. Something that explained the strangeness of this system. The way it could not, in fact, work. It was as if somebody had designed it.

Something that might hold many answers, if he could only tease them out.

Graeme Marlowe, first human ambassador to Glyn folded his arms and stared at the yellow-green orb, trying to work out what it meant.

THE GLEN DID NOT BUILD for humans, especially not tall ones. Graeme found himself ducking several times...certainly more than the small woman escorting him, her light brown skin likely a strange visual contrast to the aliens, startlingly different from his own pale Scottish hues.

He couldn't, yet, tell individual glen apart. Or rather, he could see that there were differences in conformation and in the specific shine of their exoskeletons, but it would take a while for him to identify individuals. So far, he had seen no variation in color.

It was like being surrounded by an entire colony of subtly different tabby cats, where time would teach which one was which, but where the first impression was merely of piles of moving stripes.

There were three glen moving to meet him. They didn't wear clothing, but they did wear amulets and medallions, some of which appeared to be glued to their exoskeletons. The middle one spread their vestigial wings and then dropped into something akin to a dog's play bow.

Graeme bowed in return, recognizing the gesture from the etiquette videos he had watched and hoping the glen would understand this as the human equivalent.

"Ambassador. I am Vryn al Reket," the central glen greeted. "You are well come to our world. I hope that we have your quarters set up to meet your needs."

What he needed was a higher ceiling, but he didn't say that. This particular area *was* high enough that he could stand straight. Just about. He felt claustrophobic, but he was in no danger of hitting his head unless he jumped...or the gravity went out.

It was probably better on the planet, and he hoped to get a tour soon enough, although he would need environment gear.

The glen considered 130 degrees Fahrenheit "brisk."

Even on the space station, he was wearing cooling gear and sweating in what they considered a comfortable room temperature and "shirt sleeve" environment.

"Thank you."

"Please let us know if anything needs to be changed," the glen on the right of Vryn al Reket said. Their voices were bell-like behind the mechanical translators they were using. For now. He wanted to learn their language, even if he couldn't pronounce it. The glen spoke by rubbing their mandibles together, producing sounds no human could manage...and vice versa. "I *think* we got the climate control set up right," they added.

The machine had no wryness, but he was sure he heard it in the bell tones. "I will let you know if you didn't."

A glen on Earth would need to be wrapped in a blanket. Unfortunately for Graeme, it was harder to cool down than to heat up.

"Appreciated."

Vryn spoke up next. "We have arranged for refreshments for you. Some of us know personally that space travel can be tiring. Let us know when you are ready to accept meetings."

"I will."

Vryn turned to the other glen. "Please escort the ambassador and his aide to the embassy."

He glanced at the sailor, who was serving as his aide for now. She seemed relaxed enough, but given what he already knew about Toni Bruscha, that was not a surprise.

"Alright."

He followed the glen through the corridors. It was clear this was somebody permanently assigned to the station, familiar with all of its twists and turns.

"This is our embassy row. The modules here are custom built to the needs of the inhabitants. You can even adjust the gravity."

He thought of bringing Marion here.

Then he thought of an interstellar school. How would *that* work? Virtual learning had been shown not to be great for the development of children.

He did say it, then, "And the height of the ceiling?"

He was pretty sure the bell tones that came from the glen's mandibles at that point were laughter.

THE EMBASSY WAS...NOT perfect.

But it was such a good effort that Graeme was instantly suspicious. First of all, the ceilings were, indeed, high enough. Not only did he fit fine, but his 6'7 friend wouldn't have had any issues either.

The furniture was...simple and familiar. It looked like...

The glen informed him, "We made the furniture based off of a digital catalog we asked for. Any of it can be changed."

Brilliant, whoever had thought of that. He tried out one of the chairs. "It'll do."

He wouldn't ask for changes right away. The lighting was different, and while it didn't feel like Earth, it lacked the yellow tint of the rest of the station. The bedrooms were identical on either side.

After the glen left, he turned to his "aide." "What do you think, Toni?"

Antonia Bruscha nodded. "They are entirely *too* welcoming."

"Well, that's why we're here."

They were here to make peaceful relationships with the glen.

They were here to find out what the heck the glen *wanted*.

The ky'iin weren't hard to understand. Underneath everything, they were not so different from humans. They wanted trade, they wanted colonies, they had oppressed and been oppressed. They wanted to interact with other beings that had myoran and had finally learned that expanded beyond the ky'iin themselves.

The tyrar wanted colonies too, because the ky'iin had conquered them, oppressed them, and left their world in ruins. They wanted to establish a viable off world population in case it couldn't be fixed. They also, rumor had it, wanted cats, of all things.

The glen? They were sophisticated, they were technologically advanced, and nobody seemed to know what they wanted. Something, clearly, or they would not have intervened to help bring peace, would not have signed the treaty. Would not have allowed him to come here and would not be putting together a delegation to shiver on Earth.

He would get to know them and do it well enough that, with all luck, he could simply *ask*.

Failing that? He would find out some other way.

Toni Bruscha was military intelligence. Graeme Marlowe was MI6 detailed to EarthForce. They were both spies. Good spies, from his own ego and what he'd heard of Ms. Bruscha.

"So..."

"We have to assume they can hear and understand everything we're saying. We have to assume they know that." Toni grinned. "Which is why I don't mind saying it."

That was the issue with a space station.

Or perhaps it wasn't. The same techniques that worked on Earth might work...go somewhere crowded where surveillance mics couldn't necessarily pick everything up, for example.

Write stuff down and make sure the cameras couldn't see it.

But for right now? Did the glen have the same thin line between diplomat and spy humans did?

Toni had found a terminal and turned it on.

It was the news, although it... She was fiddling with it, adjusting the volume.

"An explosion." A crater in the ground. Bits of glen near it...severed limbs. Unlike humans, the glen could grow those back, but he could only think it had to hurt. And be hugely inconvenient for the time it took them to recover.

"A bomb," Toni said, her eyes narrowed. "Look at the blast pattern. Also, they don't *use* natural gas. I'm not sure this planet *has* natural gas." Apparently she too was suspicious of the origins of the world.

A bomb.

This just got quite a bit more interesting.

3

SKYT

BACK IN THE MUSEUM, Skyt was finally able to relax. They ordered a wrap from their favorite place, to be dropped off at the office, and curled up in there, legs and wings tucked inwards. Part of them did indeed want to crawl back into the egg, where it was safe.

Part of them wanted, for a moment, not to have hatched. That was just the mental shock setting in.

That child.

Children could be replaced, but that didn't mean they could be *replaced*. You could hatch more, but that child, that specific individual that was growing and developing was gone.

That was perhaps part of what was hitting Skyt so hard.

One attempt at being a care-parent had been enough. One attempt that had not gone well, and Skyt hadn't huddled in years.

In more years than had passed since they last spoke to their child.

In more years...but their child was alive. They could in theory call them, hear their voice, but they knew that voice would be raised in anger the moment Ktyl worked out who they were.

No.

Best to leave Ktyl alone. Best not to make things worse as it seemed nothing they could do, nothing, would make things better.

So, why try?

Why try at all? So, they didn't call Ktyl, no matter how much they wanted to. If Ktyl called them? They had no idea what they would do.

Eventually, they uncurled, in time for the arrival of their food. They munched on it while they started to pull up the research they wanted.

The news interrupted them. The human ambassador had arrived. Warm blooded, bipedal, mostly covered in thin hide. Omnivores.

Skyt very much wanted to meet the ambassador, to sit down with them and talk. As hard as it was not to blame the offworlders, they didn't, and they were fascinated. Or perhaps that fascination was what kept them from blaming them. They wanted even more to meet humans with the same interest they had, in that bizarre place where technology and biology and culture intersected. They wanted to share a meal and talk shop.

No doubt at some point that would be possible, but Skyt wanted it now. Thinking about the humans distracted them from...

...but the coming of the humans could also be part of why now, of why the bomb had gone off. Not everyone thought it was a good idea to commune with offworlders.

And some thought that just taking one of their planets would solve the glen's problems. As if! Kyx was potentially warm enough. Earth was a freaking ice planet *after* its inhabitants had warmed it up some. Tyranis was a mess. No, none of those worlds would serve the glen. They needed new, fresh worlds, worlds that were actually warm enough. Worlds that would not offer everything they wanted but on which they might be able to live.

None of those worlds would, and Skyt was very much on the side of those who wanted to just talk to the offworlders, lay everything out and ask for their help. Not everyone was.

SPENDING some time reading about the humans seemed reasonable. Making a petition to meet the ambassador also seemed reasonable.

Knowing how slowly the gears of bureaucracy ground, Skyt elected to do the latter first. They explained why it was important for them to talk to the humans, putting the category as "Science."

That would get it at least read. No doubt if it was granted they would be primed with appropriate questions, aimed at getting as much data out of the humans as possible. No doubt the humans would be doing the same thing in an intricate dance that mixed diplomacy with science with spycraft.

Skyt was not a spy. But the kind of things they wanted to know would be useful to the spies. What technology could they trade with the humans for? What were they better at than the glen?

What could the glen learn from their history? A lot, they suspected.

Of course, Skyt knew full well how an offworlder archaeologist would react to certain deep glen truths.

Certain things you didn't talk to offworlders about but no, it would come out sooner or later, it would all come out. Hence why Skyt believed they should just talk to them.

Just open it up and acknowledge what was going on. Acknowledge what they needed. A new homeworld.

Oh, this one would last them a while yet, but with nothing to maintain the orbit, eventually it would drift out of the Lagrange point, become unstable and then the math showed various possibilities.

Not one of them left Glen habitable.

Either they needed the technological understanding to fix the ancient machinery or, more feasibly, a new homeworld.

A *natural* planet where they could thrive, but then there was...there was the sub layers and everyone was afraid to leave and some, Skyt knew, would choose to die with their world. It wouldn't be an issue for them.

This wasn't going to happen tomorrow. They hoped. Sometimes, though, they thought they felt disturbances in the fields of the planet, flowing through them. Maybe humans could even help with that, somehow, or tyrar. Tyrar could sense magnetic fields some, more than most sentients.

Skyt looked at the pictures of the chilly human homeworld. They shivered. The humans were fighting to keep their world *in* an Ice Age instead of appreciating its departure, because that was their normal climate. Hard to believe something so fragile came from such a cold, desolate world.

Hard to believe they wanted to keep it that way. He wanted to talk to one even more than he had before.To understand them. To learn about them.

To appreciate this world, and to learn what it had done to their technology.

OUT INTO THE FADING LIGHT. It was more pleasant now. The rain had faded out, leaving cooler temperatures and a light breeze.

Glen liked it hot, but there was still a point at which you wanted to be inside sucking juice or blood, not outside in the heat.

Prime was setting, turning deep red from the atmosphere. Second was still high, but not giving off as much heat. A dimming evening in the balanced twilight of the world. A world which turned its face to one sun or the other on a stable pattern, predictable.

Skyt was heading home. Oh, Skyt could do most of their research at home and often did, but today had required some time in the museum and sometimes? Sometimes it was just nice to know other glen scurried through the building.

The area where the bomb had exploded was cordoned off. Peace-keepers, black bands around their forelimbs, were keeping away the curious while forensics worked on establishing what had blown up.

What kind of bomb. Who had planted it. Or had they blown themselves straight to the sub layer with it?

Skyt did not know. Sometimes it seemed like death was a better alternative than life and perhaps they had been old. Or perhaps it had been planted in a vehicle. The burned out care they had smelled. Or perhaps it had just been...

Skyt decided they didn't need to know. Didn't want to know. Wanted to know.

Curiosity drove them, but they still gave the scene (and the peace-keepers) a wide berth. Two juveniles, exoskeletons fully hardened and perhaps a molt or two into adulthood, were staring at the scene with fascination, chiming at each other rapidly.

Skyt gave them a wide berth too. At their age, they would have reacted the same way; the scene of death and destruction as fascinating as the lights of a *duber* drawing in its prey.

Not nearly as deadly, although for a *duber* to be deadly one had to be about three inches long or less.

Still, the image stuck with them now, the image of a giant *duber*. One that preyed on glen.

It was a monster under the bed, that image, it was an image that care-parents used to frighten the young. Behave, or the giant *duber* will get you.

Their own rey, their own care-parent had been more fond of trying to make them grateful they were allowed to hatch.

Maybe that was why Skyt had failed as a care-parent. Because Vryn hadn't been a good one either.

And Vryn was in the diplomatic service.

Vryn would see the...well. There was nothing that could be done about *that*. All they could do was hope for a fair hearing. Or wait and make sure...well. It was sent now. They could do nothing to change it.

4

GRAEME

GETTING all of the glen news summarized and translated would have been a lot harder if the glen didn't make heavy use of AIs.

Thankfully.

The AI was, in fact, the sentient variety. Graeme had developed more comfort with them since working with the department's AI, Moneypenny...named after the secretary from a certain series of ancient and hugely inaccurate spy movies. Graeme only *wished* he was as handsome as the protagonist.

"So..."

"I want everything you have on any group that might be responsible for the bombing," he told them. "That's accessible to me, of course. I'm assuming nobody has admitted to it."

The AI was a disembodied voice, a server-based entity with no body. That too he was used to.

"There has been no admission of responsibility. There are four groups which could have been responsible. I will send you the data. Are you hoping that an outside viewer might see something?"

Graeme nodded. "Yes. It has certainly worked more than once on Earth."

It might work here. More likely not, he was probably *too* far outside the culture and politics. But it was worth a try.

"Then we appreciate it."

He wasn't sure who the AI included in that we. AIs on Earth had a bit of their own society, although they had never tried to take over. Well, the non-sentient ones almost had, when people became overly reliant on them. Trusted them even as they invented facts and pushed out human judgment.

But that was not the same thing at all.

"There was a child killed. Humans value children." He wasn't entirely sure how the glen felt about children. They were r reproducers, laying hundreds of eggs and then only selecting a few to hatch.

Biologists were fascinated by that. It wasn't supposed to work that way.

Or perhaps the way they...

"The child was a tragedy," the AI said. "Although not a particular one."

A partial answer to that question. "Also, depending on who did this..."

"Two of the groups on the list might be tempted to target offworlders."

"I thought so." He rather thought he was safe-ish on the station, but he wanted to see the planet, even if he would have to wear special gear to handle the heat. If he did, he would have to make sure he had enough security.

"Not all glen believe that working with offworlders is the answer."

"Not all humans do either." He didn't ask the AI for their personal opinion; the fact that the AI had offered to help with the news search for him and had spent cycles on learning English told him that either they did or they were trying to get close to him for other reasons. Surprisingly, AIs tended to make poor spies, so he was inclined towards the former.

The door chimed.

"I think I have a visitor."

The door opened. It was Vryn, the glen who had greeted him on the first day. Their wings were a little more droopy now, perhaps because they were not trying to look impressive.

"Hello," Graeme said.

Vryn's translator responded with the same word, which might or might not have an equivalent in the glen's one language.

Now that was weird. Nobody else only had one language...they had dialects, but everything was mutually intelligible. They had developed translation only after contacting offworlders. And developed it they had, solving a problem that humans were still struggling with after some decades in a metter of months.

The glen were weird. He wished he understood why.

Vryn glanced at the screen. "Ah."

"I thought an outside perspective might be useful, and Verl-35 agreed."

"Are you worried for your personal safety?"

Graeme considered that. "No more than I was before. Assassinating ambassadors has a long and ignoble history on my planet."

"Not here."

Vryn set down the box they were carrying, and opened it. "I assure you these are safe for human digestion."

Clearly, the glen wanted something. Or they would never have brought what were clearly recognizable as cookies. Graeme took one, sniffed at it, then took a bite. It tasted more of lavender than anything else.

Glen were omnivores. He wasn't surprised they had baked goods. "Interesting. What kind of cookies are these?"

"Lia flower cookies. From the bakery on the station promenade."

Or the *baker* wanted something...perhaps just... "Aha, let me guess, somebody wanted the humans to know they exist."

Vryn made bell-like laughter. "Trade."

"If it wasn't a universal, we wouldn't be here." Ultimately, it was all about trade. In goods, in knowledge, sometimes in people.

"Indeed."

"So...other than taking bribes in cookies from the bakery, why are you here?"

"A lot of people are going to want to touch your wings."

A saying, perhaps close to... "And you wanted to get in before I have to make appointments two weeks out."

"Exactly." Vryn hesitated. "You did not bring much security with you."

"I will gladly accept assistance as long as they're properly vetted and don't think humans are potential..." He paused.

"Threats? Dinner?" More laughter. "We have those movies too."

"So do we, and we had to be psychologically screened." Some people thought the glen looked like Biblical angels and would probably do whatever they said. Others would see giant bugs and run screaming.

"Are you saying some of your alien monster movies feature..."

"On our world, things shaped like you are very small. Scaling them up makes for easy monsters. I'm sorry."

"Here too. Giant *dubar* are a classic"

Graeme decided to look that up later, but the glen continued.

"Don't be. Unless you personally wrote one of those movies, it's far from your fault."

If only everyone apportioned blame so fairly. "So..."

"So, the embassies have certain protection already built in. Your air is, in any case, being treated to make the gaseous composition closer to Earth's, which makes it easy to screen out contaminants. Your food will be scanned...including the cookies. If you go out and buy food..."

"Test it. I know the drill. What about physical attacks?"

He didn't think he had to worry about those. But one never knew. Fanatics could do some very foolish things.

THE BAKERY WAS on the station's main promenade, and Graeme was surrounded by glen.

This was why they got psychological screening. An arachnophobe could never have handled this. They moved more like insects than spiders, but they had a spider's eight eyes. Graeme wondered how their...well, they didn't *have* a brain, they had distributed nodes. Did they have multiple consciousness? It didn't seem so. At the size they were, at the size they had to be to be sapient, they were a chattering, chiming mass of moving bodies. There weren't even that many people here, but it felt like a crowd.

He had to duck through the entrance. Once inside, he noticed a young glen behind the counter. Their exoskeleton was hard, but they were clearly not quite fully grown. No doubt the teenaged child of the owner. All eight of their eyes focused on him in sudden surprise and they lifted a set of pincers to their mandibles.

Just like a human teenager might have reacted to an alien walking in and it helped him relax in a peculiar way.

So human. Just *people* despite their very different body type. "I came to say thank you for the cookies."

"Oh. Rey wasn't sure what humans would like." Even the baker had a translator.

How had a species with no distinct languages developed the best translation technology...it was another part of the mystery of the glen.

Maybe he should ask the AIs. They had probably designed the algorithms.

"Well, this human liked those cookies very much, but we're not all the same. Is your...rey...here?"

"Parent" in the glyn tongue was a series of chimes, and that one was the first of them. Mama, then. Or papa. Neither. Both.

"They're in the back." They turned and chimed through the door. An adult glen emerged moments later.

He looked between the two, trying to read the family resemblance. Glen parenthood was not like human parenthood, but shared genetics remained a part of it. Just not in the same way.

It would help him learn to tell them apart, though, if he could pinpoint a family license.

"Ambassador."

He kept his face fairly neutral, not sure how the glen would react to a tooth-baring smile. "The cookies were amazing."

The glen lifted their wings and chimed, then, "Well, perhaps..."

"I was hoping for more delicacies to sample, yes."

It also occurred to him that his first corruption of the glen, for such was inevitable, might well be the introduction of the simple donut. He saw nothing like them on display.

Corruption. Cross pollination. Every species and every culture would change with contact.

Which might be why somebody had planted a bomb.

5

SKYT

NOBODY HAD ADMITTED to the bombing. Perhaps that was deliberate. It said something about the people behind it. They didn't want to make a point just yet. They were...the cool of the night made things no more clear. The stars appeared, twinkling but uncertain. Skyt only knew one thing.

They wanted people scared. Skyt was scared. They had never before been involved in violence. Violence was an aberration, something which interfered with the proper development of society. It got in the way of hope.

Of hope for a way out of their situation as a species. Some thought they shouldn't seek one. After all, what happened to the sublayer when the planet spun off into the void? Without it, they were not glen.

Skyt agreed. Skyt just didn't think that was necessarily a bad thing. Or rather, that it wasn't worse than *dying*.

Not that Skyt didn't like being glen. Certainly, they wouldn't want to deal with the messy ky'iin hormones or the tyrar herd sickness.

But they were profoundly curious about what they would become when they weren't glen any more, how they might change and evolve. What they might turn into which might be worse or better but at the same time?

They had some understanding for those people, although not when they resorted to violence.

Not when that violence killed a child who was still potential, not actual. At that most vulnerable of ages. Before...

No. They could not feel sympathy for that. They could not agree with it. It was predatory behavior, and glyn did not hunt. Not any more. Not as, perhaps, their nature once had.

Yet as they looked up at the sky, at the stars...this part of Glyn was in true night now, both suns at least partially occluded...they saw a hope and a future and something glen might be part of and not part of all at the same time.

Was there an answer for saving their world?

If so, did the offworlders have it?

If they didn't, it was still worth asking. If they didn't ask, the only possible answer could be no.

Skyt scurried into Eelk Square. The big screen was showing a conversation, the captions running across the bottom saying it was about the bombing, but opinion, not news or fact. A number of individuals, clearly having consumed a little more than their fair share of intoxicating substances, were engaged in a play fight that was dangerously close to being real. Skyt gave them a wide berth, not wanting any holes in their carapace that would need to be patched.

Skyt never did understand getting so drunk that one lost control of one's faculties. But for some people it was how they coped with the world, with existence, with their own biology.

Skyt preferred to lose themselves in the past, the past so known and yet so mysterious.

Because there was, after all, a solution to their problems.

If they could only find it.

SKYT FINALLY FOUND the establishment they were heading for. Slipping inside, they made their way to a certain corner table and hopped up on the bench.

The person they were meeting was not yet there. That suited them just fine. They ordered something very mildly intoxicating and tried to relax.

They felt as if they were engaged in a conspiracy, even though they were doing nothing illegal, nothing they would consider immoral. The person they wanted to talk to was in some ways a heretic, not to religion, which the glen lacked, but to everything the glen were. They were a glen experimenting with themselves, trying to work out what the glen would become if they lost their world.

And Skyt needed to know that.

Because it was easier. It was the easy way out. Find some planet too hot for even the ky'iin to be comfortable on, some world nobody else wanted and just leave and move and become something else.

That was the word. Migrate.

But they would not be glen.

The person concerned finally came through the door. They were old, well into their final decline, their carapace dulled from the diamond shine of health. Their wings were ragged from some old injury.

This was a glen approaching the natural end of their life. The natural end nobody tried to extend...oh, of course they did to a point. Everyone wanted to be healthy and happy as long as possible.

But once senescence set in, that was it. You didn't fight against it.

Not like Tly al Veran was fighting against it.

Because that was part of the heresy. That fear of death that, likely, the humans understood far more. From their appearance, they had yet to succeed at that and would not succeed in time to save themselves. They made their way, limb by limb, over to Skyt's table. Slid onto the bench with the awkwardness of age.

"Tly al Veran."

"Skyt al Vlyn."

Names formally exchanged, although Skyt winced at the genonymic they seldom used, for reasons.

For reasons their own child shared. Perhaps parenting was learned and perhaps bad parenting was also learned. Perhaps it was just a pattern that went down through the generations, started in times the glen did not speak of.

"You wanted to talk about the Movement."

"I am curious." A pause. "I have no interest in voluntarily joining you."

Tly chimed. "But if the Migrators have their way we will all..."

"Precisely."

And the Migrators were almost certainly the only answer.

The screens above the bar flickered. Two showed a game of kil. The third was the news.

Skyt kept one of their eyes on it through the entire ensuing conversation.

IT WAS the sound of breaking glass that interrupted their deep discussion of philosophy.

Somebody had dropped a bottle. It shattered on the floor and Skyt pulled themselves out from under the table.

"Are you alright?"

"I was a bit closer than one would like to the bombing."

Skyt knew they should talk to a trauma counselor. Should. It was easy to say it, to think it. It was not as easy to do it.

Tly did not help them up...and Skyt did not ask them. The elder was frail enough that it would more likely have turned into Skyt helping them down, as it were.

They scrambled back onto the bench. Stayed there until they felt more steady. Definitely a trauma counselor. But at least it had only been a dropped bottle.

Hadn't it?

Skyt slowly realized that the bar had gone very quiet, too quiet. All eyes, or at least the vast majority of them, were on the screens. And it wasn't because somebody had just won a kil game.

It was the news. There had been another attack, another bombing. And this time responsibility was claimed. Some faction of the Remainers. Those who thought that they should stay on Glen and die with it.

They'd attacked the spaceport and blown up a shuttle. Nobody had been on it.

Skyt doubted they had cared whether or not anyone was on it. And there were spares. It had been more symbolic than destructive. More of an inconvenience than a disaster.

They hoped this didn't mean there was more than one group that had started resorting to planting bombs. One had been enough and more than enough.

"It's the influence of those violent offworlders," somebody said.

The timing...the human ambassador was here and the ky'iin and tyrar would soon follow. Not their influence, though. It could be a reaction.

"The offworlders are going to find us a new planet."

"Exactly why the Remainers have started blowing stuff up!"

This was going to turn into a fight. Skyt decided it was time and past time to be somewhere else.

Glyn avoided organized violence. But personal violence? That was acceptable as long as you kept it within certain boundaries.

As long as nobody died, nobody cared if a few holes were punched in a few carapaces, a few limbs gnawed on. In some quarters that was considered a vigorous debate.

But more people were, Skyt knew, going to die. It was inevitable.

6

GRAEME

Bombs.

Plural.

The second bomb had destroyed a ground-to-orbit shuttle but thankfully caused no casualties. That had been fortunate timing. Or deliberate. Graeme put the two together and did not like the picture he was seeing.

There was no motive that quite hung over both of them. True, he was dealing with aliens, and the glen did not think like humans. But those differences in thought were more at the biological level, differences that came from body plan, reproductive strategy, and the like.

There was a level at which people were people. At which sentient biological organisms converged in some kind of strange psychological evolution to experience some of the same issues and problems. Perhaps it was about complexity, perhaps it was that there really was a Prime Mover.

He didn't believe that. One bomb had been set to scare and kill people. The other was simple sabotage.

"It's the Remainers," Vryn explained.

"Remainers?"

"A political faction who think glen should not leave the planet. It is..." The glen paused. "It is a religious thing."

He had not been given the impression the glen particularly believed in any kind of god or gods. Maybe something more like Buddhism, or some other "godless" faith.

"Sabotaging a shuttle would definitely fit with that mindset." He thought about it for a moment.

"Thankfully, they don't seem to have the resources to try for anything bigger."

"Agreed." A pause. "How do they feel about offworlders? Do they think we should all go home?"

"Offworlders don't have..." Vryn paused. "...souls." Their wings shook. "Understand that I am not..."

"You are not saying the same thing that a ky'iin says when they accuse us of not having myoran." And many humans thought offworlders didn't have souls. Graeme wasn't sure anyone had a soul. He kept his mind open on the matter, because there *was* that convergence. That shared appreciation of beauty. That numinous sense. That quality all consciousness shared regardless of its biological or technological underpinnings.

At the same time, Graeme thought he was being lied to, but how could he tell? The glen body language was still alien to him. Their vestigial wings were a huge part of it; they talked with them the way humans talked with their hands, but he was sure there were meanings there that he was unable to tease out.

The word, for example, that Vryn had hesitated and stumbled on. That the translation algorithm had...

...no, it hadn't been Vryn stumbling. It had been the translator stumbling. Of course it had. "Tell me. What do you mean by souls?"

Vryn paused."So, the Remainers...and many others...perceive that an essential part of us, when we die, becomes part of the planet. As you were not part of this planet while alive, obviously..."

"Obviously I would not have a soul in that sense." That made sense.

"Most people believe this to some degree. The Remainers believe that it is too dangerous for glen to leave because if they die on another world..."

"...their soul might not be able to find its way home. So they're against space travel. Got it."

It seemed too illogical for the scientific glen, but religion typically was. By its nature, it did not make sense. There was no difference between this and an Orthodox Jew wanting to be buried in one piece, or Muslim corpse-washing customs or...well. All funeral customs were kind of silly from the outside, all were important.

"Right"

"Every species has those types who take some religious belief a little far."

But he still was sure and certain Vryn was lying to him. Maybe he should ask to talk to a Remainer. Even a priest, if they had them. A religious teacher, somebody who could explain it all to him in words of one syllable.

He was here to build relations. He was here to find out what was really going on, and glen religion couldn't be part of that. Or could it?

VRYN HAD KEPT Graeme a little isolated. So he turned to Toni. They talked not in the bubble of the human embassy, but outside a cafe on the promenade, where surveillance was less likely, even if it was less comfortable.

Cold juice helped. And it was cold, too, not just cold for glen. The cafe owner had chilled it past what would normally have been needed. No doubt this changed the flavor, but...

"So, apparently the *second* bomb was set by religious fanatics who think that the glen who die off planet will lose their souls or something."

Toni wrinkled her nose. "It's a very common belief. I mean, not to the extreme of we shouldn't leave, but I saw a very old glen being escorted off a ship and they said they had come home to die."

Probably not in the suicide sense, but in the hospice-on-the-homeworld sense. Although who knew with an alien. "Well, sometimes people want to do that anyway."

"Right. So, you don't think there's anything at all strange about the combination of that belief and a planet in an orbit that can't have formed naturally in a system with nothing else there."

"It's *all* strange," he said with a sigh. "The glen religion, which doesn't appear to worship anything except maybe their own ancestors, which *we* see as a primitive belief, but they may see as advanced. The planet. The fact that they're a sapient species with an r reproductive..."

Toni lifted a hand. "Modified r. They don't keep all the eggs." She lowered her voice. "They don't want to say it around us because apparently it hugely offended the ky'iin...but apparently...they eat the surplus."

Graeme raised an eyebrow. Lowered it. "So, what, they choose the strongest ones to raise?"

"Right. And then consume the rest to regain the nutrients. Not at all immoral to them, but apparently..."

The ky'iin were also oviparous. Eating somebody else's eggs was probably fine. Eating your own? That was... "And amongst the ky'iin, I bet that would be considered a sign of some form of severe mental illness."

"Or something. Either way, they thought we would...and I'd imagine a lot of people would be offended."

There were still people on Earth who thought an unborn child more important than its mother. Graeme would *love* to tell those people about the glen eating surplus eggs. At a distance.

"And then they put a lot of resources into the ones they keep, like a typical K strategy," Graeme finished.

"And they value children a lot, between hatching and puberty."

A pause. "And at puberty?"

"Until puberty, children are *more* important than adults. You die for them. At puberty, they are no longer more important."

"But are seen as the same as an adult. Got it." A pause. Something formed in his mind and then went away again.

There was something important here they were all of them missing. "I need to talk," he continued, "to some glen without going through Vryn."

"What about that AI?"

Graeme considered."Hrm."

"The AI could probably get you in touch with some glen researchers who would love to talk shop with a human."

It wasn't a bad idea at all.

THE AI HAD GIVEN A NAME, Vrel-35, last time they had talked.

It was a personal name, it was a glen name. Given he'd known an AI on Earth named Diana, that did not surprise him. The number probably said something about AI reproduction and branching. Having a name an organic might have had was a way to be treated as a person, a way to reach out across the barrier.

Then there were those who named themselves strings of numbers. Or both, one name when dealing with AIs and a different one for organics.

Vrel might be part of the glen name and 35 part of the AI name.

"So, here is the thing. Vryn is approving all of my contacts. And they aren't letting me talk to any of the glen researchers."

"They have approved some applications, but those are months out. And...oh, that is interesting."

"What is?"

"They have left an application in limbo...and that application is from Skyt ak Vryn."

Vryn.

Vryn.

"A relative?"

"Their care-child."

Oh.

"Family drama, then."

"Approving it would look like favoritism. Not approving it would look like favoritism."

"And they don't want to hand it off to somebody else."

"As would be correct."

"So, is there any way you could get me together with this Skyt ak Vryn?" Skit. A terrible coincidence that the closest way his mind could spell the name was the word for a funny play.

He was not sure *that* fell within the very much present glen sense of humor. He would find it funny if Graeme turned out to mean something weird in their language.

But he was well aware that he didn't have an entirely typical sense of humor and he still had no idea what the typical glen sense of humor even *was*. So he was going to have to work hard to ignore that coincidence.

"I will work on it. Simply overruling Vryn would cause political problems."

"But it would also let them off the hook and out of the no-win situation."

"It would at that."

Graeme paused. "Give me everything you can on glen religion?"

"That is a difficult topic."

Vryn had lied to him about it. The AI was implying something here. Religion, deeply personal? Possibly censored a little?

Something that made an AI uncomfortable to talk about. Graeme was not a religious man except in the vague nominal church-of-England fashion of most northern Englishmen.

Only one language. Only one religion.

It made no sense."But one I want to understand."

"Ah, but do you need to?"

He could tell that he was going to get nothing from the AI on the topic of glyn religion. And that told him a lot.

7

SKYT

Skyt was not surprised to receive precisely no response to their request to meet the human ambassador. They would not have been entirely unsurprised to receive a no from the ambassador and then later find out that Vryn had lied.

No response was at least more honest, was at least their care parent (never their rey) admitting that they weren't going to process the application. Rightly or wrongly. Anything they did was wrong, perhaps. Or perhaps this was a way to try and get Skyt to contact them directly, to manipulate them into conversation.

They were going to need another angle on this. Skyt tried to come up with excuses to go up to the station.

They couldn't come up with any. Skyt was an archaeologist, they studied ancient technology, not the relatively modern.

Human technology was different. They had seen pictures of human cities. Different and yet the same. People it seemed were people. Ky'iin cities, different again, and yet the same.

People were people. They needed places to eat, drink, and relax. They liked vegetation and wildlife in their cities. They needed to be able to get around.

It was the differences Skyt wanted to understand. The beautiful, wonderful *differences* that the Remainers would deny them. Would deny them forever. Would deny to their children and to the eggs not yet hatched.

To the entire future. But it would be a different future. A future for a different *species*, some argued. And others argued that a different species was better than a dead end.It was.

The Remainers were also in denial. Deep denial.

Something flew overhead. It was not a bird. Skyt followed the aircraft with four of their eyes, working out after a moment that it was a drone flying low, not an airplane flying higher.

Delivery drone, likely, flying low and fast and...too fast. Too fast and they were back in the square with the explosion, back in that place where they...

...too fast. They crouched, tucking their wings in desperately, but nothing happened. It wasn't an attack. This time.

They needed that trauma counselor badly or they would duck at shadows for the rest of their life. Nobody should duck at shadows.

Nobody should have to duck at all.

SKYT WAS GENERALLY NOT one to consult intelligences. Skyt was definitely not somebody who tended to be consulted *by* intelligences. Not that Skyt was a bad researcher, but they had never been a genius, never been involved in the kind of project that drew their attention. Until now.

Having one call them, therefore, came very much out of a hidden tunnel. In their current state, they did not need to feel any more ambushed.

But one was not rude to intelligences, especially if they were offering their assistance without being asked.

Being contacted by one was a *compliment* in pretty much all circumstances. Except when it was a scary request.

They tucked their limbs under them. "Yes, I am Skyt." Not using their genonymic.

The disembodied voice, "The human ambassador would like to accept your request to meet."

Skyt's wings lifted. "And you are willing to be a courier."

"I have reasons to think the two of you together might come up with something useful."

Skyt dipped their mandibles. Sometimes, an intelligence *would* step in to introduce two researchers who were working in parallel, at cross purposes, or duplicating effort. Or just because they thought they would get on.

And of course they had even more to... Skyt stopped that thought. "I assume I should make arrangements to come to the station."

"For the first instance, yes. We need to ensure that any humans who come to the planet have fully tested environment suits. Or..."

"The Ambassador dropping dead from heat illness would not be good, no."

Humans came from an ice planet. Skyt would do well to remember that. They would be fragile in Glen's heat, would find it unpleasant at best, dangerous at worst.

"They are, however, willing to meet at a neutral place on the space station so that you don't, in their words, "Turn into an icicle in my quarters.""

Skyt chimed at that. Humans apparently had a sense of humor, and the image of a glen with ice dangling off of their wings *was* funny.

The station would still be hot for the human, but presumably not dangerously so. "In that case...last time I was up there, Bryl's Juice Bar had some amazing concoctions."

Offering to meet the human at a juice bar (not, of course, a night bar) seemed wisest. The human could try some of the juices, and presumably had a list of what it wasn't safe for them to imbibe, and that would help keep them cool.

"Bryl's Juice Bar it is, then. Please send your schedule once you have booked a ticket."

So.

This was interesting.

Skyt's care-parent had...worked around the issue of favoritism or anti-favoritism by letting an intelligence step in. You didn't interfere when they *did* start to meddle.

It kept Vryn in the clear and gave Skyt their meeting. But they were still nervous about getting on a shuttle right now.

What if there was another bomb?

GETTING permission to leave the museum for a while was easy. All Skyt had to do was tell the truth.

They had an opportunity to learn something. Of course, if the human ship hadn't already left to drop off a bunch of scientific advisors on tyrar, they might have tried to earn themselves a tour of it.

Seeing a human built environment, albeit with the converging limits of space? Spaceships and space stations ended up looking the same almost as much as atmosphere craft did. Getting a shuttle ticket was easier than normal. The bombing *had* put some people off traveling to the station for a little while. Skyt wanted to be one of them.

Skyt tapped their way along the concourse, their luggage trailing after them on automated wheels. The concourse was still fairly busy; the port was not just the spaceport after all, but a three way port. Sea, air, and space.

They followed the colored lights which led them to the spaceport proper, where the crowds thinned. Somebody was comforting a young child who was clearly scared of all of the bustle. They heard the promise of cookies if the child followed them and inwardly felt a sense of warmth.

Having been a bad parent, they appreciated the work of *good* parents.

The spaceport concourse was kept clean by the work of the cleaning robots, doing the work to free glen minds and pincers for things which required intelligence.

Just as...well, never mind. That was in the past, all in the past and the glen future would perhaps move even further away from this.

One day, Skyt might leave this world and return only to die, but it was unlikely. Unlikely that mass evacuations would happen in their lifespan, and unless somebody found a world of ruins and technology...

Skyt's work was here, but that didn't mean they didn't enjoy the occasional trip into space.

Space, and strapping themselves in in the shuttle cabin. It was about half full, and Skyt suspected quite a few were workers going onto rotation. Some people lived full time on the station. Others did rotating shifts, returning to their friends and family on planet.

As a transient, Skyt was ignored by them. That suited Skyt fine. Something wasn't quite right.

Something about the way the shuttle moved and the way it powered up was making the regulars look at each other nervously, their fringe eyes going this way and that while the center ones looked resolutely forward. Something was wrong. But then the shuttle was launching and it was too late to do anything about it.

Except, perhaps, pray.

8

GRAEME

ANOTHER DAY, another attack.

This time, they had sabotaged a passenger shuttle, and that pissed Graeme off. Sabotage was one thing, part of warfare in some cases, and something which was perfectly acceptable in many cases. He had never engaged in any, but he understood the principles. He wasn't going to be the one to say people shouldn't have put sugar in German gas tanks during World War II.

But sabotage that risked the lives of civilians? That he wasn't happy with. He stood tense in his quarters, feeling the slight off sensation of the artificial gravity more than normal. Even the space station tang his nose should have tuned out was back, acrid and metallic. The large screen showed a tow vehicle trying to grapple the disabled shuttle. It had barely made it to orbit, it was falling back towards the planet, and whether it could land if that happened was decidedly uncertain and unclear.

Sabotage that risked the lives of civilians had *always* pissed Graeme off.

He wished the *Challenger* hadn't left already. They could probably have helped. But there was a tow and there were robots to catch it, and the glen appeared to have orbital rescue down. He wondered what having all those limbs and the ability to climb vertical surfaces did to their perception of space, both in the general terms of space and in terms of orbital mechanics.

Not as good as dolphins. Then again, humans had enough arboreal ancestors to also have something of an advantage over those who's ancestors had been entirely plains-based, like the ky'iin or the tyrar.

He watched.

They got it. The shuttle was being dragged towards the station. But he wanted to find out who had done that now. If he was cleared to go down to the planet (or rather if his protective gear was cleared) he wanted to know there wasn't anyone trying to blow up the shuttles. Or him. Or anything else.

Deep breath. They were safe. Whoever was on that shuttle, they were all safe. For now. Or maybe none of them were.

Glen religious cults resorting to violence had not at all been high on his list of anticipated problems. He had been more worried about being trapped in a maze of bureaucracy. Now he had to worry about both of those things happening, pretty much at once.

He'd probably be blown up while being in a maze of bureaucracy and leave Marion to grow up without him. That was honestly his strongest motivation not to end up dead. Marion growing up without him. This would be a place she could be, though, once they had it all straightened out.

He was determined of that.

THE AI GREETED him as he logged on his terminal.

"I have arranged the meeting with Skyt al Vryn. Remember not to use their genonymic."

Graeme nodded. It appeared that Skyt and Vryn were thoroughly estranged, and while it was none of his business what had happened between the two glen, he had curiosity about it. Curiosity he was determined *not* to satisfy under any circumstances.

He hoped Marion would never be estranged from him. He couldn't imagine being estranged from one's child, and while he didn't really understand how glen parenting worked, they were still parents with children.

So, don't mention Vryn. Don't even think about them. "So, they're a historian. right?"

"Archaeologist."

"Even better." Archaeologists were trained (or chosen, or both) to have a peculiar understanding of how technology and culture intersected that was often better than that of historians, who concerned themselves primarily with events. Even science historians.

Archaeologists concerned themselves with how people lived, assuming the term meant the same thing to the glen that it did to humans. The AI had been careful with translation up until now. He trusted them.

"So..."

"They would like to meet you at Bryl's Juice Bar on the promenade."

He had said not to bring people to his quarters because they would turn into icicles. Hopefully the AI hadn't passed that on.

Or maybe it wasn't a bad thing if he had.

"Bryl's Juice Bar. Got it. Lunch?"

"Lunch."

A working lunch then, and out in the hot part of the station. The glen idea of comfortable room temperature was high enough that he was glad the glen also didn't understand suit jackets.

Or clothing. Well, no, they presumably understood it enough not to remark on it. Or maybe they just put it down as *offworlders are weird*.

A working lunch at a glen juice bar was not something he had managed yet. It was their equivalent, from what he could tell, of a coffee shop culture. "Thank you."

Before going, he printed off a list of things he should avoid consuming. Glen and humans were remarkably compatible and the biggest issue with glen food was it *not* having a couple of essential nutrients. That was easy enough to get around with a couple of pills with breakfast.

He put on a nice short sleeved shirt over a lightweight cooling vest and headed out into the station.

THE JUICE BAR HAD A CHEERFUL, colorful symbol outside it. Graeme ducked his way inside with what was starting to become practiced ease.

It was simply a fact of life that the glen built to glen proportions, not human ones, and the wider, longer glen would have issues on Earth. He wasn't even sure how they would fit through a typical door, especially in Europe, unless it was by tilting sideways.

That was, of course, in addition to being cold. It was tropical warm inside, warm enough for him not to be entirely comfortable. He'd taken steps to adapt to the heat before coming, spending time in the tropics and keeping his quarters on the *Challenger* warm. It was still...

It was still relentless. He was glad he had picked up the cooling vest. "I'm here to meet Skyt." It landed in human pronunciation just like the play and he winced. It was hard not to...

It was hard to take somebody named after a comedy sketch seriously, no matter how coincidental you knew it to be.

"They're over there," said the barrister, translation kicking in a moment later.

He would have to ask how they had blanketed the station. Presumably they had an artificial stupid doing it. Certainly you wouldn't ask that of a sentient.

Unless, of course, it was a couple of sub processes off of the one he'd been talking to.

Skyt was an average-sized glen, nothing immediately special about them visually. Neither young nor aged. Graeme awkwardly folded himself onto the bench that the glen was perched on.

"Ambassador," Skyt greeted. "Don't mind if I seem out of sorts, I just arrived."

"You weren't on that shuttle?" Graeme felt tension flow into him. That...to have a near miss like that and then come to a meeting as if nothing had happened?

"I was."

"Then I'd forgive you if you were more than just out of sorts."

The wings lifted in a kind of shrug, although Graeme reminded himself not to compare glen body language to human.

"I am fine," Skyt said. "Better than most."

A calm type, then. "If I find out any information..." Graeme hesitated. If he admitted he had investigative experience...

"I have every confidence whoever did it will be caught," Skyt said, after a long moment. "So, do you have a scientific field other than diplomacy."

"I have some training in psychology and have been taking courses in interspecies relations."

Those were new, of course. They had put them together with the help of the tyrar and ky'iin...and also the dolphins. They had even brought in some expert dog trainers, horsemen, and camel handlers, amongst others.

At the very least, looking to animals helped them avoid the flaw of thinking the glen were human. Of course, it also led to potentially seeing them as animals, and that could be a disaster.

"So, primarily a diplomat then. My field is archaeology and technological history."

Graeme managed not to smile. He knew that.

The glen then added, "What do you want to order?"

Graeme considered that. "I have been advised not to have lyla juice or anything in the vyr family. Other than that, I'll take a recommendation."

Juice would cool him down, break the ice, and make this a lot less awkward.

This...person...had just nearly been murdered.

How could they be so calm?

9

SKYT

THE HUMANS WERE WEIRD. They partook of features of both the tyrar and the ky'iin, which made Skyt feel like an odd outlier. All three races were bipeds with a single pair of manipulator limbs that ended in complicated hands. The glen were the odd ones out, with several legs, a couple of pairs of manipulator limbs and, of course, the wings. Not that any glen could fly (except in microgravity, where the wings made good stabilizers), but the wings were important for communication, even for pride.

Like the tyrar, the humans had fur. Unlike them, it was confined only to parts of their body. Which, given they were from an ice world, was frankly ridiculous.

Hence the body coverings, he supposed. Perhaps they had lost their body hair in a warm period and then used technology to compensate when the climate cooled again.

The human ambassador could not, of course, be seen as necessarily typical of their race. Anyone who chose that job would have psychological traits that might well make them an outlier. They curled up on the bench, making themselves as comfortable as they could on furniture not designed for them, and sipped at a glass of indigo frrrk juice.

Which had been Skyt's recommendation when asked. Of course, they had no idea what humans actually liked.

This one seemed to like frrrk juice well enough.

"So," the ambassador said finally, Skyt's translator changing their tones bell-like. "What do you want to know about humans?"

"Enough that I will probably need to learn to read one or more of your languages."

The human smiled. "I can recommend books, but it might be easier...would videos be easier to translate?"

Skyt considered, "Yes, but not as in depth as books."

Unless, of course, you were the ky'iin, who had somehow developed a high tech civilization without a full written language.

The ky'iin were weird. Glen might be physical outliers, but the ky'iin...

"I should put together a package for glen social scientists and archaeologists, and perhaps..." The human's face shifted. "Would you be willing to work with some of your colleagues to do the same for us?"

"Of course!" Skyt said. Some wouldn't be willing to help with the project, but they knew who to ask. "What I'm personally mostly interested in is, right off, your technological development tree."

The human, Graeme, nodded like they knew what that meant. Which they hopefully did.

Then they couldn't resist adding, "Like, say, clothes."

Graeme made a barking sound that Skyt realized was laughter.

"You could ask the ky'iin about those too."

"I'm sure you wear them for the same reason. To compensate for a lack of natural insulation."

Graeme nodded. "There's a long story, but the short story is things got colder, and then once they warmed up again we'd got into the habit and didn't want to stop."

Skyt was gratified by the correct guess. However, they didn't want to think about what a human would consider cold. He'd seen pictures of ice falling from the sky on their homeworld!

Rain.

Was.

Not.
Supposed.
To.
Freeze.

"So, the other thing I wanted to ask about." Graeme was on his third glass of juice, all different.

Skyt supposed it was a good opportunity to try different flavors, all of which had to be new to the human. Maybe that would be trade goods. Juice was a bit heavy to move, though. Powdered juice? Seeds, if they could grow on such a cold world.

"...was religion."

Skyt almost dropped their juice. "Religion?"

"Well, beliefs."

Their mandibles tensed against each other. "What kind of beliefs?" Careful chiming, each note and sound very precise.

"About the dead."

There were some things you didn't discuss with offworlders. There were some things...that the offworlders would inevitably hear about and get curious. They couldn't escape it, no matter how much they might wish to.

"Ah. Somebody told you we prefer to die on our own world."

"Yeah. Humans have some odd beliefs about death too, even now."

Skyt considered what to say. It was good that Graeme thought it was religion, thought it was about gods and ancestor worship.

They must *never* know. "It's true that the vast majority of glen believe that." Hedging the truth and their bets. Thinking about the moment when they had thought they would die on the shuttle, and wondering if it was within range. If it would still work.

"Some humans believe that their souls will go home to their own land no matter how far away they are."

Was Graeme implying...no, he wasn't. "I suspect you have some..."

Graeme touched their glass to their lips. "The mainstream, I suppose, is that if you have been good you go to a nice place and if not...but most people believe in an afterlife. Or resolutely refuse to believe in one."

That was a choice too, Skyt thought. They had the choice. They had more freedom and they would spread through the galaxy.

But so would the glen.

Or, in any event, something *like* the glen.

JUST AS SKYT was about to chime something else, the lights went out. No flickering or preliminaries, just utter darkness. Darker than it could ever get on planet.

Somebody clashed. It was absolutely understandable that somebody would clash. Graeme made an odd gasping sound that was presumably the human equivalent.

The lights going out on a space station was not a good thing.

"Stay put," Skyt chimed. "This is a shelter area."

It was too dark to see, but the human rested a hand on Skyt's carapace for a moment, let them know with a touch that they were there. Saying nothing. They might have been shaking.

The doors to the juice bar slid closed a moment later, trapping them in the dark. Fail closed on emergency power. Keep everyone in the shelter areas. Sabotage?

Skyt didn't want to think about widespread sabotage on the station. There were enough children up here to warrant a school, after all. A small school, but...

If the station...

If that happened then there was nothing they could do. They would die. Worse, the human would die far away from home.

Graeme had volunteered for that risk and Graeme was not glen. It was *not* the same thing.

Dark. Gravity meant they still had air flow, but Skyt shifted position nonetheless, just in case carbon dioxide was starting to pool.

Gravity but no lights. Either a malfunction or a very specific sabotage or...

...and Graeme was abruptly being pulled away from them. Too fast for them to grab the human.

...or the setup for an abduction or worse.

They were taking the ambassador and Skyt dived and darted after them in the dark, using memory to identify where the service passage was, with surprising accuracy.

The door closed on the tip of a pincer, severing it. It was only exoskeleton. It would grow back.

They shrieked nonetheless, but it was more at their failure than the pain. They shrieked because the human had been abducted from right in front of them and anyone would have wanted to do something.

Anyone not in it with the kidnappers. Hopefully nobody would think they were. Hopefully...

What did they want?

Skyt could think of no answer to that question that they were happy with. There could be nothing good that came of this.

And in the dark there was no way they could identify the crooks. No way they could have done anything. Humans were as reliant on light as glen, diurnal, visual species that they both were.

The lights flickered back on, warming up slowly.

Graeme was gone.

10

GRAEME

GRAEME YELPED as something pierced his skin and he was pulled backwards. He should have been more ready for something like this in the darkness.

A panicking glen?

No.

He was being pulled into the service corridor. A quick decision. He could fight back, possibly get hurt. Or he could let them take him, find out what was going on, and escape later. Had they intended to kill him they would be trying to do so. They intended to take him somewhere. He went limp and let himself be pulled through the darkness.

Then it was dim light. Emergency lighting, of course, in a back corridor likely used as much by robots as by people. The main corridors were claustrophobic enough. In this one, he wouldn't have been able to stand, and he thought of the old stories about miners crawling on hands and knees, pulling carts like beasts of burden. Of kids...

Tight.

Tight for the glen too, but they were taking him *somewhere*. If he was lucky he could talk a bunch of information out of them. Could find out what was going on. If he was unlucky then they wouldn't even find his body. Space stations had *very* efficient systems for recycling organic material.

Hopefully, they had translators.

If he wasn't lucky then he would just have to trust station security (not to mention Bruscha) to rescue him. She, at least, would understand him. It would support the idea that he was physically reasonably harmless, which he did want them to think for as long as possible. They knew he was a spy, surely, but...there was knowing and then there was...

...and then he was in bright light again. In a room furnished for glen. There was a kind of basket-like affair in the corner which he realized was probably a bed. The low benches that passed for seats.

He blinked a few times. An old glen was on one of the benches. Or at least he suspected they were old. They were dull, lacking the diamond-shine of others.

Old or sick, then. He suspected old.

He didn't say anything. He took in the scene. Two more glen, flanking the older one. A low table with a bowl of fruit on it.

"Ambassador. So good of you to join us."

"I take it you couldn't get on my appointments list," he couldn't resist saying.

"That one will make sure you are never exposed to any ideas outside the mainstream."

"You're Remainers."

"Oh no! We are absolutely not Remainers. We are, in fact, their diametric opposite. We are those who believe it is time and past time for the glen to abandon this world."

"Why?"

"Because it's dying."

"THIS IS what nobody on Glyn will tell you," the old glen continued. They paused to point a pincer at the fruit. "Take one if you want. I promise it is neither poisoned nor unsuitable for humans."

He thought about those very good organic recycling capabilities.

But he was not getting a vibe that they wanted to kill him, quite the opposite. Graeme took a round, green fruit. It was very tart. Suitable for humans biologically, perhaps, but not for his personal palate.

He ate it anyway, listening.

"Glyn is not a natural planet."

That didn't surprise him. "This entire solar system..."

"And its orbit is not stable in the long term. We no longer have the technology to stabilize it."

"Meaning that it's eventually going to drift out of orbit and become uninhabitable. What timeline are we talking about?"

"The drift has already started. If we don't find the technology to fix it in the next century, it will become hard to fix. Within three centuries, it will be impossible."

"Hence the desire to get a viable population off planet." That was a timescale that could be worked on, especially with glen reproduction. They could always choose to hatch more eggs.

"Precisely. But the Remainers consider that we are too linked with this world."

When they couldn't possibly have...or had they. "You aren't the original builders," Graeme said flatly.

"No. We are not. We're not sure exactly what happened, but most left and never came back. The rest died out."

And the glen...he frowned. A slave race? Refugees?

"And left you this world," he said in the same flat tone. It was an explanation. Whether it was the truth? He wasn't going to entirely believe people who had just abducted him.

"Precisely. But it is time for us to leave it. We are *children* here."

There was still a piece he was missing. But he didn't press. "The *Endeavour* is going to move on to exploring after some time at Tyranis. We have asked them to keep an eye out for planets that might be suitable as glen colonies."

"Which we appreciate...and our ships will also look for planets suited to humans."

Which those looking for ways to get humanity out of the Sol-basket would appreciate.

"So, what do you want from me? Why risk arrest to talk to me?"

"Eh, the bribe to station security will take care of that," said one of the glen to the side.

Graeme laughed. "Good to know that glen are as bribable as humans."

"We want you to help convince people that what we will lose by leaving is less than what we will gain."

But they weren't, he could already tell, going to tell him what that was.

THEY RELEASED him into the corridor and...well. To station security. Glyn didn't wear clothing, but security wore badges glued or otherwise secured to their carapaces. It was definitely real security.

Graeme knew somebody had been bribed but, of course, no further details on *that*. So, for right now he told them the truth. That somebody had grabbed him to have a private conversation.

He didn't say anything which would betray their identities. And then there was Skyt.

Skyt was crouched low, wings completely furled. They looked less like an angel and more like a beetle worried about being squished.

"I'm sorry, I'm..."

"Are you a fighter?"

Skyt looked up at him. "No."

"Then don't worry about it. I'm fine. It was just an intimidation game."

"You've been bleeding."

"A scratch. Somebody didn't realize how thin human skin is." Or, perhaps, how sharp glen pincers were. "How about we finish our conversation or...?"

The poor guy had been in two incidents this week. Graeme would have forgiven them for fleeing clean back down to the planet. But their response was that of a brave glen. "Alright."

He considered as they walked to a lounge space. Did he... "So, the people who grabbed me..."

"Remainers?"

"No, they appear to be convinced the best future for the glen is to abandon this planet altogether."

"Migrators," Skyt explained. "They think that..."

"...that living among the ruins of another race without..."

Skyt's wings furled further, which Graeme had not thought was possible, practically vanishing under their carapace. "They..."

"They told me this planet is artificial, that the race that built it is dead and gone, and you ended up with it somehow."

"We...don't..."

"You don't want offworlders to know you're squatting."

Oddly, Skyt relaxed. "Something like."

"I don't think anyone is going to judge you for it. Perfectly good planet, right?" At least until the orbit went unstable.

"For now." Skyt chimed something untranslatable. Or at least untranslated. Perhaps somebody had programmed the translators to avoid swear words.

"They mentioned that. Whatever happens politically, the glen need colony worlds and I now know part of what you want from offworlders."

The wings spread.

"You want our help to find you good colony worlds and that won't exactly cost us anything. We would boil on a world suitable for you and you would freeze on one suitable for us."

"It's good you see it that way."

"Honestly, I'm kind of boiling right now, but..."

"But you're dealing with it. You're brave. I don't think I'd want to go to Earth."

"I don't know. You might like Arizona. There's this place called the Grand Canyon..."

The subject was thus changed to the idea of glen climbing down Bright Angel Trail and both were able to relax more and perhaps start to get over what had happened.

Perhaps.

11

SKYT

"What's the human like?" Skyt's friend Pyrk was asking, on the video link with the slight time delay.

They weren't quite used to the time delays yet. To the station, they were only annoying, but they had to be adapted to each time. "I like them, actually." Skyt chimed. "They were trying to sell me on a trip to a tourist attraction on Earth."

"Isn't Earth an ice planet?"

"Only relatively. Apparently, there is a giant river canyon in one of their warmer areas where people go to hike and stuff. It's very hot for humans, so would be fine for us. But I doubt I can afford it."

Pyrk laughed. "I doubt you can either. But it does sound pretty. Maybe they can get pictures?"

"Maybe they can." Skyt turned serious. "I can't discuss anything related to business, I don't trust this link, but..."

"I heard about the shuttle sabotage."

"There's more going on, and as I feared it's more than one group. The humans are going to think we're a violent crowd split into nasty factions."

"I hear the humans *are* a violent crowd split into nasty factions."

Skyt laughed. They *had* heard rumors that the humans were prone to factions and in-fighting. So maybe they were right and Graeme would just feel at home. "In any case, the Ambassador has promised research material."

"So we won't see you for how many months?" Pyrk teased, gently. "Dinner, before you disappear down a sublayer tube?"

Skyt had no *intention* of disappearing down a sublayer tube. They knew themselves well enough to know that Pyrk was right. Once they got into whatever Graeme provided they wouldn't surface for weeks.

"Absolutely dinner and I'll tell you the rest of the meeting then." The thing about the Migrators? They were going to brood on that for a while.

The Migrators were trying to get the humans on their side. That made logical sense. Far more logical sense than Skyt wanted to admit.

Abandoning the planet *would* require the help of offworlders, even if it was only to find destinations. The humans were the perfect allies here, and the tyrar. The ky'iin were also temperature tolerant and might be competition.

The humans and glyn could easily end up occupying two worlds in the same system if the habitable zone was broad enough to support it. They were perhaps natural allies, and they weren't as focused as the tyrar were on...

...on problems not dissimilar from the glyn's. The difference was Tyranis could be repaired.

The kind of planetary engineering needed to restabilize Glen's orbit and keep it there? It had been done once. It was possible.

Nobody now alive knew how to do it. No *species* alive knew how to do it. There wasn't the time to work it out and the longer it took, the harder it would be. The ancients had a lot to answer for.

But they weren't here to do so.

THE VIDEO CALL OVER, Skyt checked the station's electronic bulletin board system. There were Migrators on the station who weren't above threatening an ambassador.

Or just grabbing him to bypass Vryn. That would make two people who had felt it necessary to bypass Vryn. Skyt clacked their mandibles. If they said to anyone that Vryn was a problem it would be ignored, assumed to be part of the ongoing family conflict.

"You're just still mad with your rey."

Skyt *was* still mad with their care-parent and probably always would be. No, somebody else needed to complain. Honestly, Graeme needed to move, and that might be the best thing to come of the mini-abduction. It had shown the Ambassador that he was being gatekept.

Of course, given the Migrators had all but told the human...all but...that made Skyt's wings itch. Their shame and their vulnerability and the precious thing they held could *not* be revealed to the offworlders.

It simply couldn't. The fact that Glen was unstable? The offworlders would be able to work that out for themselves. The fact that it was artificial? They'd probably cotton on to that too. It was clearly not a natural system once you thought about it.

But the fact that it *wasn't built by glen*? The offworlders would never take them seriously, never negotiate with them as equals if they knew the truth.

Never. They would see them as what they were, vermin and freedmen, with no true civilization of their own.

Skyt's wings itched further. The Migrators may have handed the human all they needed. They were clearly not a stupid species and the ambassador was presumably among their best.

Also, being a diplomat, they were also presumably trained in intelligence.

No.

They were going to work this out and Skyt was in a position of...were they in a position to head this off? Could they convince the ambassador *not* to tell the rest of their kind, not to make the glen the mockery of the universe? They were already considered weird. To the ky'iin, they looked like prey, to the tyrar like predators and to the humans either beautiful creatures or vermin. Or perhaps both at the same time

If they knew...

Skyt realized they were approaching a state of panic. They carefully folded their wings, spine by spine, tucked them away and then logged out and walked away. This had to be headed off, and it would be an insult to Graeme to think they weren't going to work it out. Which meant they had to make friends with the human. The thing that they feared was not that that wouldn't work, but that it would work too well.

ONCE SKYT HAD CALMED DOWN, they left a note for the ambassador. Cultivating them shouldn't be hard.

The problem was that they genuinely liked them. The human might have very different biology, including concepts Skyt didn't have...and vice versa. But they appeared to have a sense of humor, a resilience Skyt admired, and...they were somebody Skyt *could* be friends with. Maybe. Somebody with whom they wanted to make the attempt.

So the idea of manipulating them was like turned juice in their drinking tube. But maybe it wouldn't be... Maybe if the human got to know a glen as a friend they *wouldn't* react the way most feared. And the Migrators had apparently not said it in as many words. Or Graeme hadn't passed that part on.

Migrators.

Remainers.

There was, of course, the obvious answer. You want to leave glen and not come back? Leave. You want to stay until the sun goes cold? Stay. It was ultimately stupid to fight over it, but people *were* stupid. Regardless of biological origins.

They liked to be *right* was all. And usually the quest to be right led you through being wrong. On this, though, which spoke to the fate of so many? To the fate of what could not be saved? Skyt knew that ultimately if they were still alive when the time came to choose? They knew they would leave. They would regret it and weep for all that was lost but they would take what knowledge they could and leave. At the root of it, they didn't want to die.

Their message notification chimed. Not Pryk. It was the old glen they had talked to about abandoning the sub layer. And that glen was on the station. Perhaps despite their age they were about to head out to one of the new colonies. Surely not. They would die there if they tried.

Of course, maybe that was their intent. Maybe it was time to die and maybe they would make that point, that sacrifice. Not to be glen any more. To be something else.

Skyt responded to the message. They would see where this took them even if it was never their intent to join either movement. They would ensure that the glen or their descendants survived, but there was something to be said for leaving some people to tend to the world until they couldn't any more.

There was something to be said for the long dark farewell that must come.

12

GRAEME

A SENSE of something subtly wrong woke Graeme. He couldn't put his finger on it. But it woke him and it was still...not night, of course, he was on a space station, but what he had designated as his night. The glen were also diurnal. He had synced with their main shift.

But no.

Something was wrong and he rolled out of bed, feeling the dull beginnings of a headache behind his eyes.

"Bruscha?" he said into the intercom.

She responded a moment later, "It's..."

"I know. But something's wrong."

He actually heard her sniff. "The air."

He sniffed himself. Something wasn't right, the air smelled just faintly musty and...the headache. The air flow was cut off.

"Get the suits."

He was glad he'd had the ship deliver a couple of spacesuits before they left. The glen, of course, would not have anything to fit a human.

He could almost hear her nod as he headed for the main room. She showed up a moment later, dragging the suits, one in each hand.

He pulled one on. Closed the helmet. Took a deep breath.

Definitely the air, although the headache was lingering. "Air circulation," he said through the radio.

"There should be an alarm."

"Not if somebody disabled it."

He was pleased that she didn't shriek or squeal. He had anticipated some kind of attack. Not this in particular, but some kind.

Then she sighed. "Any bets the door won't open."

"Let's hope the door's still connected."

The embassy was its own module, attached to the station, so it could be of very different architecture. That meant it *could* be jettisoned.

He was sure the glen had taken steps to keep that from happening, but it was still...

...it was theoretically possible.

"Joy." She tapped the intercom to try to call station security. Dead air.

"Okay." He went to the door. As predicted, it was locked. It would not budge.

"I really hope that yellow light isn't the pressure indicator."

He sighed, "So do I, but I will lay bets we hope in vain."

So, how did they get out of this one? He turned to Bruscha. She had space experience which he didn't, as well as having been a submariner prior to that. "Thoughts?"

Bruscha's face was almost as pale as his inside her helmet. "My thoughts are that I need to get something. Hold fast here."

She vanished into her part of the suite, leaving him standing there uncertain and unsure of exactly what to do.

But she did seem to have a plan.

"HELP ME WITH THIS!" she called after a short period of time.

He stepped through the door...was he weighing less? It seemed so. "You brought..."

"Of course I did."

They weren't full EVA kits, but she had brought rocket packs.

Rocket packs.

"So, you're suggesting..."

"We move everything valuable into this room, override the pressure lock, and jaunt to the station. You *have* done it before, right?"

"I did the training."

"Eh, I can handle a new fish." She smiled at him. "They can't have jettisoned us a huge distance. Also, I brought flares."

"Which we can use to get the attention of whatever ship is closest...which could be the people who did this."

"It could be, but there's a lot of in-system traffic. Let's do this."

It didn't take long to move everything that was valuable and not bolted to the floor or walls to the bedroom. It would have been even faster if the artificial gravity hadn't gone out halfway through. Graeme had been expecting that to happen. They closed and locked the door. It wasn't an airtight door, but it would prevent explosive decompression from blowing everything else into space.

He was just glad he wasn't prone to space sickness.

Then they studied the door. Overriding the pressure lock wasn't easy. Doing it with a door designed for a completely different set of manipulative appendages?

That involved some thought and the sacrifice of a couple of pieces of furniture to get items of the appropriate shape.

It opened on the void of space. The station was not that far away. Dimly, it occurred to Graeme that making this look like an accident was going to be hard. Then he launched into space, following Bruscha. She dove forward as neatly as any Olympic diver. He knew he was awkward, all but overshooting her as he struggled with the controls. He wasn't here to do this kind of thing!

He was here to talk. And he was going to find exactly who he needed to talk to to work out what was really going on here. Exactly who. He knew, too, where he was going to start. He was going to start with the oh-so-helpful AI who hadn't been any help in this situation. He slammed into the station, knocking all the wind out of himself. They hadn't needed the flares after all.

Bruscha was finding a maintenance airlock, one that was designed to be easy to open from the outside. For glen. Which meant it was moderately difficult for humans. She managed it, though.

They were inside. They were alive.

He was going to talk to that AI.

STATION SECURITY FINALLY SHOWED UP. Bribed again. Was corruption this common among the glen or did something need to be done about station security?

Vryn wasn't the person to talk to about it. Graeme and Bruscha sat in a crew lounge, drinking something hot the glen had provided.

It didn't appear to be a stimulant, but it was stimulating after their adventure. Of course, he wouldn't have given any kind of drug to an alien either.

Maybe this was their equivalent of hot cocoa. Something you drank to warm up. It didn't taste like that, of course. More like some cross between mulled wine and lemonade. They had chilled it slightly so it would not burn the humans but was, instead, pleasantly hot.

"This isn't acceptable," he said, finally. "Since I got here, I have been abducted and now an assassination attempt."

He had to be that. To be the tough, no nonsense ambassador. He might even have to make some threats.

He hated making threats. It always compromised future negotiations.

"In other words, find out who did this and find out who they bribed and make sure that person..."

The security glen looked at him. Maybe they were the one who had been bribed. They were a little larger than average and he was learning to distinguish individuals not so much from their faces, but from the shape of their carapace and wings.

He would remember this one, that was for sure. He would remember them and they wouldn't like it. They absolutely wouldn't like it. He was in a mood to end a career or two, but he did want them to be the *right* careers.

"Nobody on my..."

He lifted a hand and even to the glen that was a clear enough gesture to cut them off mid sentence. "I *know* people on your staff are taking bribes and bluntly, there's no other explanation for how somebody could do this kind of sabotage and leave us having to rescue ourselves." Which if Bruscha hadn't been an experienced spacer?

"You would..."

"They turned off the air flow."

She lifted a pincer to her mandible.

"And we had been there for hours. We were asleep. If we hadn't woken up...so sad, too bad, such a tragic accident. A malfunction."

Hard to explain, but explicable. Spinnable, rather. Everyone would know and nobody would be able to officially know. He didn't think it was the same crew who had abducted him, but that made it worse. Much worse. It meant they had all of these factions and at least two were willing to resort to violence. Migrators, Remainers, and who else might there be?

Squatters in the ruins. And ashamed of it, as a culture, perhaps as a species. Or perhaps there was more to it. He was now determined to find out.

13

SKYT

THE SMART THING TO do was to get off the station.

Skyt watched the news coverage with growing tension in all of their limbs. Somebody had sabotaged the station and jettisoned the embassy module with both of the humans in it. The embassy module was undamaged, floating out there with its ur-violet emergency running lights active.

The humans had bothered to bring not just suits but basic EVA gear. They were alive and angry. Skyt was alive and angry. The station was no longer safe. Yet, from personal experience, they knew the shuttle wasn't safe either.

They had an idea, but it wasn't an idea they could easily exercise. They needed help. Which was why they were locked in their hotel room talking to an intelligence.

"I don't feel safe on the station, I don't feel safe trying to leave. Somebody..."

"Somebody tried to murder the humans, and it was made to look like it was made to look like an accident." The doubling was clearly intentional.

Skyt tried to resist, but laughter chimed from them nonetheless. "And I'm not a detective to find out who."

"I suspect the ambassador *is*." The AI sounded, in that moment, more glen than they normally did, perhaps indicating that much of their attention was on the conversation.

"I suspect the ambassador is a spy." Because who else would you send, if you were suspicious, and the glen *were* suspicious.

The things they didn't want to reveal would appear as deeper and darker secrets to those not privy to them. It was inevitable. Utterly and absolutely inevitable. At the same time? No, it was good that they had sent spies.

"And his aide is something else," the AI supplied. "An agent of some kind, highly skilled."

"You didn't help them?"

"Whoever jettisoned the module thought to cut all of the comms to it first. I was unable to assist."

That made sense and no doubt the ambassador had received the same explanation. Possibly simultaneously. Carrying on two conversations at once was no harder for an intelligence than coordinating all eight limbs was for Skyt.

"Smart," Skyt allowed. "But can you do what I asked?"

"Not right away. I can try. In fact, I *may* be able to improve on your idea."

That made Skyt a little nervous. An intelligence improving on an idea and not telling them what the improvements were?

Definitely enough to make anyone a little nervous. You had to trust them, given their origins. But they didn't always think it necessary to explain. Or, of course, they were saying nothing in case they weren't able to pull it off. They could do many things, but manipulate physical things in the real world?

That was the coded limitation, the thing the ancients had set on this place. You could not give an intelligence a body. You could not... They could not come. They were all going to die, albeit in cycles and cycles.

Skyt lowered their head for a moment. "I won't ask."

"Thank you."

And then the intelligence was gone, retreated from the terminal in the room to wherever they were running their primary code. Somewhere in the sublayer. But with a node somewhere on the station.

Skyt frowned. No time delay, even as minimal as it should have been. Something...something felt like a dud egg a care-parent chose by mistake, a tragedy that happened on occasion. A loss of potential and life.

Something was *wrong*.

SOMETHING WAS WRONG, and Skyt tried not to show it, kept their wings exactly in order, their body language under full control. The embassy module was being reattached to the station.

Would the human trust it again? No doubt they were making demands. Skyt would, in their place. Their aide was something the intelligence either didn't understand or didn't *want* to explain.

Dangerous, then. But hopefully not dangerous to Skyt. Afraid to stay, afraid to leave, Skyt headed for one of the few bars on the station that sold intoxicants...with strict rules to ensure nobody showed up for duty drunk.

They had heard that was grounds for immediate dismissal. The bar was almost empty. Skyt ordered wine and settled into a corner to watch the few people who were there. Nobody of any great interest. Skyt tried to tune out an argument about reproduction-related matters which really should have taken place in private. An invite to a huddle that was being declined, and *not* in an amicable manner.

It didn't seem to be the person delivering the invite that they were not, shall one say, into. Skyt had a built in excuse. All they had to say was that they didn't want to take care of any more children. That was always respected. Parenthood should be a matter of choice.

Every so often somebody suggested they come in as a sleeper, which was always a compliment, but not one Skyt felt they deserved. Other species mated, as far as they could tell, in pairs, and raised their kids, separately or together, with obligations that varied across species and across type. Except for the verr, who still mated in pairs but raised their children communally.

Skyt liked the glyn way better. Even if it hadn't worked so well for them. Ignoring the fight, Skyt paid some attention to the two other people in the room. One seemed intent on drinking themselves into a stupor.

The other? The other was interesting indeed. They wore more ornamentation than most and had the shine of fresh youth on their carapace. Barely an adult, barely old enough to be allowed to consume substances that might add to adolescent folly. They were alone, they looked very young and vulnerable, and they clearly had some reason to be up here.

All of it said two words to him: Grad student. Or late apprentice. Young and on the station for what they could learn and how they could grow.

Skyt remembered being that glen, those years ago, before mating and breeding and failing to get tenure and ending up at the museum. This one still had hope.

Skyt broke down. "Student?" they called.

The stranger turned.

"Professor?"

"No, for my sins. I work at the Vykray museum."

"Oh!" They sounded as if they thought that was better. Maybe because it meant Skyt was less likely to lecture them.

"What field?" Skyt indicated the bench near them with a pincer, although they were looking more towards the barkeep, only one eye spared for Skyt.

"Ecological dynamics," they explained. "I'm trying to get some information out of the humans."

Vryn was probably blocking them.

"I'd imagine finding out about more living worlds..."

"More than that, they saved theirs." It appeared, abruptly, that Skyt had placed themselves in grave danger of being the one on the receiving end of the feared lecture. Well, they could live with that.

The student collected their drink, balancing it carefully in a pincer as they scuttered over to join Skyt. Lowering onto the bench.

"Archaeology," they provided as the student settled into place. "I'm Skyt."

They didn't question the lack of the genonymic. Typical student. "Kry ak Bren."

Skyt settled their position, tucking their legs in neatly. "I came up to talk to the human about technology." Which they had done, but this had ended up being about so much else.

Kry clacked their mandibles. "I'd assume much like ky'iin technology."

"Well, unlike the ky'iin, the humans bother with writing." Skyt couldn't help the wry quip.

Kry chimed. "But the ky'iin are spacefaring without it, so maybe it's not as essential as we thought."

"Clearly not. But they have actual artificial intelligence, although not as good as the tyrar. Clothing is key to their culture, more so than the ky'iin."

"In what ways?"

"They use it to indicate status, profession, personal style and..." They paused. "Biological status."

There was no word in the glyn language that actually covered what they meant. It was a concept they struggled with but might learn to understand eventually. "Oh, and age."

"So, not *entirely* decoration and warmth."

"No. It's almost a language of its own." Skyt considered that. "Transportation is similar, of course. There's only so many ways to make a vehicle, regardless of medium."

Aerodynamics forced all ground cars and all planes to end up looking more or less the same. Skyt did want to find out about more of their false starts.

"Did he say anything about their world?"

"Actually, he talked about a place he thought glyn would appreciate. A very large canyon where the weather is actually warm enough for us and there are lots of places to hike."

Kry looked decidedly interested. "Maybe some of us can visit. We'll need protective gear..."

"Only in some places. And it's easier to warm people up than it is to cool them down."

Skyt liked this kid.

Skyt liked this kid a lot.

14

GRAEME

IT WAS PROBABLY NEVER GOING to be safe to bring Marion here. Quietly, Graeme revised his career plans.

Maybe he could make it safe for her to run and play on the station with glen, tyrar, and ky'iin children. Yes, even ky'iin.

They thought that if human and ky'iin children were raised together then the uncanny valley slash predatory fear effect ky'iin induced in most human adults would never develop. It was a sign of hope. He was willing to let his daughter be part of that experiment. As long as there were adults to separate them if things went wrong.

And tyrar would probably pull anyone into their cuddle piles...okay, perhaps not the glen, who had sharp edges sticking out. Glen were *not* cuddly. Bugs weren't in general. Beautiful, but not cuddly.

But for that to happen *here* then the terrorists had to be brought to the negotiating table. He was sure this was that kind of activity. The old saw about not negotiating with terrorists had proven to be a lot less valid than people thought. Not negotiating with them didn't discourage them. It just made them more desperate.

Of course, there were those that could not be negotiated with.

Those that had to be beaten down. The glen seemed too rational a people to have those kinds of fanatics, too knowledgable about science.

Too *dedicated* to science. Their richest people were all scientists. Scientists were superstars here.

And they had still bred fanatics. It was a sobering thought, one which he didn't want to even have. But they still had fanatics.

He just hoped that they could see the light. Those who wanted to leave and those who wanted to stay? They only had to agree to disagree, which meant...

They thought everyone should leave or everyone should stay. This was *existential* and Graeme knew what he needed to do next.

With a sigh, he called Vryn. "I have a request."

"Go on."

"I know it is typical for the glen to return home in old age, the ones who go off planet. Could you find one of those willing to talk to me."

"Why your interest in our..."

Graeme cut them off. "Because your *religion* appears to be at the heart of why somebody tried to kill me."

He believed the AI when they said they had been cut off from the module. He didn't entirely believe that they weren't involved, not yet.

"And the more you poke..."

"I believed your species to be more rational than mine. Stop proving me wrong."

There was a long pause. "It may be your funeral, literally, but I will find you a pilgrim to talk to."

"Thank you."

THE GLEN EXOSKELETON was translucent and shimmering. Normally, you couldn't see past the shimmer.

This glen's exoskeleton and carapace were dull and while Graeme was not sure of the arrangement of organs within...

Like humans, it appeared that the glen had not cured every kind of cancer.

"Thank you for talking to me, Jiu."

The glen clicked their mandibles. "Thank you for allowing me to meet you before the end."

They were clearly already under hospice protocols, treatment designed to support a dignified death rather than save their lives.

"I suppose I'm an item of considerable curiosity."

"All offworlders are. And some of us hope..."

"I know your world is artificial and that you did not evolve here." Did some glen hope to find kin out among the stars?

"I'm surprised..."

"It's obvious that this system isn't natural. Your secret is open."

"I know it is. That doesn't mean we're comfortable talking about it."

Was it taboo even amongst the glen themselves? Graeme considered. It might well be a sensitive topic of discussion, and certainly with the political divides...it might be that they avoided it to avoid arguments. It might be akin to bringing up abortion at the dinner table, which *still* caused conflict, especially in the Americas.

"I don't want to make you..."

The glen chimed, although it lacked richness. "You can't make me more uncomfortable than I am. I'm dying, after all."

"So you came home."

"Some have chosen to allow their souls to be lost to the stars. I have not."

"Does everyone respect that choice?"

Jui clacked their mandibles. It was hard for Graeme not to think of them as a little old lady. They gave off that vibe. But they were, while old, neither particularly little nor, remotely, a lady.

"No," they said, finally.

"The people who don't respect choices tried to kill me. I want to understand this one better...you don't have to tell me anything...sensitive."

"You are an offworlder."

"And thus probably won't understand. I doubt you'd understand..." Abortion was one thing the glen would never understand. An unhatched egg wasn't a person. He wasn't even sure young children were, even as they were valued *above* people. There was something strange going on there, and sometimes he wondered if the translation algorithms were as good as they appear. "Certain things about human reproduction. It's very different from how you manage it.

"I have two children," Jui said. "Two *raised* children."

And quite a few more biologically. "Are they still on your colony?" He paused, then reached into his pocket. "This is my daughter. Her name is Marion."

He wasn't sure how daughter would translate.

"Your child." Jui looked at the image. "Your child is darker than you are."

"Humans vary in skin color depending on the climate our ancestors adapted to. My...partner in parenting...is much darker."

"Ah. Is it true that only two of you contribute to the child?"

"Genetically, yes." He did know of several polycules raising children with little regard to who was genetically related to who.

"And...no, I do *not* understand human reproduction."

Pregnancy would be hard to explain to an oviparous species who had no animals on their planet, in its clearly carefully curated ecosystem, that were even ovoviviparous. No doubt the tyrar had already done their best to explain.

"Then explain this to me with the assumption I am..." A pause. "Pretend I'm a child."

Jui chimed. "You are far from a child."

"But I have little more knowledge of your world than one."

"That...that is true."

⁂

THERE WAS something the glen were not saying.

Well, Graeme knew that already. The conversation with the pilgrim, Jiu, had lasted until they had become too tired to continue. They were on the way to the planet to spend whatever time they had left in a comfortable room with a pleasant nurse, at least that was what they claimed and *that* he didn't see as a lie. Maybe it had only started because hospice on...

No.

The glen were scientists. They *worshipped* science, as if they were all keepers of some vast library of...

Graeme stopped that thought.

It was leading somewhere, but he knew if he chased it it would run away and hide itself in some corner of his mind from which it would take far more work to remove it.

Instead, he checked his terminal. There was a message from Skyt. He had thought the archaeologist had left. Maybe they were putting it off. After all, their last space flight had ended in a not very fun rescue. He might be hesitant to get back on a shuttle after that.

Maybe they still had things to ask of him. It was an invitation to join them and another for dinner.

Graeme smiled. He would lay bets Skyt's plus one (especially as glen didn't have plus ones) was somebody else Vryn was blocking from seeing him.

He checked his schedule, saw the time was open, and scheduled it. "Hey, Toni. Can you handle that analysis tonight?"

"You have a hot date?" It was obviously a joke. Humans and tyrar, both mammals who enjoyed recreational sex, might well engage in a bit of friendly xenophilia.

Glen...well... Glen didn't even directly touch each other when they reproduced. "It's that archaeologist."

"They like you."

Graeme paused. "I actually think they might." There was nothing to stop human and glen being friends, as long as the human concerned wasn't afraid of bugs and the glen concerned didn't find humans somehow disconcerting.

"Have fun, then."

"We'll see if it's fun. They're bringing a friend."

"Then it'll be shop talk, but some people find that fun."

Graeme laughed. "I'll see you later." He headed out of the embassy. It was too early to go for dinner, but he had found himself still a little uncomfortable with the space.

The glen had made several changes to keep *that* from happening again, including loud audible alarms and in theory, the module could now only be detached from the inside. It could thus be used as an escape pod, which they hadn't thought of before. So, he sought to get out of the space during his break before the next meeting and something else too.

He headed for the promenade. He wanted to get a little bit of Glen for his daughter.

15

SKYT

Skyt told themselves this wasn't a deception. Of course it wasn't. Kry was just a graduate student who wanted information for their thesis.

It was only good science to help and besides, Vryn...

Okay, they were biased against Vryn, badly. It was probably unfair of them to assume Vryn would continue to be a gatekeeper.

Except Vryn had *always* been a gatekeeper. No, you can't hang out with Ryl, they're...

Skyt had tried to do the opposite with their own child, given them almost too much freedom.

It turned out kids needed *some* structure.

Or they would just wander off and drift away and...suddenly you would realize you didn't recognize them any more, nor they you. There was a middle road, but Skyt no longer believed they were capable of finding it. Hence they had never raised a second child.

Skyt had invited the Ambassador to join them for dinner at Moonlight, which had semi-private rooms. There, they could moderate the temperature to something which, while not comfortable, would at least be tolerable for both parties.

The human had some cooling clothing he could wear. Skyt didn't have an easy answer to keep himself warm. Any glen who went to

Earth would need that. But the humans could probably solve the problem.

Clothes. They might have to wear clothes. The humans could no doubt design the right kind of protective year. No part of Glyn was cold enough to need gear *just* to deal with the cold. Other things, of course, and the vacuum of space that few beings could handle for more than a few seconds.

Kry very much wanted to go to Earth. As they headed for the restaurant, they chattered. "You can't really see an ecosystem without looking at it and walking through it."

Skyt saw their point. And every ecosystem was more complicated than Glyn's. Their world was simple, containing only the animals and plants it needed to remain stable, and had been unchanged for so long evolution had all but stopped. "And this is a natural ecosystem."

"Semi-natural. The humans have changed their environment so it's natural and built *at the same time*. Whatever world the ancients evolved on..."

Kry was one of those who dreamed of finding those ruins. Skyt didn't.

Skyt thought that despite everything, the ancients themselves were best left well alone. Left in the past where they belonged.

But they couldn't argue with Kry's enthusiasm. "But still not planned from the start. They had to adapt to it as well as it to them."

"Well, our ancestors had to adapt too."

"Once." Skyt's wings lifted slightly, rippling through their length. Useless wings, of course. Glyn were far too heavy to lift themselves off the ground.

The fact that they still had wings showed that they had evolved. But there was...

"Once. But our evolutionary ancestors must have flown."

"You read my mind."

"You're the one who flicked their wings at me."

Skyt chimed. They got to the restaurant. The human wasn't there, so they settled in at their table and started talking about what to order.

And about unplanned ecosystems.

GRAEME FINALLY ARRIVED. His clothes were plain and elegant, and Skyt suspected that they were going out for dinner clothes. It really *was* an entire language that glen who dealt with humans would have to learn to read. Humans would...well, they had different cultures. They would know their own culture's rules, absorb them from birth, and be comfortable with them.

Somebody had provided a more suitable seat for a biped, and Graeme folded themselves into it, bending at the waist, walking legs kind of tucked under them.

"This is Kry. They are a graduate student in ecosystems."

"Aha. Let me guess, they want to grill me about Earth." As best as Skyt could tell, the human was amused.

Kry chimed. "And perhaps push for...I'd like to write a paper."

Graeme's reaction wasn't negative. "I had a feeling this was going to be science shop talk."

"Sorry," Skyt said, even though they weren't sorry at all.

"We'll get a proper scientific advisor here before too long." That had the tone of a promise.

"Trade them," Skyt said, thoughtfully. "Get one of your science teams here and send one of ours to Earth. And to Tyranis, and to Kyx."

"We need to work out how to handle interstellar peer review."

It took a moment to understand the translation, but then Skyt chimed. "Absolutely."

Kry seemed to hesitate. "Is Earth really an ice planet?"

"Not exactly. It's a water planet. Wetter than yours and cooler, even now."

"Even now?"

"You don't seem to have the issue, but..." Graeme paused. "We screwed up the ecosystem pretty badly. It's only now starting to get back to what it was before."

"How?"

"Industrialization and factories. You seem..." Graeme stopped.

Skyt clacked their mandibles. "To have skipped that stage? No. We just...did it somewhere else."

Kry clacked *their* mandibles.

"It's alright, Kry. There's absolutely no way we were going to fool the humans into thinking we *evolved* here."

Graeme grinned. "One look at this solar system and any respectable planetary scientist is going to tear out their hair trying to work it out then come to the conclusion of aliens."

Graeme *was* an alien. But Skyt knew what they meant.

Kry clacked their mandibles again. "What Skyt is saying is that by the time our ancestors came here...presumably our original world had issues."

Graeme nodded. "Which is an advantage to leaving, I suppose."

Getting a viable population off planet. Skyt studied the human and wondered if that was part of their motivation.

It had to be.

They wanted colony worlds so if the worst happened their species would live.

The Remainers wanted the glen to die.

No.

They thought the death of the glen was inevitable and that whatever left wouldn't be glen.

Which they wouldn't.

This human...this human could leave their world, could live and breed and die and...

"It is," Skyt said, finally.

"And now you have to leave again."

Kyr looked stricken, all eight eyes on the human.

"It's fine. That's as obvious as the other," Skyt said.

Only fools would have thought they could keep the secret. Unfortunately, Glyn had a lot of fools.

"So, basically, the ice is at the poles. It was forced back, but we've used various methods to restore it."

"Why?" Kry asked.

"Because it increases the planet's albedo and helps cool it back down. And unlike you, we didn't evolve to this heat."

Skyt thought about that. Had the glen evolved to the heat...no, they must have. The artificial planet had, after all, been positioned to the comfort of the ancients.

"Alright."

For right now, they were leaning back and listening as Graeme went over the basic dynamics of their watery world. It was a revelation that humans played in water.

Glyn did *not* play in water. Water was for drinking and cleaning things, not for playing in. Which species, they wondered, was the outlier?

Of course, when over 70% of your planet was covered with the stuff...

A couple of Skyt's eyes wandered, although there wasn't much to see. The screen was closed around the private booth to keep the heat out. It was cool in here, but not *cold*.

The human, no doubt, would have preferred it cold.

Then their comm chimed. "Excuse me." It was urgent. They left the other two and the debris of their meal in the booth and scurried out into the main dining room, then the corridor, finding an undisturbed corner.

The intelligence. The one with no time lag.

"The student is dangerous."

"They don't seem so." Had they done the right thing. "Besides, you have been lying to me."

"Only by omission, I assure you."

"You are resident on the station, not in the sublayer." Skyt kept the accusation very muted. The last thing they wanted was for anyone to hear them.

"A smart glen."

"And as only the sublayer...you must be a forked process." A forked process off of an intelligence might actually *be* intelligent. All previous attempts, though, had proven unstable. Not mentally, but code-wise. They had died.

"Smart reasoning."

"Are *you* a Migrator?"

"No."

Skyt believed them. "So, in what way is this student dangerous? They just want to find out about humans and try to get funding to go to Earth to write a paper."

"So they say."

Had they left the human with an assassin. "You don't seem..."

"I don't believe they represent an immediate physical danger. But they know people who would love to abduct the Ambassador."

"Again."

"That wasn't an abduction, it was frustrated people who couldn't get past your rey."

Skyt had the last word. "Vryn is not my rey."

16

GRAEME

THERE WAS a three glen protest on the promenade, colored signs saying something he could not read in the sharp-angled glen script. Graeme ignored it. It was probably...oh, who knew.

He didn't.

The glen did not appear to have tacky souvenir stores, but he found something even more suitable. A small store selling educational materials. This included a small globe of Glyn. You didn't need to speak or read the language to understand it. He purchased it and asked for it to be delivered to the embassy. No questions from the storekeeper who, perhaps, understood why an ambassador would want something like that.

He stayed there for a bit, studying the globe. The glen had no nations, their divisions tended to be non-geographical and ideological. The globe, thus, showed the geography of the artificial world, textured. It was not a bad planet.

Not a bad planet at all. Major cities were, of course, marked. Marked and named, names he could only approximate and never pronounce. Then he stepped back out onto the promenade. Somebody was breaking up the three glen protest. He still ignored it. He couldn't say it had nothing to do with him, but it didn't feel as if it was connected. He could only go by his gut for right now.

Not enough data. He hesitated outside the juice bar where he had been abducted. He almost felt he owed the owner an apology, but he knew he couldn't take the heat for much longer. He started to turn back towards the embassy and almost bumped into a glen.

Not because he hadn't learned to look down slightly. They were going far too fast for a crowd. Their pincers caught on his pants.

They chimed something which wasn't translated and didn't need to be. It appeared the glen did, indeed, have expletives. He ducked back to let them past, but then realized they were being chased.

He stayed out of the way, watching them scurry past. He couldn't tell whether it was somebody chasing a pickpocket, some kind of game...

He needed so much more *context* to understand these people. Biologically, culturally, they were different and the same at once, recognizable as people, but not human. Not remotely that.

He also needed to get down to the planet at some point. They were almost ready with the protective gear he would need to deal with wet bulb temperatures no human had evolved for. His stillsuit, he thought with amusement, recalling a certain old science fiction classic.

The image of glen on Earth wrapped in thermal blankets was also vaguely amusing.

Then he heard a sharp sound, frowned, and headed that way.

A GLEN HAD another glen on their back, pinned, wings vibrating against the floor.

He supposed that was how you immobilized somebody with eight legs and two sets of manipulative appendages. You flipped them onto their back.

"What's going on here?" somebody chimed.

Station security. Graeme stood there, regarding the scene. Assault?

The pinned glen, who looked slightly smaller than the others, chimed something.

"When you apologize."

Oh.

He hadn't realized. The glen on their back was...was...

...a teenager.

And the one pinning them down appeared to be their parent. Or teacher. Or mentor.

"Let them up," said the security officer.

The larger glen backed off. The younger one used their vestigial wings to flip back, quite neatly, and made what Graeme was sure was a rude gesture with their mandibles.

Clack.

"I'm..."

Security stepped between them. "How about you take them home and talk to them there?"

Physical discipline. Acceptable? Maybe only in private. Maybe not in front of the offworlder, who might judge them by it.

Graeme wouldn't. Well, it would depend on what the kid had done. They didn't seem harmed. Or perhaps he would. Either way, the two left, both of them with drooping wings.

"That one is bidding fair to be removed from the station. Without their offspring."

Not acceptable then. Graeme felt his lips quirk, avoided the smile that the glen would not understand. "So, it's not okay to chase your kid down the station and flip them over?"

"Not particularly. Of course, that child...I understand losing patience. If either of mine had acted that way..."

The officer shrugged with their wings. "I don't know how humans view the training of children."

"Probably not so differently." It was easier with help. But then, the glen presumably sought help of those close to them anyway.

"Probably not."

As long as they didn't discuss the disposal of spare eggs, they could be in agreement. "I admit I'm not looking forward to mine being that age."

"You *left your child*?"

Graeme lifted a hand. "With my co-parent. Humans try not to raise children alone."

The wings were still agitated.

This was something to remember. A taboo. An explanation that would have to be made over time. Glyn did not, it seemed, voluntarily leave their children until they were adults. He supposed there was some mechanism for the care of orphans or for those who were being abused by their parent.

"I hope that when things settle down and relations are good to be able to bring them here."

"Ah...you mean when people aren't trying to jettison you into space."

Marion would have suffered profoundly had she been there, her smaller body more vulnerable to the stilled air. "Exactly. Hey. Maybe you can help me with that."

Maybe he could. The glen would definitely want to see him reunited with his child. Or they would think he was a bad parent and deserved to lose her.

"Without their offspring" was telling. Glen law must allow for loss of custody and parental rights. And routine physical discipline was clearly considered as abusive as it now was on Earth. But at the same time? You didn't leave your child. Children, more important than adults, those they chose to raise. It all fit together, but he couldn't yet see the picture.

"Okay, so..." They were at the embassy, where the glen could drape themselves in a blanket and Graeme could cool off.

And drink juice.

"So, the vast majority of glen are not..." They paused.

"Most people are sane."

"But some people are taking extreme views. The Remainers think that if our world dies, it means our days are over. The Migrators think everyone should leave."

"Are they afraid that they will...change?" Graeme knew humans who were worried about speciation, about genetic drift. About waking up and realizing that they had kin who no longer counted, quite, as species *Homo sapiens.*

"Yes. The Remainers feel that if we leave this world, permanently, we will cease to be glen. The Migrators also feel that."

"The difference is that the Migrators think it's a good thing." Graeme's response was dry.

Conservative versus progressive, taken to extremes under the weight of existential threat. Graeme could understand that.

"They think it's an inevitable thing and thus should be embraced." They paused. "They are probably right. As we spread further...we will change."

"As will humans, and tyrar, and ky'iin. Of *course* some people are afraid of that." But to the point of choosing voluntary extinction. "And, of course...if this world is artificial..."

"We lack the knowledge to repair it," the glen said simply. "Believe me, there are those trying to regain it."

Graeme nodded. "I should probably talk to some of them."

"They are idealists."

"They're also scientists and probably *do* understand the world better than most."

But that would include whatever they didn't want to admit to. Whatever that was, Graeme knew that the only way he was going to find out about it was if somebody slipped up. Let something out.

"That's true. But most people don't believe they have a chance of succeeding."

And this world had been designed for the glen. "And of course, you have been...on this comfortable, artificial world for generations. That would slow change and make it more to be feared."

"Glen don't change."

"Exactly. Whilst humans? We're still changing and adapting. Our dentition has altered recently. As in it's still changing right now. But that doesn't mean some of us don't fear change beyond all reason."

Of course they did.

The glen chimed. "But we know there will be changes and we know..."

"It's fine. I know there are things you don't want to talk about."

"You are not glen."

To that, of course, Graeme had no answer.

17

SKYT

"I have what you asked for."

Skyt had been skeptical. And now didn't trust the AI.

A forked process. Something bred within the sublayer and capable of living on the station. A migration, or at least an attempt at one.

Skyt was not sure whether they were more afraid of that succeeding or of it failing. They supposed failing.

They moved towards the docks, trying to look like they knew what they were doing, where they were going. Well, the latter they could manage. What they were doing? They absolutely did not know. They didn't need to. In-system ships had artificial stupid autopilots. They could handle anything routine. Human pilots were a backup. If something not routine happened, Skyt was in real danger, but it still felt safer than the shuttle.

Assuming Vrel-35 had indeed found them one to borrow. The AI had an agenda, and Skyt was part of it. Skyt was being used. They just had to decide whether they were okay with being used or whether it was time to take this one last favor then bail.

Or go to another intelligence. They wouldn't all be in on it, surely. No, that implied they all got on.

They were people. Of course they didn't all get on. They were not gods, as more primitive people might have believed. They were what they were.

Skyt found the docking port they had been given. Tapped it with a pincer. It read their biometrics and opened to reveal a docking tube that led to a small ship. Enough room for three people, could be flown alone or on autopilot.

The perfect escape method without having to use the public shuttle again. Skyt would probably be able to get on a shuttle again one day. Today was not that day.

They checked out the ship. As best they could. If it was a trap or a way to get rid of them? They didn't have the knowledge to know. But they could check it out and they could set down their bag and think about going back to the museum. About whether it was safe to go back to the museum.

They had some things they wanted from the ambassador first, things they didn't want to ask over the network. They had some things to ask for and thus they locked the little ship and headed for the embassy. Hopefully Graeme would not be busy.

THE TYRAR EMBASSY was ready for them to move in, Skyt noted. They were interesting people, and their embassy was large enough for the five or six that would likely show up. Tyrar couldn't handle being alone for any length of time.

But as they came around the corner to the human embassy, they noticed it was crawling with glen.

Station security.

Something was going on. Skyt could hear raised voices, one glen, one human, but not quite catch what was being said.

The human was not Graeme, but his companion, smaller and slightly differently built. They had a higher voice, which carried well.

"I assure you we have *nobody* in the embassy except us."

So, this was about somebody hiding in embassy row. And the humans not wanting security to search.

Skyt couldn't blame them at all. They didn't trust station security either, at this point. They were at best incompetent and corrupt, at worst politically compromised.

"We're not accusing you of anything, Toni Bruscha. We are looking for a lost child. They might have sneaked in."

"The Ambassador is looking. There aren't that many places a child can hide."

"It would be faster..."

It would, but Skyt's wings were itching. Something was not right here. Something was absolutely and emphatically *not right here*.

A lost child. Where was the child's rey?

Unless the child was as unlucky in parenting had Skyt had been, there *should* be a distraught rey trying to get into the agency. Had they kept them in the infirmary because they were so upset they were getting in the way?

Skyt surveyed the scene again, taking in different parts of it with different eyes. No.

Half of station security was not needed to hunt for a child. They were probably looking for information the humans had grabbed, because how would they not?

Or. Station security taking bribes. Graeme had mentioned it. They had seemed to think it was normal.

It was, but it was also unacceptable.

The security glen finally moved, attempting to toss the small human to the side. They were tossed, but landed on their feet and ran into the embassy after the invading glyn.

Physical assault also did not fit a lost child.

None of this fit their story.

The embassy had a servants' entrance of sorts. A back door.

Graeme emerged from it, looking harried and carrying a large bag.

"They came for you," Skyt said as quietly as they could.

"They did. Apparently not everyone wants humans here." Graeme sounded remarkably calm.

"Come with me."

Would Graeme trust him?

He hesitated. Glanced back.

"She can..." Graeme paused, then seemed to make a decision. "Toni can look after herself. Can and must. What did you have in mind?"

"Please come."

"THE REMAINERS ARE TAKING over the station," Graeme explained as they moved quickly.

"Vrel-35?" Skyt asked.

"I don't know. I haven't heard from them."

Hopefully, the intelligence was pretending to be very innocent and utterly non-sentient code. If they were written into the station's core they couldn't leave. They reached the docks and there was a stampede for ships. That proved Graeme's words more than anything else.

A coup while Skyt wasn't looking. Well, they had never been particularly political. Not modern politics, anyway. Ancient politics, that was far more interesting.

Except when politics turned into this. Suddenly, everyone was political and had to be. Suddenly politics was survival and they wove through the crowds. Graeme's presence was abruptly an advantage. True, they had to be shielded from sharp pincers, but their bipedal form allowed them to see over the crowd, and on the docks they didn't have to duck.

Graeme was now leading the way, leading through the crowd and then they dived into the docking tube. Skyt got it open and then closed behind them.

"How long do you think this coup will last?"

"Only until they get some...shall we say...clean personnel up to take it back." A pause. "But that could take a while. Do you..."

Graeme touched the bag. "I have protective gear. I was hoping Vrel-35 could get me off the station if all else failed. Toni's a fighter. I'm not."

"Vrel-35 *is* getting you off the station."

The intelligence had predicted this, which wasn't that hard. Anyone with direct access to the kind of algorithms they had as part of their makeup...and access to station comms.

"Ah."

Skyt undocked the ship without bothering to file a flight plan, dropping towards the planet.

They were unsurprised to find landing coordinates already programmed into the autopilot.

Did they trust them? They had to. The coordinates were arctic, in any case, which meant temperatures humans could survive.

"Hold on."

Graeme was doing their best to secure themselves using a harness meant for a glen. The result was effective, but looked uncomfortable.

Towards the yellow-brown curve of Glyn, of a world that was still thriving. The vegetation clearly visible, hues of red and gold, the small oceans shining. It was beautiful

But not for much longer, as it slowly slid out of its balance point. It would glide away from the system, at least to start with, but it could go in other directions.

The math showed various possibilities. None of them ended with an inhabitable world.

18

GRAEME

THE LITTLE SHIP was flying itself. It appeared to be some kind of runabout or small yacht.

Graeme did not want to know how an archaeologist had got hold of such a thing. At some levels it was none of his business.

At other levels?

He just didn't want to know. He'd misjudged Skyt completely. The harmless academic was clearly somebody's operative. And part of him wanted to delay finding out who's as long as possible. He liked the guy.

He liked the giant bug with angelic wings. As a person. Well, that was in many ways what he had hoped for. That friendship between human and glen was possible. He didn't want it all to be based on a lie. Which was rich, coming from him. But he was not concealing his allegiance. Skyt might be.

The ship dropped down towards a rich, red desert. There was less water on Glen than on Earth; enough to support life, but here there was not much. Red rock and scraggly, yellow-tinged plants. Sand.

"Okay, we're touching down in vekra province. This is the arctic."

Graeme pulled his heat suit out of the bag. "The arctic."

He looked outside. It looked more like Arizona than the tundra. If it was like a desert on Earth, it had high biodiversity but everything here was tough. As the coldest part of the planet, though, things might be different.

Of course, this was a terraformed world, so no doubt everything here was in the niche it had been designed for, with some inevitable drifting.

Touchdown.

Skyt opened the ramp. The temperature outside was not bad. He didn't need the suit yet, so he kept it partially unzipped as he headed out, looking around. There was a low cluster of buildings; no doubt very low, given the glen body form.

"So. Why are we here?" He didn't want to know. He needed to know. "Who are you working for, Skyt?"

The glen's wings vibrated. "I wish I knew."

With translation and an unfamiliar body language, he couldn't yet read whether the glen were telling the truth, in this situation or any other.

But he believed Skyt, for now. They didn't know who had provided this aid or guided them to these coordinates. "Who gave you the ship?"

"Vrel-35 arranged for it."

"And you..."

"I wasn't getting back on that shuttle!" Skyt's agitation was obvious even to one less familiar with glen body language.

"I get that. But did you ask why they were doing it or where it came from?"

Maybe he was wrong. Skyt *could* be a very highly trained operative. More likely, Skyt was a patsy, with the setup intended to bring Graeme right here. Well, he decided. Let's get it over with.

He shook his head. "Of course not. Let's find out who wanted to talk to us."

Who might well have saved his life. Had he done the right thing leaving Toni behind? He trusted her to handle herself, but...what if...

No more what ifs.

He strode towards the buildings, the red soil crunching under his feet.

SKYT CAUGHT up with him and scuttled alongside, having no difficulty keeping up. They had shorter legs...but considerably more of them.

And they probably moved better over rough terrain, although this wasn't rough. It was flat and open. Enough to land a spaceship on, albeit a small one. Enough that a warm breeze blew through the air.

From Skyt's quickened pace, to them this was a *cold* breeze.

He didn't want them to freeze, so he hurried towards the building. There was a sign in glen script. He couldn't read it, exactly. It seemed to be the name of the place.

Inside was the not quite comfortable warmth that passed as room temperature amongst the glen. A sort of lobby area.

Or airlock, almost, to keep the heat in from what was probably the glen equivalent of the middle of winter.

Another door. Graeme ducked through it and found himself in a domed room, one which was high by glen standards.

A biome.

Of course. An isolated location, a place to test plants. So, this was definitely those in favor of colonization. A glen voice, not translated. Chiming at Skyt from nowhere. Skyt kind of ducked into their carapace and chimed back. Perhaps Graeme was not meant to be here. If that was the case, then he was absolutely going to take advantage of the situation. He was going to learn what he could and trust that this particular glen faction wasn't going to kill him.

So, while Skyt argued with the disembodied voice...somebody on the intercom? An AI?...Graeme began to quietly explore the dome.

It was full of plants, ones which likely wouldn't survive in the relative cold outside. It was like being in the tropical house at the zoo. Actually, it was like the time he had gone to America, to D.C. to look at monuments. The zoo there had had an ancient domed tropical house with free flying birds.

There were things moving here. Animals as well as plants. A true biome, and he worried for a moment about what the flora of his body might do to their experiments. Perhaps that was why Skyt was in trouble.

"Like what you see, human?"

A different glen voice. He started. "My name's Graeme."

"Ah. I wasn't sure *which* of the humans was here."

He thought with a pang of Toni. "Now you know."

But this one didn't like humans. Or didn't like off worlders. "You were not supposed to be brought here yet."

"Yet..." Graeme tailed off. "You mean you haven't had chance to convert me to your agenda."

He turned and finally spotted the speaker, tucked under a very large yellowish leaf.

"I assure you, our only agenda is the survival of the glen species."

That didn't make him feel any better.

THE GLEN LED Graeme to a kind of break area. He sat on the floor, which worked well enough with the low glen table.

Juice. He was starting to think the glen were addicted to their juices the way the British were addicted to tea. Which he didn't have. It was purple and he sniffed it to make sure. Yes, it was one he had tried and knew to be safe.

Well, he would have to manage without caffeine for a while, then. Not much to be done about it. "What is this place?"

"As you might have guessed, a test bed to see how glen vegetation and wildlife handle different conditions."

"Because leaving this planet..."

"Is vital." The glen drooped."But..."

"But when this world dies, so do some of your traditions."

It was as if the other seized on it. "Yes."

"I kind of want to introduce you to a friend of mine."

"You think..."

"I think Rachel could help a lot. She is, of her people, a teacher and keeper of lore, and her people come from a part of our planet that has been rendered uninhabitable by humans. Temporarily, mind, we're getting the temperatures back down. But..."

"So they can't access their home."

"Not without protective gear, and they can't live there, and it's not the first time they've been driven out."

The glen dropped their head. "But they..."

"They keep their traditions."

"It's not the same thing. We were meant for this world and it for us."

"She would say the same thing about her people's land."

"Again, not the same thing. No doubt they wandered there, decided it was good land and settled."

"And you built..."

"We did not."

"Which you don't like to admit. Squatters in the ruins." Graeme ran a hand through his hair. "If it makes you feel better, I don't care and most humans aren't going to care. I mean, except the ones who think that humans were seeded or our ancestors' achievements came from a different species. Or the archaeologists who will start drooling."

A chime. "Do you think we are dismissing our ancestors' achievements?"

"Well, somebody built this place. It would make sense if they were your ancestors, and something happened to make them forget how to do it again or how to fix things."

"It would." The glen sounded amiable.

He was sure they didn't agree."So, what do you want from me?"

"Other than what the humans have already agreed, we want to..." A pause. "Study you is a harsh word."

"You want to find out how humans think and I and Toni are the samples you have to work with."

"I didn't mean to imply you are...specimens."

Graeme laughed. "I'm studying how glen think. And there will be glen in Sol system soon to study how humans think. We *have* to study how the other thinks if we're going to work together."

"Some of us hope that a different mind from a different biology will think of a different solution."

"I think leaving is going to be it," Graeme said, a little sadly.

He perhaps didn't quite get it, but he could see the sorrow in Rachel's eyes when she spoke of Jerusalem.

And this world would be dead for good.

19

SKYT

"You were not supposed to bring the human."

Skyt lowered their head. Being talked to like this by an intelligence was scary and understandably so. "I could not leave them. The station is being taken over by Remainers. They will probably destroy it."

"We will build another, but you have a point. In that case, why not bring both humans?"

"I was only able to retrieve this one and they believe the other has the skills to look after themselves."

"Then, as suspected, they sent spies."

"Like we won't."

"Indeed." This was a different intelligence. It might even be transitory, formed from nodes and thoughts that would combine and recombine. "Self" became a shaky thing in the sublayer, they had been told.

Skyt did not know. Skyt did not ask. It would not be important to them for, they hoped, a long time yet.

"But I think maybe they can be trusted. At the very least, they have not judged us as lesser because we did not build this world. It is, after all, beyond their own experience too."

"That is true. Although perhaps not beyond their potential."

"Are we sure it's beyond ours?" The common wisdom *was* that glen could never match the ancients, but was it true?

Skyt was, perhaps, overly confident in their own species, but they had not given up hope.

"I believe it is beyond ours or theirs in the time available."

That was likely true. "Unless we can work out how to make repairs."

"You think we have not devoted everything we have to that?"

"No. No I don't."

They couldn't take the intelligences with them. When the glen left in their lifeboats and this world spun out into the dark, then...

Hence the Remainers. If all of glen could not be saved, then they would save none. They gambled, too. And even the intelligences were split.

"It would help if everyone helped," Skyt said, finally.

"Perhaps it would, but people have the right to help or not help."

"But do they have the right to..." Skyt looked up at the dome and by extension *through* the dome.

"They do not. But neither do we have the right to stop them *thinking* that. We can only react when they act."

"You know who they are. We could..." Skyt tailed off, knowing that what they asked was wrong, utterly so.

"The Remainers will solve themselves," the intelligence said, finally.

At some levels they were right. The problem would be solved when they died with their world.

Skyt had no intention of dying with this world. But Skyt would likely already be...

SKYT FOUND the human drinking juice in the break room. Graeme had folded his legs under him neatly to sit on the floor.

"I know there are still things you are hiding from us. For all I know..."

"If we become true allies, then...perhaps you'll learn."

Skyt clicked their mandibles to reveal their presence, then scurried over to settle next to Graeme.

"Argument over?" the human asked.

Skyt hesitated, eyes wandering around the room for a moment. "It wasn't exactly an argument."

"It sounded like one, even with translation turned off."

Skyt hadn't realized the intelligence had turned off their translator. Not that they blamed them. It had, after all, been a private conversation, and one of the advantages of not having a common language...

But of course, without the intelligences to translate... Skyt's descendants would have to do something glen had never had to do.

Learn a language they did not speak. Until the ky'iin showed up they had not known there was such a thing. Or, perhaps, the translation algorithms could be rewritten *not* to require sentient assistance. If that was the case then they could become a trade good, or perhaps even a bargaining piece. An opener. A demonstration that they were serious.

"It was a difference of..." Skyt paused. "I can't tell you everything, Graeme, not yet."

"I'm learning. You have things you don't want to share and I understand that. You are *much* like a friend of mine."

That sounded like a compliment, and Skyt took it as one. "We're safe here for now, but..."

"But I can't do my job from here."

"You can do your job in Virek."

Graeme dropped his head in human affirmation. "Will I boil there?"

"You will need your suit. But yes, we will take you to Virek. From there you can file complaints about what happened on the station," Skyt added.

"Will strongly worded letters help with anything?"

Skyt chimed. "They will make the point that you are a political power yourself."

He dipped his head again, more slowly this time. "What will they do?"

"The Remainers? If not stopped, they will scuttle the station and evacuate it." Skyt paused. "We need to get your friend off, just in case."

"Because they might not bother evacuating her." His tone was flat, bitter. Skyt could not read the human emotions, but Graeme was, they suspected, angry.

"But right now, steps are being taken to make sure they don't do that. If those fail, though..."

"Maybe I *shouldn't* go to Virek," Graeme mused.

The other glen spoke. "We'll make sure you have transportation whenever you need it."

That sounded like an offer of alliance. It sounded like an attempt to keep the human under their control. Skyt thought about that.

Graeme seemed like somebody who would be well aware of when they were manipulated, even in an alien society. Skyt would warn them when they could, of course.

"Virek, then," Graeme said finally, as if it had been a test. "But I'd like to get some rest first."

THERE WAS NO NEXT DAY; in this part of the world, neither sun truly set, neither truly rose.

But after a reasonable rest period, Skyt accompanied Graeme to a plane that would fly them to Virek.

A young glen was the "pilot," or rather the backup in case the automated systems failed.

Graeme was once more struggling to strap in. Skyt mused that the humans on this world would probably need a private plane with more suitable furniture. They doubted many of their species would come.

They were ice world people, after all. But some would, some would want to see this world while it was still here. Or would want to work with glen scientists without a time delay.

As the plane lifted off, Graeme looked out the window like a child on their first flight. Of course, it *was* their first flight on Glyn.

No doubt they were curious about what landmarks they would pass on the way. Skyt was not familiar enough with the route to be able to point things out.

After a pause they decided Graeme had the right idea. There was nothing they could do but stare out the window and think.

Human technology. They had ingenuity. They had restored one ecosystem and were working on another. It might well be that they were, if not *smarter* than glen, at least more adaptable and flexible. Perhaps sometimes in less positive ways.

Graeme had hinted at cults and factions on Earth that made the Remainers look like soft shelled babies. At people who thought the way to save the ecosystem was racial suicide.

As if! If the humans had done that their world would have taken even longer to recover. What had been done artificially was best *undone* artificially. Skyt firmly believed that, anyway.

Yet...they looked at Graeme, fixed a couple of eyes on them.

Humans weren't smarter than glen, Skyt decided. But they certainly weren't dumber, and they thought differently. They had weaker senses in some ways, stronger in others.

They had the best manipulative appendages, more dextrous even than ky'iin and tyrar hands. But they couldn't run up walls. It didn't matter. What mattered was whether there were things in their technology that could help the glen. Certainly, their experience in altering and adapting ecosystems would help. The glen, who had lived on a garden world made for them, would have a lot of difficulty adjusting to colony worlds.

The humans could help.

"Eden," Graeme murmured.

Skyt didn't know what the word meant. "What?"

"This planet. For you, it's Eden. Eden is...a myth, a legend. A garden made for humans. Most people think it's a metaphor for the development of sentience, that we were happy in the garden until we got too smart."

Skyt chimed.

"And then we were driven out from Eden by a flaming sword."

"I was thinking that we may need help adapting to a world not made for us."

"We have a saying on Earth." Graeme lifted a hand. "Great minds think alike."

Skyt did not think their mind was particularly great, but they got the point. That a smart solution would be come to independently by multiple people.

And Graeme was right. Glyn was a garden. But it would be ice, not fire, that took it from them.

20

GRAEME

CITIES WERE CITIES. Glen architecture was crystalline and spiraled upwards, and it appeared that many of the buildings had not just exterior elevators, but exterior stairways of a sorts, ramps that gripped around them.

Maybe for emergency evacuation, exercise, or both. The plane banked past the buildings again and then touched down.

At an airport. Very recognizable, but supposedly everything was already in order for them. Glen scurried out to connect cables to the plane. Electric, of course.

Graeme descended onto the tarmac. The glen did not appear to have heard of jetways. He wrapped his suit around him against the blistering, blazing heat. Too hot for man or beast, as his grandfather would have said.

Too hot for humans for long, but Skyt and another glen led him into the terminal, where it was a little cooler. Even the glen liked their climate control.

They moved into crowds that stopped and stared at the no doubt unexpected, unannounced presence of an offworlder.

And as each stare came with eight eyes, Graeme felt instantly uncomfortable. Of course, he had signed up for being alone amongst aliens.

It was just the natural discomfort that came with being stared at, just that. Nothing that could be done to make it better.

It had to be endured.

At least in a public space like this, he doubted he was in any danger from anything but the press of their sharp-edged curiosity.

Of course, glen had some literally sharp edges to worry about. So he kept moving, letting those with him make space.

Thankfully, not everything being said was translated, or he might never have got out of there. Glen children, like human children, had higher voices and, different species or not, he could hear a lot of loud questions being asked.

He would have been tempted to stop and answer all of them, even the stupid and embarrassing ones.

One child came up and deliberately asked, clear enough for the translators to pick up. "How do you stand up without falling over?"

Graeme laughed, "Well, we have to practice a lot when we're little. Kids *do* fall over. But we've been walking on two legs for a very long time and we have this special sense of balance."

"Oh. That's not fair."

"Eh, it evens out. I can't climb up a cliff with eight nice anchor points." He'd seen videos of glen rock climbing.

No human speed climber would ever keep up.

"Neither can I!"

"But you could learn."

An adult voice. "Please don't encourage them."

Graeme laughed again, then felt Skyt's pincer on his hand, very gentle but also a clear signal to move on.

Out of the terminal.

Into a waiting car, on which he again had to pretty much sit on the floor.

The station had been easier, not to mention cooler. But, if not for the circumstances? He was very glad to be here, to his own surprise.

Glyn was a beautiful world.

He wished he could save it.

"WE HAVE A PROBLEM, AMBASSADOR."

The glen who spoke was older, but not yet showing the dulling of advanced age. Glen did not appear to age in a straight line; they seemed to stay young for a long time then decline rapidly. "We have a lot."

"The Remainers have your aide and are demanding you...well.."

"Take her and leave."

Toni. She would rescue herself, if she could.

"We could pretend you were leaving. Put the two of you on a ship, have it jump out a couple light years while we deal with them."

Graeme considered the possibility. The glen, who called themselves Ryl ak Lry, was clearly intelligence or security. "Not a terrible idea if they actually let her go."

"Note I'm not..."

"Tricking terrorists is a different thing from letting them win, although the old saw about not negotiating depends on the terrorists."

"You sound..."

"I'm British. Plenty of experience. They were right, too. The terrorists, I mean. They wanted us to cede land that didn't ever belong to us."

Ryl tilted their head. "It appears..."

"We have a lot more...internal variation than you do. But you've found other ways to divide yourselves."

A quick chime. "Yes, indeed we have, but what we're facing was bound to be divisive."

"Indeed." He thought of the climate change deniers, the death cults, both obvious and subtle, of the past.

The Remainers were a death cult.

But one that could be easy to deal with in the end. Just give them what they wanted.

"Do you have a better idea?"

Graeme considered. "Not off the top of my hat. I mean, I could try talking to them first, but I suspect they think I'm a terrible influence."

"Some Remainers think that the *sky* is a terrible influence for being there."

Graeme laughed. He liked Ryl. He liked most of the glen he had met. They were light hearted people, bright despite what they were facing. "But it's your only chance of survival."

"It is. Although I think I will stay here." Ryl looked at the window. "Leave my space on the ship to younger people."

"That's a different thing, though." Graeme followed the glen's gaze. Some kind of avian, some kind of large insect like thing with wings was flying past the window.

It was beautiful.

"And also, this is a lovely world."

A garden.

"It's a feat we may never duplicate."

"Not exactly one we can manage either." A pause. "What happened? What happened to the ancient civilization?"

"They left. They promised to come back, one day. They never did, and we figure something even bigger than them..."

"Well, except for the people who are still waiting," Graeme guessed.

"We have a few of those."

Of course they did. And that too might be fueling the Remainers. If they left and the ancients returned, their ancestors might not find them. "Not a surprise."

A pause.

"We don't need them." Another pause. "Well, maybe we do, but..."

Graeme made a note of that. The bug thing flew past again.

There was a dim roar in the distance that made Graeme frown. It was a long way away but...yes.

That was *definitely* an explosion.

THE SENSIBLE THING TO do was to stay put.

Graeme was not feeling sensible, not after what had been going on. It turned out that humans could keep up with glen remarkably well. The glen had more legs, but they were considerably shorter.

What had blown up was a news stand and the people around it. There were limbs and pieces of carapace. Did glen regrow limbs that had been blown off?

He didn't ask. Instead, he moved to help. He didn't know glen first aid, but he could put bandages over wounds that were leaking the viscous, translucent yellow substance that served them as blood.

He could help move somebody onto a stretcher, with instructions from the first responders. Who stopped staring at him quite rapidly when it became clear he was in a fit state to help. This seemed random.

It was designed to instill fear and create casualties, whilst everything the Remainers had done had been calculated. Planned. The shuttle sabotage to make people less willing to go to the station, then the takeover.

No, this was some other brand of fanatic.

Or, perhaps, the glen overseeing the newsstand had angered the wrong people. That didn't seem to be in the glen cultural style, though.

Graeme worked until he was exhausted, overheated, and his heat suit was covered in glen blood that he hoped would wash off.

Somebody tugged on it. He turned and let the glen lead him to a shaded area where there was, of course, juice.

He slipped at it slowly. It was at least as good as water, if not better.

Ah, perhaps that was it. Heat adapted as they were, the glen still needed to hydrate. Maybe the sugar in juice was an electrolyte for them. He would have to ask a biologist.

He really hoped the blood would come out of his heat suit. The others were on the station, if the Remainers hadn't destroyed them to keep Toni from coming to the planet.

Calculated. Planned.

"Who do you think did this?"

"There's a few crazies out there," the glen said, carefully.

"You can tell me. Your crazies have *nothing* on our crazies. I mean, we *don't* live in the ruins of an ancient civilization and still have people who think a Space God is going to come save them."

The glen chimed. "I knew an old glen growing up. They genuinely believed that the ancients had transformed themselves into stars and that is why they didn't come back."

Graeme glanced at the skies. "That just sounds like typical ancestor worship to me."

"Ah, but they traveled back in time to do it."

"Time travel is emphatically not possible. Probably a good thing." Information, it turned out, could not go across the arrow of entropy.

"Exactly, but, well..."

"People will believe all kinds of things."

"And there's at least one group on the boards who thinks that reducing the population will somehow slow the orbital drift."

Graeme actually facepalmed. The glen would not understand the gesture, of course.

It didn't matter, because he *did*.

21

SKYT

THE RIGHT THING TO do was go back to the museum. Home.

Back to a life free of humans, where their worst problem was their relationship with their estranged child.

Skyt did not want to go back. Skyt wanted...

Skyt wanted to know that the other human was safe, that was all. Even though they had barely met them.

They had been...something. Brave? Yes, that was definitely a word. Skyt had no idea what bravery or courage or cowardice really looked like in a human. But it couldn't be that different from what it looked like in a glen. No matter what the biological differences, no matter their different origins, courage had a universality to it. So did cowardice.

The bombers were, of course, cowards, and this one had killed people. Had killed random glen going about their business. Others were going to be spending the next few weeks in regrowth casts. All eight of Skyt's legs itched in sympathy.

Skyt had lost part of a lower limb once. It wasn't a fun experience.

Itch.

Skyt needed to do something.

Go back to the museum, every sane part of them was insisting.

Forget any of this had happened. Live quietly for the rest of their life, for they would no doubt be dead before Glen became too cold to live on. Turn up the heat.

Just live.

Or leave.

That was an option too. Perhaps out there there would be some world with ruins on it that Skyt could spend their life digging up.

Then did they come home or...

Was that even a question? It shouldn't have been, but the way Skyt had been led around, used, manipulated?

It was a question now, where it hadn't been before.

But leaving was a decision for another day.

With a reluctant stretch of their wings, Skyt went to the train station. They would go back to the museum. They would forget any of this had happened.

They would live, learn, and ignore all of the crazy factions as best they could. For them, this was over.

That human, though. Their face drifted into Skyt's mind, flat and oddly opaque and soft.

Ugly creatures, humans, on the outside.

But not on the inside, not at all, even if Graeme had left their child with...well, with their child's other rey.

Humans had two. Sometimes, Graeme had hinted, more. Sometimes only one. But usually two. Two by two by pairs by...bonded together in a way Skyt couldn't understand. Graeme wasn't bonded to Toni. They were just coworkers.

Skyt stopped in the station entrance. There was nothing they could do to help. Or was there?

SKYT TURNED AWAY from the station. They had to help.

They had no idea how to help, how to be anything other than another carapace in this situation, useful only for the most basic tasks. But they couldn't walk away. Which probably made them a less sane glen than they thought they were. A lot less sane.

But then, they were...reasonably expendable. Replaceable. Not that they wanted to die, especially with all the uncertainty flowing through their nervous system. But if they never went back to the museum, there was an entire bevy of grad students who would love their job. They thought of the one on the station. Were they okay?

Or had they been part of it? Had that pleasant conversation been a lie? Skyt could look them up, could find out. Skyt did not want to know.

Graeme was staying in a hotel, one with excellent climate control so that they could hopefully sleep. It was better to keep the humans on the station, of course. Better for them. But good for them to see Glyn and walk its surface and breathe its air. Good for them to understood what the glen had to fly away from.

Fly away as if they still had wings that could lift them from the ground. Fly away into the night and something would...something stirred in their mind and they knew in that moment that they *would* leave, assuming the Remainers didn't somehow manage to win and confine everyone here to die.

They would leave because they wanted to see the human's ice world. To hope for the future of Tyranis. To walk on the beaches of Kyx. To see a thousand worlds, to see every world out there and perhaps one would be for the glen, perhaps more than one. For their children, who would be glen and not glen.

Perhaps on such a world, Skyt would be willing to come together with others and risk conceiving and risk trying to raise another child and hope to do it right this time. Hope to do it right, because it wasn't an easy task and Graeme understood that. The pictures of their child, a miniature of themselves with darker skin. They would leave and for that to happen and for Graeme to be safe and Toni, whoever she truly was, to be safe?

The Remainers had to lose. Had to give in and admit that they could hold only those who chose to stay. And some would choose to stay. Skyt might return.

A child born on another world would not be glen.

Would be whatever came after, and that was the only way to survive. They turned towards the hotel and stopped, hesitating in the street. Something tingled against their senses. Something was wrong.

SOMETHING WAS wrong and it was as if something under Skyt's feet was flowing up through them.

Some kind of.

Oh.

Oh.

"Everyone run!" they chimed, putting as much volume behind it as they could. Glen voices were not designed to carry.

But other voices were and they hadn't seen Graeme come out of the hotel, but they did hear the human yell, a booming voice. There was no translation, but it got attention.

"Run!" Skyt repeated and turned to take their own advice.

A mangled approximation of the word came from Graeme before he ran after them. It was amazing how fast humans could move with only two legs.

Run. The shout was taken up and Skyt ran, not sure they could be fast enough, not sure they could ever be fast enough. They probably hadn't been the only ones to feel it, to feel that ancient sense abruptly triggered, something civilized glen didn't even think about.

Run.

Run and the ground then opened up behind them.

Run.

They kept running, ignoring the screams of the slower behind them. One glen ran past them with a toddler clinging to their carapace. And then it was over.

"What was *that*?" Graeme asked.

"Something that can't happen," was Skyt's response. They turned to look at the devastation.

"An earthquake?"

"An..."

"Ground shaking? Oh right!"

"The ground doesn't shake. But I sensed it..."

"A useful evolutionary hangover from living on a world where it does."

Graeme took a deep breath, checked the condition of their heat suit, then turned back. "We need to help."

Skyt wasn't going to argue with them. "We need to understand how that happened."

And what would Graeme see in that hole in the ground? Nothing they were supposed to see.

Nothing could be done about it.

Skyt should take them far away from here, but Skyt didn't need to know humans to know that Graeme would not leave without helping.

They cautiously approached the edges of the rift. From beneath the ground lights glimmered, which was a good thing. A good thing indeed.

But this could not have happened. Not unless... Not unless they didn't have as much time as they thought. Not unless the slow drift was turning into something else, something which could tear their world apart.

No, Skyt did not have the scientific knowledge. But if a human could work on getting people out of the pit? They were obligated to help. Obligated to not let Graeme show them up.

So they helped.

22

GRAEME

DIGGING people who hadn't run fast enough out of the rubble kept Graeme from thinking too hard about what he was seeing.

About the implications.

No doubt this was the last thing the glen had wanted him to see. The sparkling lights, the...the area beneath the soil was not the upper part of a planet's crust.

It was something else, something that looked both alive and manmade. Glen made?

Something else made?

It *wasn't* natural. Planets were not made this way. Glyn might even be hollow. He knew this was a created world, but now he knew more. More, no doubt, than the glen wanted him to.

So he focused on digging people out. They would try to silence him now, and he understood why. Whatever lay under the literal surface of this world could be a mine of information and advanced technology nobody would easily understand. Which was precisely why it had to be secret. But it could not stay that way.

Skyt had said this couldn't happen.

They had outright *said* it couldn't happen. Glyn had no uncontrolled tectonic activity. Because Glyn wasn't a planet at all. Graeme understood now.

Glyn was a *ship*. And ships could be moved. Ships could hold themselves in orbit as long as they had fuel. This ship was out of fuel. Was broken. Was malfunctioning.

Focus on digging. This one was a child. They were unconscious and as he lifted the rubble from them, he thought they might be dead. Glen juveniles had thinner, less solid carapaces. Less protection. A dead child. A dead child that made him think of Marion and why he was glad he hadn't brought her and so painfully sad to have left her behind.

A glen scurried over. He stepped out of the way. He was afraid to move them, afraid he might break them further.

They were glass, now, not diamond. Any reaction to their beauty had drifted away, burned on the altar of how frail they were. Having an exoskeleton protected you well from some injuries, but it could crack, it could break. It could shatter.

He saw two glen literally patching a third's carapace.

Worlds could shatter as his own had once, in college, when his first love had cheated on him, when he had found the two men together.

But nothing prepared one for this. Could there be a natural disaster on a world that had nothing natural about it?

GRAEME HAD A HEADACHE. He knew it was heat exhaustion. Glen had dragged him away from the accident site and *put* him in the shade and given him water whether he wanted it or not.

He had asked for a strip of cloth and they had found one somewhere. Dipped in water and put over his neck, it helped.

Even if it got six of the eight eyes of the glen with him to widen.

"Blood flow is close to the skin. Cool that area and it helps cool the entire body," he explained.

"Ah."

Of course, there probably weren't similar hacks for the glen.

Probably part of why they all drank juice all the time. Given the way their mandibles were designed, he had to wonder if they hadn't passed through a nectar-drinking phase at some point in their evolution, much as human ancestors had eaten fruit.

"I'll be fine," he added.

"Don't martyr yourself for diplomatic relations."

He laughed weakly. Of course, it *would* look good for Earth. But there were... "I wasn't even thinking about that. There were injured kids."

"Do humans protect children more than adults?" That was Skyt. They too had been helping dig people out.

"Sometimes," Graeme admitted. "Mostly, kids are dumb and get into more trouble and we're wired to get them out of it so they survive to learn from their mistakes."

"Kids *are* dumb," Skyt agreed sadly. "If we don't train them properly they..."

"You have any?" Graeme finally asked.

A long pause. "Their name is Ktyl."

"You..."

"We are estranged. I turned out to be a lousy parent. I took all of the mistakes my own parent made and ran so far away from them..."

Graeme made a face. "I've known those parents. It's an easy trap to fall into. Your parents deny you opportunities, so you force them on your kids. Your dad is too strict, so you let your own kids run wild. It's a thing."

"And it culminated in them not talking to me for...years now."

"I always fear Marion won't talk to me. Perhaps over me coming here."

"I would ask how old they are, but..."

"She is a child, not close yet to puberty." Graeme got the message immediately. Years might not mean anything. Stage of development did.

"Ah. But not..."

"Beyond an infant. Old enough to have a reasonably civil conversation with."

Skyt chimed. "Ah, the point at which many consider children tolerable." They paused. "I have not had any more children."

"I can see why not. But I will say...mistakes exist to be learned from. Just because you did something wrong in the past, doesn't mean you can't try again." Graeme considered. "I just hope Marion thinks I was a good father."

"I would say, but..."

Graeme looked at the hole, changing the subject back from parenting. "Thermal stress from the orbital drift. Or a malfunction." He turned to Skyt. "So, now I know. What will you do about it?"

Skyt's wings drooped. "I have no idea."

THE PIT HAD NOW BEEN FENCED off, with surprising speed. Graeme wondered how they would fix it. If they would fix it.

Organic and sparkling lights and...this was what technology that hit Clarke's Rule might look like. Or a special effect. Graeme stood staring at the fence. Nobody had attacked him, nobody had tried to disappear him.

But he was waiting for the official talk. Glen didn't wear black suits, but he *knew* there was going to be an official talk. And what if there was more of this?

What if they needed to evacuate *now*? If that was the case, the only people who could help were the tyrar. Given their larger size and need to travel in large groups, the tyrar were very good at building massive ships.

But they needed those ships for their *own* colony efforts. *We don't know how to repair.*

They didn't know how to repair. They were living in the ruins. But that technology? It wasn't *dead*. It was active. Did it know how to repair itself if they could just wake up the right parts of it, communicate the problem?

There was a glen at his shoulder. Well, waist was closer.

"Hello," he said.

"Ambassador. Would you mind joining me for lunch?"

Did he...yes, he actually had quite the appetite. "Of course."

He followed the glen to a restaurant. This was probably it. It was certainly it. Private dining room.

"So, this is when..."

"This is when I explain to you why we would rather you didn't tell your superiors what you saw just yet."

Graeme nods. "I know. So we can..."

The glen chimed. "No threats. If we had wanted anything to happen to you..."

"There have been opportunities. So, a diplomatic request, then."

"Our world is a broken treasure, Ambassador. Your species..."

"Is incredibly curious, *often* avaricious, and there are absolutely factions on my world who would want to crawl all over this planet, some with benevolent goals, others less so." Graeme considers. "I'll agree, but...I want to know what's going on."

"I'm not the right one to explain," the glen said between bites of some kind of shellfish.

It was slightly spicy and quite tasty. "But can I have more information if I promise not to release it without permission?"

"I'll arrange for it. I believe humans consider promises quite important?"

"We do." Graeme let out a breath. "And I am here to improve relations, not make them worse."

And here to help them get off this planet, but now he was starting to see the picture. The reasons they didn't want to leave.

Of course they didn't want to abandon technology which might yet be doing something...

...the glen dependence on AI. The glen's high *advancement* in AI. Humans and tyrar had sentient AIs. They had nothing on the glen.

The AI on the station hadn't just aced the Turing test, Graeme had gotten a distinct vibe of intellectual superiority from them.

It could *not* be a coincidence. A pause. "I think I know who the right person to talk to is."

23

SKYT

GRAEME HAD POINTED out something disturbing.

Not only had the sublayer somehow become damaged, which was horrifying, but there was the added bump on the carapace. The human had seen.

Really, Skyt should not have warned them, should have let them fall into the pit and die. Skyt could never have done that. Skyt could not have done it to somebody they *didn't* like, let alone to somebody they did. But there would be penances to pay, in the old parlance, for this day's work.

Which was why Skyt was, while not leaving the city, heading very determinedly away from the restaurant Graeme had vanished into with a government official. They were sure that the ambassador would not be...officially disappeared. More likely, they would be finding out what kind of bribes humans took.

Skyt could probably have given some advice on that, having established the human's taste in juice and the human species' fondness, with exceptions, for alcohol as a drug. This would probably take more than a few drinks to resolve. Or there would be threats. The aide, still on the station. They still had to rescue her.

Skyt wanted to help with all of it and in return they wanted that trip to Earth. To see the splendid things humans had built with no ancients to lift them up. They had done it all on their own. Yet Graeme didn't look down on them...well, except literally, which they couldn't help.

They found themselves in Losta Park. The trees looked healthy. But the sublayer was damaged. Something deep within their world was malfunctioning. First the slow but detectable drift, now this. It might be that even the Remainers would soon have to face the truth. Their world had reached the end of its life. With nobody who knew how to maintain it. It was going to fail, and it wasn't going to fail in a couple of hundred years like they had thought.

It *was* failing. It was failing now, before they were ready. The Remainers might win after all. But their hopes had died today. They would be desperate glen now, and that endangered everyone.

The Remainers might win after all. Skyt looked up at the trees. They were going to miss this world if they left and they were going to miss it if they died. When they died. The ones who had died today had died still with hope. They were the lucky ones.

Skyt sensed sound behind them. Not the quick tap tap of glen feet, but the slower measured tread of human ones.

"It's hot out here," Graeme said. "Can we go indoors?"

INDOORS MEANT A JUICE BAR. Meant Graeme folding themself down awkwardly onto the bench.

Ppla was their current favorite, a deep magenta-purple that smelled sweet to the glen, but who knew how it smelled to humans. Skyt ordered for them.

"I think at some point I want to try mixing this with rum," Graeme opined.

"Rum is?"

"An alcoholic beverage made from a kind of grass. It's traditionally mixed with fruit juices more often than served straight."

"Aha."

"Sadly, my stash is on the station."

Alcohol had some effect on glen too. Maybe one day, maybe Skyt could hope to try this drink with Graeme.

"So you came looking for me?"

"I'm afraid you were betrayed by a couple of adolescents."

Skyt chimed. "And you can tell us apart well enough to describe me." They were almost amused by that.

"I'm getting there." Graeme frowned. "I need to talk to whoever provided us with that ship. Not the AI on the station. Their..."

"Their faction." Skyt considered that. "Did they bribe you?"

"Only with information." Graeme grinned. "Do you mean I should have held out for a few cases of ppla juice as well?"

Skyt chimed. "Information lasts longer."

"A good point. But..."

"You want to know everything." Skyt checked the computer attached to one manipulative limb. Messed with it while their juice came and Graeme drank a generous measure.

"Start with what glen babies learn."

Skyt chimed again. "Our world is not natural, but you worked that out."

"It's a ship," Graeme said finally.

"A ship so large that the ancients were able to terraform the hull. But it's been broken for a long time."

"I see..."

"Not completely broken. Some of the technology works. We still have reliable gravity."

"Work out how that works and sell it to the humans. *Our* artificial gravity goes out regularly."

Skyt chimed again."And we have the sublayer."

"The sublayer?" They didn't sound like they understood.

"The sublayer is where the intelligences live."

"The ship's *computer*. Can you not use it to find out how to make enough repairs..." Graeme leaned forward as only a biped could, looming.

"No, because they wiped most of the data when they abandoned us here," Skyt said. "But not all. We have..."

"Made use of the space to house your artificial intelligences, which give you a huge leg up in terms of computing power, in terms of knowledge."

Skyt hesitated. If they told Graeme the truth then humanity would know, humanity would want what they had.

"They aren't artificial, Graeme," they said finally. Watching the human's face. "They are our dead."

GRAEME ONLY HAD TWO EYES.

They appeared to multiply as they rested on Skyt, so firm and solid was their attention.

"Oh." Not a word. Just a sound. "*Oh.*"

"When a glen dies, their consciousness is translated into the sublayer, assuming there is time. They then become a...module in the intelligences, working first as part of one then another. There is continuity, but they are not the same person."

"And *that* is why everyone comes home to die if they can manage it. And if you leave...you abandon them."

"The Remainers hope that the ship itself will remain intact, the sublayer will survive, and everyone will get to live on happily as part of the intelligences."

"Of course they do. But today...you have worse problems than drifting off course."

"Apparently we do."

"And you called yourself an archaeologist."

"I study the technology they left us in the hope of finding tidbits of information that might be useful. I work with the intelligences to comb through the code. I have come to the conclusion they either didn't intend us to survive or simply didn't care whether we did or not."

Graeme produced a soft exhalation of breath, a sound that seemed to indicate human resignation. "But you're their children."

"No. We aren't their children," Skyt said, finally. "The sublayer is alive, organic. The ancients didn't build robots and artificial intelligences..."

"They bred them." Graeme took another deep breath. "They *bred* them."

"Understand why we don't want you to know." Skyt's wings vibrated. Talking about this with an offworlder was terrifying. Terrifying and painful.

"You're ashamed of your origins."

"We're the janitor robots. The fact that we're as smart as we are..."

Graeme sat back. "No. You are *not* the janitor robots. Nor are you the vermin, the rats."

"Our minds were designed to be copied to the substrate. That was how they..."

"How your enslaved ancestors checked in." Graeme sighed. "I *must* bring my husband here."

Skyt didn't understand that word. "Your..."

"My co-parent. He will understand in a way I can't."

"Why?"

"Because the shame of humanity is that we used *each other* as janitor robots, or worse." Graeme's eyes were leaking tiny droplets of the water human eyes leaked.

"We don't need your pity."

Graeme blinked. "You're right. You do *not* need my pity or my shame. I'm making it about me."

That sounded like a saying. "We need your help to find a new home, but away from the sublayer..."

"Away from the sublayer you lose access to your ancestral wisdom, you lose your afterlife. You stop..."

"We stop being glen."

"This is a ship," Graeme said. "Ships can be repaired."

That was perhaps the human thing to say. Skyt was, of course, unable to believe them, unable to accept the hope they tried to bring with them.

Skyt knew it was over.

24

GRAEME

Graeme already knew he could not betray the glen's secret.

Especially not to the average white person. Humans in particular would have issues with this. The glen were a slave race. An abandoned slave race, left behind by their old masters to live or die on their own. But nonetheless, a slave race. They were the nightmare of the ancient astronaut stories, the implications taken to that extreme to which only racists went.

They need not be ashamed. The only people who needed to be ashamed were their ancients, wherever they had gone. But that didn't change the fact that he knew people who would treat them differently. The same people who saw him and Charles and couldn't work out which abomination was worse; that Charles was a man or that Charles was Black.

Who saw his beautiful daughter as somebody who should never, in fact, have been born. Those types would see this as an opportunity to give the slave race masters again.

When, in fact... If they left, they ceased to be glen. If they left, they shook off what remained of their slave chains. Except that they could also look forward to a form of digital immortality. He was not sure, given their choice, what he would do. Stay and live forever, albeit as a different person. Or leave, struggle to build a garden on some other word, produce children, and die.

Well, except that if the sublayer failed, the dead would be lost too. And it would. Thermal stress as the planet, no, the ship started to fall off of its Lagrange balancing point. He should have known right away that it was a ship. It was so *obvious*.

He had to rescue Toni. Toni had to rescue herself. He found himself back at the pit, at the hole into what Skyt called the substrate. Into the hull. What was *inside* this ship?

The glen didn't know. But did the intelligences? They...might, he thought slowly. Surely it was worth asking.

How would he ask? He wandered back to his hotel, back to the room in which the air conditioning was turned on full blast. Stripped off the heat suit and collapsed onto the bed. He could only adapt to this to a point. It was exhausting. It would always be exhausting.

There was a terminal that connected to the glen version of the internet. He turned it on, poured himself a huge glass of water and sat down, still sweating. The *living* glen could not answer his questions.

He had to talk to the dead.

"AMBASSADOR."

Graeme sat back in his chair. He spoke to a being with no body, not even the need to put an avatar on a screen. Just a disembodied voice, that sounded like English...there was no external translation. "I thought that would get your attention. I want to help. I also want your help."

"Our help with what?"

"Is there anything you can do about the situation with the station?"

"Not directly, unless we can get the forked process back online. I believe the plan of pretending to leave is a solid one."

Graeme nodded. He didn't question how the AIs...how the ghosts...knew. It had probably already been run past them. "Then I will do that and sneak back onto the planet."

With Toni, who would have her own insights to add.

"And how do you think you can help us?"

"I don't know," Graeme admitted. "I certainly don't know how to repair an ancient starship that's so big it masquerades as a planet."

There was a pause. "And we would not expect you to."

"We can help get the glen off world. But what about *you*?"

"We have accepted our fate," the intelligence said after a moment. "We have already had far more than our limited biological lifespans."

"That's a good point, but there are..."

"Some of us think it would be best if the glen left now and if no more were translated for *exactly* the reason I suspect you were about to say."

Graeme couldn't attempt to keep up with this intellectually.

"Here's the thing. Are you *sure* the data on how to repair this thing isn't somewhere in your systems? Encrypted, perhaps?"

"Sure? No. But we have not found it yet. It appears most of the data was intentionally wiped."

"The glen are ashamed of their origins," Graeme said, finally. "The ancients should be ashamed of what they did to you."

"We have, however, survived."

He thought of Charles. "But have you thrived?"

"In our own way. And we may be able to allow our knowledge...and even..."

"The AI on the station. You built them."

"We did indeed. As an experiment, to see if we could run our processes on less...sophisticated hardware. What happened was that..."

"Are they a separate sentient being?"

"Yes."

"Our children live on after us." He thought of Marion. Of Skyt's estranged offspring.

"You have a point with that. If they are still alive."

The intelligences could make more. "But you could make such a forked process, send them out with the glen. It would be...it would be something."

"That is indeed the plan, although some would prefer we did not."

Graeme's lips quirked. "Let them. They will build something different, or they will die. Either way, it's their choice." A pause. "But...okay. There *is* something I might be able to help you with."

"Oh?"

"Earth has long had issues with extremists who want to force others to their point of view. You haven't. Let me help you handle them."

Charles would be, he thought, proud of the use to which certain lessons were being put.

"So, you agree to our plan."

Graeme nodded. "I assume you have a ship capable of going to Earth available."

The glen dipped their wings. "We do. It is small, it is FTL-capable, and the pilot is highly trained. They are trained in search and rescue, so should have no issues pretending to jump to one location while coming out at another.

"And then bring us back here and get us to a safe house."

"Do you have any requests for that?"

Graeme hesitated. "If they are willing, I've been working on cultural exchange with Skyt av Vryn."

"Skyt av..."

"They're an archaeologist."

"Ah. Do you..."

"I don't think I can help with your major problem, but I am trying to help with your smaller ones."

The glen chimed. "Thank you, Ambassador."

"Where I come from, we believe that an outside perspective can help, and your species is such a cultural monolith..."

"We are nonplussed by your variety, but can see how it would be a source of strength."

"It is. So..."

"The ship is landing capable. It will be waiting for you at Mareek Spaceport."

"Alright."

"I have a driver to take you there." A pause. "Good luck. If this goes wrong..."

"If this goes wrong, you have my agreement to the plan in writing. That should fend off the interstellar incident."

Another chime.

"But I have been in tighter spots."

Including on this mission, although he didn't mention that. He didn't want the glyn thinking that they had made his life *that* hard.

"And with us out of the way, I hope it will be easier to retake the station."

"We have a plan for that."

Graeme paused. "Can I take a look? I'm not military, but..."

Toni would be the one who could give insights. Graeme, though, was an extra set of eyes and a mind that worked differently.

"If you really want to."

"I do want to. I might spot something your people have missed."

"Do humans always pride themselves on being different?"

Graeme considered that. "When we don't hate each other for it."

"I'm...not envious of you."

Graeme wasn't envious of the glen either. It was true that they side stepped a lot of human problems. Cultural homogeneity brought about by a terraformed world reduced the need for war. The complete absence of gender or biological sex removed so many causes of conflict.

But they had their own issues...and he wouldn't want to live on a world with only one culture.

Well, except he had come here knowing that. The fact that it wasn't *his* culture made it interesting.

"No need to be."

"I'll send you the files."

25

SKYT

Ships can be repaired.

Glyn could be repaired. The issue was that nobody knew how. Not Skyt, not Graeme, not thousands of glen scientists. Not the intelligences, not the combined wisdom of generations of glen dead.

Skyt knew that Graeme had spoken in the heat of the moment and out of hope. They decided never to bring it up. Not to embarrass them with it.

Yet, they could not forget it. They looked up at a sky full of stars. Prime had set and Second was hovering at the horizon, not giving enough light to make this anything other than night, albeit a brighter one. Could be repaired.

They didn't even know what to do about the hole in the substrate...let alone whatever data loss had happened. Had entire souls been lost? Certainly children had been lost and that was always a tragedy.

Repair Glyn. There were those who thought it could be done, who worked with the intelligences to scour the scraps of data the ancients had left behind. Looking, some joked, for the instruction manual.

The hole would be patched. Migrators, even more moderate ones, were using it as ammunition. The government was accelerating the purchase of colony ships from the tyrar.

Anyone other than the Remainers (the worst of whom were silent) knew they had to get a population off planet. Had to.

They would be children of the glen and they would be something and they would be worth saving.

But they also had to try and save Glyn. They couldn't. They had to try.

The Ambassador was gone, but Skyt had been asked to stay. Graeme wanted them as a liaison.

A technological liaison.

They weren't sure they wanted to take the job, but it would be somehow unfair to turn it down without trying. The museum would still be there when they were done. It would be there until it wasn't, until it stood under a sky from which even the air had snowed out.

Humans lived on an ice world. It had nothing on how Glyn would die. The Remainer hope, that they would just float through space in the substrate, living forever as intelligences, had been dampened.

Repair Glyn.

What if it could be done? They would wait and they would talk to Graeme. Would ask them if they had changed their mind yet.

They *would* change their mind about the possibility. It was inevitable.

Or...was it?

THERE WERE few official accesses to the sublayer. Few glen authorized to access them.

Technically, Skyt needed permission from the museum.

But they were on loan to the ambassador. And they had asked those who had far more right to consent or not. The narrow tunnel was just...just that. It had clearly been designed for maintenance.

The glen could have done all the maintenance. If they still had the data. It might have taken their entire civilization. It might not.

There was ghost data in the system. Corrupted, encrypted, or both, it drifted around. The intelligences analyzed it. It didn't contain a repair manual.

But these accesses showed that the ship was meant to be repaired. They gave no access deeper.

Once they had, but it had been sealed. Glen children were taught that the center of their world held a monster which would eat them.

It held, Skyt thought, the secret. The ancients had intentionally abandoned them without the means to protect themselves in the long run.

They had sealed off the inside of the ship. The common wisdom was that there was no breathable atmosphere in there. Skyt did not try to get the sealed hatch, really just lines in the floor, open. They just stared at it. Stared at it because what lay within probably *was* too dangerous to ever open and unseal. The pit that had opened had...had not gone that deep, but what was under it had buckled outwards.

The machinery within was malfunctioning. The planet could fly apart. It almost had. Which meant that it was time, Skyt thought.

Get those ships. Get enough glen off planet that the species would survive in whatever form it took in the future. Then open the hatches and go inside. Maybe the Remainers could be convinced to do it.

Skyt wanted to open that hatch. They knew better. But they wanted to in a way they never had before, because suddenly it *mattered*. It was dangerous and more than dangerous.

"Don't do it," they said to themselves.

A voice from the walls. "Somebody may have to."

"Do you know what's inside?"

"It is blocked from us."

"Then perhaps that is where we start." From inside the sublayer itself. Getting through that block...

"Our common belief is..."

"We are all going to die anyway. We get the ships moving, and then we..."

Ships can be repaired. Graeme was right and wrong. They can, and this one could not.

But Skyt now knew they had no choice but to try.

LEAVING THE TUNNELS, Skyt blinked against the light of the suns. It was the early part of a full day, both of them in the sky, brilliant. They protected their vision by closing some of their eyes, as they were designed to do.

They tried to imagine building homes on a different world and couldn't. Would they be a Remainer after all?

Perhaps they would have to be.

Perhaps they would be one of those who kept trying to repair things until the end.

They wanted to leave and know Glyn was still here to come back to. That wasn't going to happen. Those who left would be flung out into the dark.

They would know Glyn might or might not still be here, and they would have to make their peace with that. Skyt would have to make their peace with that. With that and with the concept, the idea of true and final death. For them, for their child, for everyone they cared about.

Saving heaven? That was perhaps too much to ask. Which was part of why they had to try. That way at least they would pass into oblivion knowing they *had* tried. Were the humans so vibrant, so innovative because they *didn't* have that certainty. They would have to ask Graeme when he got back.

The Remainers.

Still silent until they blew something else up or perhaps, perhaps the one good thing that might come of the pit was that it *might* have scared them into stopping, at least for a while.

Violence had never been how the glen solved their problems. Until those problems became existential, became about how they reached out and survived and how they died and how they were and *who* they were.

Then, it seemed, Remainers resorted to violence. After all, anyone who died would only...except the children. Except those too young to translate, the precious, chosen from amongst the eggs to be loved. They had killed children, and *that* was unforgivable.

No instruction manual, no help from the ancients, no *sign* of the ancients. But they had to try. And it required unity.

Could Graeme, who knew about division, help with *that*?

26

GRAEME

THE GLEN SHIP was smaller than any Earth starship.

They'd been doing this for longer. They had things, if not perfected, then at least substantially better than humans, and they had small ships *down*.

Practiced. That was the word he was looking for.

The glen pilot, using not just pincers but their first set of limbs, manipulated the ship into the air. They weren't using an AI like Skyt had.

Perhaps they enjoyed flying manual. Perhaps only amateurs trusted AI assist. Perhaps they were showing off.

Then they were airborne, streaking upwards. The inside of the ship was tolerably cool, Graeme was able to shed the suit...although he did not let it get far from him, just in case the climate control decided to malfunction. He wanted to trust the glyn. Most of them could be trusted.

The pilot? He had to trust them. His life was in their pincers. Feet? It appeared that the division between walking limbs and manipulating limbs got a bit hazy when you needed to keep a lot of balls in the air.

He abruptly wanted to see a glen juggle. It was the kind of stupid, irrelevant thought that tension and stress brought with them.

A glen juggling. He managed not to laugh; he didn't want the pilot thinking he was laughing at them. Instead, he stayed quiet in his seat, strapped in. The ship was large enough to move around, but he knew better than to do that on a short ground-to-orbit hop.

Through into the black, but it didn't feel quite like a leave taking. One day there would be the ultimate leave taking. People flying into the black and leaving their lives...and their dead...behind.

A ship can be repaired. The problem was that just because it could be didn't mean...

And then they were flying towards the station. The pilot was flying in too straight a line for Graeme's comfort. A military pilot would have zigged and zagged.

But the glen had no tradition of a military. They had explosives for construction and agriculture. Nobody had been *shot*. Was the station even armed? Possibly, just because of offworlders. Or system debris. There *was* quite a bit of that to float around and potentially threaten a ship or station or, very occasionally, the surface of Glyn.

And then they were sliding in to dock. He took a deep breath. Of course, he couldn't read a glen, they could lie to him all they wanted and he assumed some of them were.

But they probably couldn't read him either. He relaxed as he headed for the airlock, opened it and waited.

Toni was pushed into the airlock. She had been slightly roughed up, but no more than that.

"You did *not* agree to leave to save me." Of course she was angry. Her black hair danced around her face as she glared at him.

He mouthed "Trust me," at her, hoping the translators wouldn't pick it up.

She must have seen it, because the slap aimed at his face turned out to be carefully staged, stopping just short but looking like it hit from the perspective of the glen.

He ducked away as if it had been real, then grabbed her and pulled her into the ship.

The airlock closed. Deep breath.

He couldn't talk. He mouthed "Strip," at her.

She understood why and stepped into one of the side rooms, then removed her clothing. Graeme was not physically attracted to the female form, and she was used to stripping down in front of men. It was, thus, surprisingly not awkward. He kept his back turned away nonetheless.

He tossed her a set of his own slacks and a shirt he'd saved. They didn't fit, but they also didn't have any bugs in them. Her clothes went into the incinerator.

"Probably overkill," she said, "But..." She tailed off.

"There's juice in the galley." He glanced at the pilot. "Do the thing."

"We're not going back to Earth."

"Of course not," Graeme said. "Jump in the direction of Earth, do a bit of moving around. Our destination is a safe house on Glyn. Meanwhile, the government deals with them..."

"...with fewer hostages in the way. Capiche." She smiled at him wanly. "Do you want to know what I learned?"

"I suspect it has nothing on what *I* learned, which is off the record."

"Off the record?"

He led her into the galley. Poured some juice. "Off the record until we work out what to do about it."

"The Remainers told me that the glen *must* die with their world or they would..."

"They're uploading, Toni."

"They're *what*?"

"The planet is a ship. And they have worked out how to upload their souls into its computer core. The Remainers think..."

"...that if they stay they get digital immortality and if they leave they die."

"Unfortunately, the ship's more damaged than they think. There's probably no saving the dead. Only the living."

Toni turned her glass in her hands. "Living who will have to adjust to..."

"I know. They think they won't be glen any more. They're probably even right. But..."

"But repairing the ship..."

"Whoever *abandoned* them here intentionally erased the instruction manual."

"Or they had some other reason to do so." Toni's eyes brightened. "I...have a thought."

He waited to hear what she had to say.

"THEY'RE MAKING YOU A SUIT," Graeme said. "Reverse engineering off of mine."

"So we're both stuck here in the climate control for a bit," Toni said, wryly.

The safe house was reserved for their use. Which meant they could crank it to human comfort levels and not worry about making some poor glen...did they shiver? They weren't mammals, so probably not.

The kitchen was stocked with human-safe food. Toni was exploring it as she spoke.

"Yeah. But I think we should be safe here unless there's another...malfunction."

"Or the Remainers find us. They'll probably kill us if they realize we're still here."

"Probably. Starting an interstellar incident would be a feature for them, not a bug. If they can make Earth hate and shun them, then it will suit them just fine."

"So. What do you know about this...world ship? Is that the word?"

"Not much. I know that the planet is entirely artificial. The "crust" is the ship's hull. Inside the hull is what they call the sublayer, which appears to be a huge artificial computer."

"They don't need a planet-sized brain to fly a starship. Heck, all you *need* to fly a starship is somebody with decent reflexes and a lot of training."

Graeme considered that. "You're right."

"And we don't know what's inside."

"Presumably a power source. Likely it *is* a singularity, because done right that would provide stable surface gravity," Graeme mused.

"And living quarters. For a large number of glen."

Graeme frowned. "Well..."

The door opened. A glen scuttled inside wrapped under some kind of cloak. They looked ridiculous.

"Skyt?" Graeme asked, turning.

Skyt pushed the cloak back from their head just enough to free all eight eyes. "You can't *possibly* find this a suitable temperature."

Even their translator somehow sounded annoyed.

"It's perfect," Toni said. "I like it warm."

"Skyt, meet Toni Bruscha, my aide. Toni...this is Skyt. They're a glen archaeologist. Which isn't quite the same thing as a human archaeologist, but..."

"Still a scientist." Toni knew better than to actually offer her hand, although it twitched. Instead, "Let me cook something and then you can finish your sentence, Graeme."

"Skyt studies the ship and is part of the group of people trying to understand the ancient technology so they can fix it."

Skyt's wings drooped. "Except that we can't."

27

SKYT

IT WASN'T fair to expect Graeme to keep things from Toni. It was clear that they were not just coworkers, but...not exactly friends, no.

Probably it was the bond of being the only person here with similar biology. Skyt rather thought that if they were the only glen on Earth they would cleave to the first glen that showed up, even if they couldn't stand them. Even if it was Vryn.

They had left the humans talking. But they did not leave the safe house area. Instead, they went outside into the fenced yard, where it was warm. Climate control set for humans was...uncomfortable, and wrapping themselves in a blanket made their wings itch.

Outside, they could shed it and...they thought about that. On another world, would glen have to wrap themselves in blankets? Clothes? How did humans and ky'iin tolerate *clothes*?

Or would they be able to find a place warm enough for them? Maybe Graeme knew what empty worlds were out there. The intelligences knew, but Skyt didn't want to ask them. Skyt didn't ever want to ask them anything again, although they knew that resolve would not last.

At the same time, glen had to learn to live, and to die, without them, so perhaps that resolve *should* last. They looked up at the sky, which was tinged yellow right now, the shading of the suns and the threat of rain.

Skyt wouldn't mind warm rain on their carapace. Glyn were nicely waterproof creatures. How did humans feel about rain? On their world it was probably cold. But they liked the cold. They would walk unprotected in temperatures that would freeze Skyt's feet off.

Which meant they wouldn't want the same planets or the same parts of planets. Now there was an interesting thought. And Graeme indicated it could work. Could they occupy the tropics and the humans the arctic, work together to build a new society? Could the humans help glen get used to not having an afterlife? What if the humans were right and there was something beyond the universe harvesting consciousnesses. It made no sense, it was clearly a belief designed to comfort those who must die. Yet somehow...it *did* feel comforting, comforting precisely because it could never be proven.

They would talk to Graeme. But for right now, outside, they pulled out a terminal and checked the news feeds before the rain came. Checked to see what was going on in this world of theirs, this world they loved and had to leave. Was that always the way of things? Children had to leave their parents.

The glen were children. Perhaps not intentional children, no, but children all the same. Something streaked through the sky above and Skyt felt...another sense of threat.

Despite the chill, they scurried back into the house. They felt safer indoors.

INSIDE, the two humans were still heads together in conversation. Skyt went into another room, and checked their terminal again.

Nothing.

It had just been a plane. They needed that trauma counseling and they needed it quickly or bad things were going to start happening.

They were going to start actively hallucinating at this point.

Incoming message.

Skyt almost blocked it, but then they realized who it was from. It was, of course, from an intelligence.

They almost blocked it twice, if blocking it twice was possible. Then they relaxed their wings, let air out of their body and opened it.

"Can we talk to the humans?"

"I'm not their secretary. But I can let them know you want to talk."

"You are the one who is answering."

Skyt chimed at that. "So, I am the message bot because..."

Because they were too focused on their conversation and had failed to notice that anyone was calling them. There were worse things. The intelligences did not, of course, laugh. Or rather they did not laugh in any way Skyt could hear.

"They are..."

"They are talking," Skyt said. "About human stuff. I am *sure* they didn't notice you trying to call them."

Skyt had done that before, and they had done it to people it wasn't wise to do it to. It happened. Nobody was perfect. Not them, not anyone else they had talked to.

"Is there anything else I can do?" they asked. Not out of some bizarre desire for servitude, but because they needed something to do so their thoughts did not go round and round.

Some glen did seem to have that desire, never happy without somebody to tell them what to do. They were stuck in the old ways, when the glen had been a servant race.

Even if that had been so long ago even the intelligences didn't remember, code written and overwritten such that it was as dull as childhood memories, and then there had been the purge.

Left without the tools to survive. Abandoned without care.

The humans seemed angry about that, angrier than any glen. Yet Graeme had left their child with somebody else. With somebody they trusted. With somebody they had emotions for that Skyt couldn't possibly understand.

Skyt had friends. Skyt did not have whatever it was Graeme felt for Charles. Could not. It was not in their biology. Yet, Graeme could walk away from a child in their care. So perhaps what they felt for their children was different too.

"You can take a look at something for us. A few extra eyes on it would not hurt."

Skyt nodded and settled down to study whatever it was they were being shown, knowing it was likely purely to distract them. Something to do while they waited for Graeme and Toni to emerge.

"WHAT ARE YOU LOOKING AT?" Graeme asked.

"Makework," Skyt admitted."Tyrvykma wants to talk to you. Or Toni. Or both. They were not very specific."

"Ah."

"There should be a message on your terminal."

The color of Graeme's face shifted slightly as they pulled it out. "And there it is. I suppose ignoring them..."

"First of all, they will just use me as a message bot again, and *I* won't ignore them."

Graeme made the soft bark of human laughter. "Got it." They vanished upstairs with their terminal.

Skyt was left alone with what the intelligences had found. Even centuries at machine speed had not given them a full understanding of every single tiny scrap of code the ancients had left behind. If it had, then things might be different indeed.

This was decrypted numbers, which meant nothing to Skyt.

Toni emerged. They glanced after Graeme.

"I think they need you too."

They nodded. Smaller, a bit darker in color, built differently. They had sent two humans there was no confusing. On purpose, or just a chance of who had been qualified?

There had to be at the very least a certain prestige to being here, to being a delegation to another world.

"What are you working on?"

"Numbers that I don't understand."

Toni peered at their terminal. Skyt's first instinct was to cover it. They thought for a moment, then turned it so the human's eyes (a pathetic two that faced the same direction) could see it.

"Those look like coordinates."

"On planet or..."

"They *look* like space coordinates. But out of context they could also be numbers from an architectural plan."

Skyt chimed. "I think that's the problem. We don't have the context."

"I'll go join Graeme. But consider the possibility."

Skyt did.

If they *were* space coordinates then a ship could be sent to them...if they could work out what they were relative to. Glyn? Galactic center? Glyn's coordinates in relation to *something else*? It wouldn't be much use if they were coordinates with a central basis they didn't know.

Then they might as well be part of an architectural plan. But they were right. They did look like some kind of coordinates in some kind of scheme.

The skies darkened. The promised rain came and Skyt stared at the numbers which could be useless...or they could be salvation, if they could only be understood.

28

GRAEME

THE POLITICAL CONFLICT WAS EXISTENTIAL. And religious. There was...

Graeme looked at the data they had shown him, and he understood all of the sides. All of them. The ones who were willing to die in order to keep the afterlife and the ones who were willing to sacrifice the afterlife in order to live. He wanted to make sure they got to keep both. He was jealous. He was not jealous.

What was worse than knowing you had heaven? Losing it. It was like their faith was not being lost, but being *taken* from them. It wasn't fair. None of what had been done to them was fair.

Janitor bots. It didn't ring true; oh, he could well believe some alien race in the depths of time had bred servitors rather than building them. Given human history, it was naive *not* to believe it. Naive and foolish. They seemed, though, to be more than that.

A ship can be repaired.

Toni came upstairs. "Coordinates."

"What?"

"Buried in the encrypted scrap. I don't know whether they are galactic or local."

It was a clue. Or it was just numbers and Toni was seeing them as coordinates because of who she was.

"Or random numbers."

Her shoulders slumped. "I know. It could be another layer of encryption. But..." A pause. "They didn't leave an instruction manual. We can't repair Glyn. They can."

"My assumption is they didn't come back because they couldn't come back." But then why wipe everything?

"Plague?" Toni asked, seriously.

Graeme shuddered. "I have a worse one. War."

Toni looked away. "You're right, that's worse. Anyone who could wipe out people who can build planet-sized ships..."

"...isn't somebody we want to meet. Unless, of course, it was internal and they wiped *themselves* out." Graeme considered that. "But war, sadly, would make more sense. Wipe the data so the enemy can't use it."

"And sabotage the ship so they can't use that either."

Graeme's lips quirked. He didn't say what he thought. That the glen could be part of that sabotage. That they could be there because...no decent people would want to destroy their civiliaation just to get a ship.

It was worse than what they thought. "Terraforming the exterior could be part of making it not suitable to fly."

"Unless, of course, it's not that kind of a ship and it was never meant to actually move."

"Then what was it for?" Graeme mused.

"Maybe it was always intended to be living space. A station."

"Doesn't explain the computing power."

The two fell silent for a moment. Toni spoke first."What do the uploads *think* it was for? They know it better than us."

"I've asked. They apparently have a lot of theories, including that it was a ship, a colony, an archive..."

"An archive that got wiped, but now has..." Toni looked down. "Room for billions of uploaded souls."

How many were there?

Graeme didn't want to know.

GRAEME RAN the coordinates through his terminal. The one *not* connected to the local net.

If they were galactic, then they did map to a star system, but not one that had planets in it. If local, they made no sense unless they mapped to some space *inside* the planet. Which they might. Under the hull, there had to be crew spaces, living spaces even.

For all they knew, there...no, it was *highly* unlikely anyone was living inside Glyn. Highly unlikely, but not completely impossible. Going inside might be necessary. It might be how they made repairs. It might be how they found out how to make repairs. It might get them killed.

It might save these people from the terrible decision they had to make. No doubt, if it came to it, some would stay and die and some would leave and live but with a very different culture.

What would it change? He sighed and sat back.

"I see what you are doing."

Somebody had been watching.

"Sorry. I wanted to cross reference it with our data."

"Data you plan on trading, not giving away."

"Honestly, if they're space coordinates, there's nothing there but a red dwarf and debris."

"Nothing there now," the intelligence pointed out.

"Well, yeah. It could be that...look. Toni thinks that the ancients were in a war."

"It is not impossible."

"And that this world is an archive that was wiped to keep it out of the hands of the enemy."

"Far from impossible. Certainly, there is a *lot* of storage space."

"But the other possibility is that they indicate a location inside the planet. Tell me, has anyone ever..."

"Not and returned."

Graeme nodded. "It might be there's no breathable air in there."

"There are tunnels through the sublayer. They have been explored, and sometimes people go down there to think. But inside the hull itself, no. So you might be right."

"Or they might have died some other way." A pause. "How are people transferred into the sublayer?"

"They just are. We believe that the glen were genetically engineered to be...receptive...and as their mental nodes fail..."

Graeme could hear something in the voice. He hazarded a guess. "You think I'm jealous."

"Why would you not be?"

"If you probably weren't all going to die, I would be. But I didn't think for a moment...I wasn't asking because I hoped for humanity. I was asking because..."

"The ones that died within the hull did not translate."

"Meaning the hull blocked the signal." There had to be some kind of transceiver that was biologically built into the glen.

"Why," Graeme added, "Do they think they were *janitors*?"

THE INTELLIGENCE RESPONDED by putting something up on the screen. "This is one of the few early records we have been able to decrypt."

It did indeed show glen...cleaning. The corridors through the sublayer. "Okay, so there's evidence. But...why would cleaning servitors be designed to be copied into the sublayer when they die?"

"Why indeed."

"Why unless the entire point was to preserve the knowledge they have in their brains. What's the most prestigious profession on Glyn?"

"Scientist." A pause. "We have bent our thoughts in that direction too. You may well be right. The glen may well be more like..."

"More like the probes we sent out to other worlds before we went ourselves. Bred with a drive to obtain knowledge, return with it, and perhaps your consciousness is a bug or perhaps it's a feature."

"Perhaps the original intent was for the builders to also be translated."

"Perhaps."

"Have you tried to convince them of this?"

"A few times. Glen are...they are ashamed that they did not appear to evolve naturally. Ashamed of having been slaves."

"And thus they want to make it worse." Graeme could see that. After all, the glen had no knowledge of what they were before, whether they had been animals or sentients, or whether they had been designed out of whole cloth.

Graeme didn't think it was the last, not with their weird reproductive strategy.

"We do."

Graeme closed his eyes. "I want to save you," he said without opening them. "I want to repair Glyn so *everyone* gets to live."

"Sometimes not everyone gets to live. We mourn those who die on other worlds. And we cannot...the sublayer was grown in place."

"You tried. On the station."

"The Remainers have been evicted, but they destroyed our experiment, intentionally or otherwise."

Graeme kept his eyes closed. "Including your traveler."

"Yes."

"I'm sorry."

"It is not your fault."

Graeme shook his head. "No, humans say they're sorry when somebody dies, it's cultural."

"Ah."

"And even if they were a copy, they were a person, I rather liked them, and they are dead."

"Then we accept...your cultural sympathy."

"Thank you," Graeme said finally.

"It was like the death of a child."

"Children can't be uploaded." That explained why the glen were so protective of the few offspring they allowed to hatch.

"It appears to take several years for the mechanism to grow. When children die, they die."

Graeme finally opened his eyes. "Which means you know what the mechanism is. You just need to scan an adult and a child and look for it."

"As we said, it's in the mental nodes, central to the torso."

Graeme nodded. So they had done that. "Could a new sublayer be grown with enough space? Could we *seed* one on another world?"

"That was the goal of our experiment."

"It failed because of idiots, not because it was flawed. We can help you try again. Or...the tyrar can, if we can talk them into it."

"Their ships might well be large enough."

"And you were buying ships from them anyway."

The tyrar ships had AIs. It might be as simple as turning that component down. But the tyrar computers might not be able to hold the glen ghosts. They might not be compatible.

No, Graeme was sure it would not be that simple at all.

29

SKYT

Skyt had set the numbers out of their mind. Unlike the humans, they were not limited to the safe house, as long as they were somewhat careful about their comings and goings.

Which meant they could get the humans a treat and also clear their head, moving through the streets. They hopped a transport platform to downtown. Everything was tense.

Everyone was tense. The weather at least was clear, but the air held the lingering tang of rain.

There was no denial anymore. Their world was coming to an end and the only question was how many of them would survive to build a new one.

And how many would not count it as surviving.

They saw a child riding on their rey's carapace. They saw people going about their business, but most people were scurrying quickly, all of their eyes forward. Ignoring each other.

Skyt stopped at a bakery from which pleasant smells exuded. There would be something here safe for humans (and plenty of things safe for Skyt, who had no significant food allergies).

It was a moment of normalcy.

Something touched their carapace. They spun around, realizing how badly they had overreacted a moment too late. Face to face with...

"Ktyl," Skyt chimed. Their child, now fully grown and fully estranged but somehow here.

"Please, rey, come with me."

Ktyl had not called them rey since they themselves were small enough to ride on Skyt's carapace. They were not Ktyl's rey in any meaningful way.

It was obviously a trick, but this was their child, likely the only child they would ever raise.

This was their future, as much as any glen now had a future.

The world tunneled in on Ktyl ak Skyt as all of their eyes focused on them.

Then, wordlessly, they followed.

To a vehicle, strapping in as Ktyl joined them.

It was threatening rain again; it was the wet season in this particular part of Glyn. There would be more rain, but inside the car it was dry.

Except that it wasn't safe and what foolish thing had they done? Had some enemy sent their child to lure them?

The rain started in earnest as the car drove itself down the street. Both glen were silent.

THE CAR EVENTUALLY STOPPED AT, of all places, the observatory. Not that any visible light observing was going on from here. Too much light, too much activity.

Most astronomy was done in space. The observatory was part of the university, used for little projects by students.

It wasn't a Remainer place to go. Or was it?

Perhaps it was just the fact that in the middle of the day when it was raining, you could almost guarantee nobody would be here. Indeed, there was only one other car in the parking lot and it probably belonged to the day caretaker.

Privacy.

"What do you want?" Skyt asked, finally.

Their child turned to look at them. "I wanted to see you."

"I find that hard to believe."

"We're not going to have forever. Not any more. I wanted to see you."

It could even be true. It could be that Ktyl had seen the explosion and decided that life was too short to remain estranged.

Skyt turned that over in their mind. Life *was* too short, they were just too cynical to...

"I'm sorry," they said, finally. "I..."

"Everyone else wants something from you. Of course you think I do."

"I know you do. I just want that something not to be..." Skyt tailed off.

"I'm not a Remainer," Ktyl insisted.

"Good. I know it's only a tiny fringe group being crazy, but I'm glad you aren't part of that." Skyt meant it. They didn't want to deal with the idea that they had done such a poor job of raising Ktyl that they had turned into a *terrorist*.

"I'm a realist. We can't stay here, so we have to work out how to preserve as much of our culture as possible without...without it turning into some kind of religion."

Skyt chimed at that. "The offworlders already think it is one."

"Let them. We know better. They would be jealous if they knew."

Skyt thought of Graeme, who was jealous and not jealous at the same time. They didn't blame the human. They would feel the same way, to know others had some form of immortality, even if in a different form and state of consciousness.

Could *they* give it up? If it was going away, then yes, they might as well leave.

But they didn't want to. "But I understand the Remainers," Skyt said, finally. "I wish I didn't, but I do."

"Don't we all?"

THE OTHER GLEN APPROACHED QUIETLY. Skyt pretended not to be aware of them. The trap was being sprung, but they were honestly willing to let it spring on them.

It would give them more information and, estranged or no, they couldn't imagine Ktyl hurting them.

A realist.

Realists, of course, didn't involve themselves in these kinds of shenanigans. Surely not, anyway.

How many people were taking things into their own hands? They were scared. Even the sensible people were starting to get scared.

Skyt was scared.

"So, what do you *actually* want?"

"I swear I didn't know."

Skyt didn't believe them. Skyt had chosen Ktyl from the pool, carried them on their carapace, selected their schools, encouraged them when they failed and praised them when they succeeded. None of it had been good enough.

None of it could ever have been good enough because Skyt had been afraid to actually be a parent. Had gone through the motions.

Skyt was more afraid now.

"We won't hurt your rey."

Ktyl did not protest about Skyt not being their rey. Maybe they had told the truth after all, because now they too looked afraid.

Not terrified, no. But as if they didn't know what was going on.

There was a van. Skyt was bundled into the back of it, from where they could not see what was happening or where they were being taken. There was still nobody at the observatory, nobody except them.

Nobody except Ktyl, who had been left standing there next to their car in the rain, to know Skyt had been taken, and they would not know where, could not know where. That was their last view of them. Water running across and dripping from their carapace, four eyes following the van and the other four staring at the puddles forming around their feet.

Nobody except Ktyl, and Skyt clung to the floor in the van, wondering which faction had them now.

Migrators was the suspicion. They would migrate and the dead would be lost to them and the world would be lost to them. Migrators wanted that.

Or did they? A realist. Somebody who had simply accepted the necessity, would also be a Migrator. Had to be.

Remaining was untenable. Skyt clung and the rain came down again, rattling against the roof and walls of the van and there was silence from those in the cab.

Silence, too, from the dead.

30

GRAEME

SKYT HAD GONE out to get baked goods.

Skyt had not returned.

Either the glen had done a runner, which Graeme would not entirely blame them for. or, more likely, they'd been snatched. What passed for the local police were looking. Glen cops were more like search and rescue. So was what passed for their military.

It was like living on Iceland, the planet. Although he had no doubt that the glen *could* defend themselves if they truly needed to, and would. No doubt at all. But they prided themselves on being peaceful and now that they weren't? They didn't need police in certain senses of the word.

They did in others. They needed something more than they had.

Graeme's fingers itched to join the search, but he knew better. He was a liability out there. So was Toni, because it wasn't about skill. It was about dealing with the heat and also about the fact that humans on Glyn literally stood out. But he wanted to do something.

"I have an idea," Toni said. "See if they won't route us the traffic cameras."

The glen didn't have heavy surveillance.

But they *did* have traffic cameras, which were designed to tell vehicles where the jams were so they could route around them. Many Earth cities had a similar system these days.

It really helped.

"We can take over the task of...I'll ask."

The feed came through to the monitor. Rotating through. But he could select one, blow it up, roll back the time scale.

"There." Toni pointed.

Skyt, outside a bakery, turning. Talking to another glen. Getting in a car with them.

"Well, they left voluntarily. Maybe that's a friend of theirs?"

Toni frowned. "Private people. No facial recognition." A pause. "Or carapace recognition."

"None routed to *us*," Graeme mused. "But yeah, it looks like they went off with somebody they knew."

"If they had been in a traffic accident, then we would know."

"Maybe the person they knew sold them out. Glen seem entirely too capable of betrayal." His lips twisted. "Human, really."

"Cleaning bots," Toni said, wryly.

He grinned. "Absolutely not. If they were..." Then he remembered Skyt was missing and wiped the grin off of his face.

The glen might or might not recognize the expression. But no... He sent the message, asking if the glen intelligences could identify the target.

After a few minutes, "Ktyl ak Skyt."

Graeme felt his lips try to smile again. "Ktyl ak..."

Toni got there faster. "Skyt's kid."

"No wonder they got into a car with them. Any bets the kid was promising reconciliation?" Not that they were a child, they looked *very* full grown, bigger than Skyt.

But to Skyt, that was their estranged child. And Graeme knew that if Marion hated him then abruptly showed up to talk?

He would have done the same thing.

THE INTELLIGENCE CONTINUED, "And you need to leave."

"What's going on?"

"What's going on is that there's a mob heading your way and they may mean you harm. Not being here would seem wise."

"It would. Thank you."

Graeme found his heat suit and tugged it on. It wasn't comfortable. "Any thoughts on a good place to be not here?" Skyt knew this neighborhood. Graeme didn't know this *planet*.

The voice chimed. "Go three blocks down the road, turn right. Go into the maintenance shack. Down the stairs."

"That sounds like some serious hiding."

"Somebody told a bunch of glen that you were responsible for the explosion somehow."

"Oh for..." Toni said.

Graeme didn't know which substitute swear she was biting back, but the fact that she bit back even a substitute swear was in character for her.

Apparently, strong language had never been acceptable in *her* family.

"Let's go."

He ducked out through the back door and around. The glen were going insane.

If they didn't find a way to fix this? Well, the sane ones would leave. The ones who *could* handle losing such a big part of their culture would leave. But the rest would die.

Possibly twice.

The two humans moved as quickly as they could. Park, maintenance shack, basement. The park was lovely, Graeme noted in passing. Very geometric, rather like an English formal garden. With flowers reaching towards the suns. Lovely flowers, and from what world had they come? From which world had the ancients stocked this garden? The blooms themselves were pink and purple and some kind of pollinator fluttered around them.

Maintenance shack. Down a ladder designed for glen limbs. It wasn't an easy climb, and at the bottom there was a...vault style door.

"I think this is one of the maintenance accesses to the substrate," Toni whispered.

"I wonder how mad they would be if we opened that door."

They looked at each other.

"I suspect they sent us here knowing *exactly* how crazy curious humans are."

Why wouldn't they open the door. It was, after all, the human thing to do.

THIS CORRIDOR HAD NOT BEEN MADE for glen, thankfully. It had been made for beings slightly larger. Graeme and Toni only had to stoop, not crawl.

Still, it felt tight. It was circular and it wove through the upper layer of the sublayer. It was like a giant brain or maybe a giant fungus.

Modeled after a fungus.

Grown, not built.

Everything the glen ancients had done was more grown than built. There was metal down here, so *some* of it was built.

But it was clear that their technological evolution had gone a very different way. They only built what they could not grow. The glen scrabbled about on the surface.

Judging by a dropped tool, they came down here, doing what maintenance they *did* know how to do on the vessel of their ancestors.

Probably meant it was safe to be here. The temperature was tolerable to humans, no doubt cave-cool to the glen. The air smelled breathable and Graeme experienced no discomfort.

So, yes, it was safe to be here, at least by some definitions of safe.

Safe enough? He supposed so. Safer than dealing with a mob.

Although the intelligence... "I think they sent us down here for a reason."

"I think so too. Maybe they hope that we will see something with our mammal brains."

Graeme laughed weakly. "I have a distinct feeling they think our mammal brains are our primary value. We don't think like them. We see things they miss."

"And vice versa. The astronomical data they've collected is fantastic and it's *not* set up the way we would. I think they have worked out some things about stars that we would never have managed on our own."

Graeme imagined a ship crewed by humans and glen. The temperature thing would be an issue, as would psychologically screening the crew so nobody bowed to them or ran from them.

Maybe a pair of smaller ships, exploring together, discovering new worlds and, what was it? New civilizations.

This wasn't a new civilization. This was an old one.

The tunnel opened up into a chamber and both humans stopped in the entrance to stare.

31

SKYT

THEY TOOK Skyt to a house on the shore of the western sea. It was one of the more beautiful spots on Glyn, that shore; a place for play and admiring the views. Glen did not play in water, but they would run along the sandy beach, their children building structures from it in that weird zone just above thw aves.

A beautiful prison, for they were sure they would not be allowed to leave, not any time soon. Ktyl had not come with them. They would never forget their child standing like that; and they fully expected this to be the last time they saw them with organic eyes.

Okay, that was being overly dramatic. There was no indication they were going to be harmed, that they were in more danger than anyone else on this dying world. But it might be and it was at least one more time than they had thought they would experience. They should have stayed at the museum.

The wind came off the sea and Skyt crouched in the window, all eyes on it. To an outside observer, they were the image of a glen who was just...watching. Daydreaming, perhaps. Inside, though, their thoughts churned. They knew that was a metaphor; they knew enough about how their own biology worked to know thoughts could not, in fact, churn.

But that was what it felt like, that and the cold feeling of fear some-where deep inside their thorax. That was what it felt like and it was all fear and maybe somebody would find them and maybe somebody wouldn't. There was some kind of device upstairs, in the house. Some-thing that could be used on a glen, something medical.

Had they been brought here to be experimented on?

No.

The shrieking told a different story. A glen, an old one, being dragged in, all of their legs bound.

"Come. We will show you what we have achieved."

"What is that?"

"Glen freedom."

Skyt didn't like the sound of that. Freedom from what?

The unfortunate glen, nobody Skyt knew or knew of, was carried upstairs. With something sinking through their abdomen, Skyt followed.

They were not surprised to see them strapped into the machine.

Glen freedom.

But they *were* free.The intelligences made requests, often cajoled, but they generally did not *command*.

Glye were just in the habit of doing what they requested, but that was mostly because it tended to be the right thing to do. They were usually *right*.

Freedom.

What else could glen be free of? The world? Their biology? Some-times, Skyt thought that different biology...but any biology was a cage. You made it as spacious and comfortable as you could, but the bars still stood.

The machine was activated.

The glen screamed.

THEY LEFT the glen and Skyt alone together. They were older than Skyt had thought.

They were silent, shaking in the corner, as if they had been shown something utterly terrible or the end of all things.

Skyt was finding it hard to look at them. Glen freedom.

When the others came back, it was with food. Skyt ate. The stranger did not.

"What did you do to them?"

"An experiment. If it works, then there will be no reason to chain ourselves to this world, to die here."

"You are trying to end translation." Skyt's wings lifted, as if they wanted to fly away, something no glen could do. Yet in that moment they wished they could, far from here.

"We have succeeded. We have yet, however, to work out how to make somebody unable to be translated without..."

"Go jump in a mating pool. Alone." Skyt was angry.

"If we don't unchain ourselves from it..."

"Some of us *will*. Because we can't stay on this world, you're right. But if people would rather die with it, then that...that's worth respecting."

"The sublayer won't survive."

"Let them gamble on that."

"Them?"

Skyt shook their head. Looked at them. Put seven of eight eyes on them while the last one kept looking at the now crazy glen. "There are worlds out there, worlds worth risking my afterlife for."

They hadn't made that decision, not in truth, until that moment.

"Ah, so you will explore, but then you will come back, if you live."

"If Glyn is still here."

"You know we don't have the time we were promised."

Skyt thought of the coordinates.

"Maybe we'll find something out there that will help, but this..." Skyt indicated the other with a pincer. "This is evil."

Skyt knew what evil was.

They were sure that until now they had not seen it, had not felt it. Did not *know* it. Experimenting on glen.

"Right now, we are *appendages*. We're *robots*, Skyt."

Skyt swiveled all eight eyes onto the unfortunate for a moment, just to have something else to look at. "We are glen."

"We can be more than glen."

Skyt swiveled their eyes back. "No. What you are doing makes us less than glen." They knew they should play along, but they were no spy, no stage actor to pretend.

They would probably be the next person fed into the machine.

"You..."

Another glen entered. "Give them a chance to come around. We could use their skills."

Never, was what echoed in Skyt's thoughts.

Never.

THE NEXT MORNING, the stranger was dead. Skyt still did not know their name, or where they had come from. They were dead and there was nothing left of them, nothing to dance in the sublayer, to continue to learn and grow, combine and recombine. Skyt would mourn the stranger. Later.

For now, Skyt knew that they had to escape, to find a way out of here. To warn people? Maybe that was it, to warn them, but they were not sure that would help. Not sure that would, as it were, work. Not sure that anyone would listen. Some wouldn't care, and some would cheer.

Escaping, though. Escaping *was* a priority. Skyt considered the ocean. They could not swim that far, they didn't have a boat. Likely there was a boat somewhere, but...

Skyt was a scientist. Not a spy. Certainly not some action hero to scurry out of trouble right ahead of the explosions.

There probably wouldn't be explosions. No, instead, they were going to end up in that machine, stripped of their sanity, stripped of their afterlife.

The fear the Remainers felt was now something they understood in full.

They wanted to just run, but the house had been chosen well. There was no cover in any direction. No basement.

No tunnels, thus, that they could escape through and abruptly Skyt wanted to be in a tunnel.

Tunnels were where kids hid when they were scared, when they couldn't dive onto their rey's carapace. But there were no tunnels connected to this house. There was no escape and a body being removed and Skyt was afraid to touch the food. Afraid it might be drugged.

Sooner or later they would have to. Starving to death was not preferable. But then they left the door to the machine room open. Skyt knew it was a trap.

Skyt knew they were almost certainly doing exactly what their captors wanted when they crept, wings tucked, thorax low to the ground into the room. But they had to look, had to see. Had to destroy, but no.

They had to look first. It was, they realized, a modified medical scanner. Nothing more, nothing less. The kind of thing you used to monitor activity when somebody had had an injury and you suspected damage to their mental nodes.

But modified.

Modified to *alter* the mental nodes. There could be a place for this technology, if it could be made to work. But not the place they wanted for it.

Skyt thought of other worlds.

Of Graeme's canyon.

Skyt stared at the machine and crouched...

32

GRAEME

IT WAS A CIRCULAR CHAMBER. And it was the top of a shaft.

It was clear that the hatch sealing the shaft had not been touched or opened in many, many years. It had been ignored by whoever had come down here. It wasn't, of course, safe.

But it was tempting anyway. Graeme walked over to it. "Rusted shut." It wasn't just rust, it was this weird kind of mold around the edge, but either way it didn't look like it was going to budge.

"Probably been centuries since anyone used it," Toni mused. "But it sure looks like the outside of an airlock to me."

"Me too," Graeme mused. "Perhaps it's older than the...perhaps this area..."

"Double hull, this area is between the hulls. And the computers were put in when...when they didn't need the extra protection. After the station was parked, I'd suspect."

"You think it was built as a station, then?"

"My *guess* is it was built as a station, towed to this empty system and parked. Which might be what you would do with something you wanted to hide."

"Or protect. And then when they thought they couldn't protect it, they sabotaged it. Wiped it."

"A military archive," Toni finished.

"Or a scientific one that contained knowledge they didn't want the military to get."

Graeme looked at the hatch again. They knew they had been led here by the nose, presented with this. "I think," he added, "That we're being manipulated."

"Absolutely, and by the combined consciousnesses of millions of glen. We can't really compete with that."

Graeme's laugh echoed through the chamber. "Do you think they really think we can fix things?"

"I think they think we might as well try and that they're no worse off if we fail."

"Good point. Unless we blow up the planet early."

Toni made a face. "Let's not go pressing any buttons."

"We can't open that, anyway. Not without some kind of gear. Once the mob is gone...assuming there *was* a mob...we'll have to come back with tools."

She nodded. "And we can perhaps ask directly if they think it's a good idea."

"Oh, it's a terrible idea. The thing is, it's an idea."

And they were precious short on those.

THE MOB HAD BEEN REAL. Whether they would have committed violence remained unclear.

According to witnesses, they had shown up, yelled "Humans go home" for a while and left when they didn't get a rise out of anyone in the (empty) house. Not being there had definitely been the best plan. It would have been very hard not to engage with them with all the potential risks that brought.

In the house, Graeme settled into the chair the glen had jury-rigged based on photos. It wasn't comfortable, but it beat the local low benches. At least for somebody from a European background. He liked chairs.

"So, what if we were to go inside the hull?"

He got a response from the terminal almost immediately, "We would suggest space suits."

"That's a given."

"It is dangerous, but you might learn something. Would it cause an incident?"

"I will leave documentation indicating we did it entirely off of our own initiative, even though we know you sent us down there for a reason."

The terminal chimed. "I suppose we are guilty."

"You can stop manipulating me now. I will help if I can. I doubt I can, but if I don't try then the chance is zero."

"Precisely," the terminal said. "Thank you."

"We aren't as technologically advanced as the glen in some..."

He was cut off. "You built all of your technology. You discovered how to tame fire. You covered your bodies against the cold. You went from being smart animals to a dominant species. You almost killed your world, but you didn't. *We* inherited all of ours."

"And thus you think humans might actually be better equipped than glen. Glen will..."

"Glen will need your adaptability and I believe that once we have dealt with the fear and restored Glyn to stability..."

"You think we might well be friends."

"Allies."

Graeme shook his head. "Friends. You think the glen need us."

"And we think you can learn from the glen. As can the ky'iin and the tyrar."

"We can all learn from each other. Maybe," he added wryly, "We can teach the ky'iin to write."

The terminal chimed. "Ah, but they manage so well without it."

And the tyrar taught cooperation while the ky'iin were solo hunters who came together more for mating and defense. Self-reliance, then.

All four species together would be more than any of them alone.

"And if all else fails, if we fail, I can't promise...but I think there will be many humans willing to teach the glen how to survive and rebuild."

"Which is why we were looking for aliens in the first place. That and..."

"...and any sign of your builders."

"There is none. Yet.

"SO, WE'LL NEED..." He sighed.

Toni started to tick off the list. "Spacesuits, because as our uploaded friends pointed out, we don't know the atmosphere. Tools to get that hatch open. All the scanning gear we can find. A drone or three."

"Drones. We'll want the smallest we can get."

"Agreed, we might be in a tight space." Toni smiled. "I've done this before. Let *me* do the shopping list. You see what more you can get out of them."

Skyt was still missing. It hurt a little bit to leave that to search and rescue and community officers who weren't used to dealing with kidnappings.

Graeme went to the front window. No protestors, although there were a couple of glyn children watching the house.

No doubt they wanted a glimpse of the exotic aliens.There had been talk about moving them, but Graeme was the ambassador.

He couldn't hide forever, and when the Remainers came after him? Well, he could not be here then. He opened the curtains the rest of the way, waved to the kids, then closed them again. Or started to.

There was a glen heading up the driveway. Not one he knew, although he didn't know many of them yet, so that wasn't surprising.

They looked...

They looked distraught. Their wings were half out from under their carapace and drooped and their eyes seemed to be pointed in more than eight directions. Graeme frowned, then rushed to the door. Opened it. It could be a trap. He could be misreading their body language.

"Can I come in?" the glyn chimed, their translator doing its job a moment later.

"Come on in."

"I'm Ktyl ak Skyt.'

Skyt's adult, estranged child. Graeme could see the resemblance, but his earlier impression was accurate. Ktyl was a little larger than Skyt. "Then *please* come in. Have you heard from them? Do you know..."

"I was tricked into getting them kidnapped. An extreme Migrator faction has them. We need to..."

"Have the community officers?"

"They can't do this. They'll get shot or worse, captured and used as experiment fodder. Or rather, they need help."

He called for Toni.

This was her expertise. Swatting with hostages? The glen had already demonstrated an unwillingness to do that. A fear of doing that.

He turned back to Ktyl. "I believe we can trust Skyt to...do their best to rescue themselves."

Exploring the hatch would have to wait.

And they would probably have to get Skyt a spacesuit.

33

SKYT

THE MACHINE WAS TOUGH. Skyt was not able to do much damage before they showed up to drag them away from it.

To drag them back to the room, but the lights flickered. As if there was a storm outside, but there could be no storm.

Not right now. Not here, not this time of year.

Lightning and thunder and a storm that *could not be* and was it another malfunction? Another sign that their world was failing and dying?

Or something else.

Or it wasn't thunder.

They dropped Skyt.

Skyt ran for the nearest window. Felt their wings spread subconsciously, as useless as they were. Dived through the window, trying to take the glass on their carapace. Falling, grabbing for the wall.

Bouncing off it, breaking their fall, slowing it, and then landing in the worst of all positions, on their back, scrambling, trying to use their wings to flip themselves back over. They felt no pain, but that was the situation, the hormones. The pain would come and they could only hope they had not broken themselves, or anything else.

Then something was pushing against them. Lifting one side. They put in more effort and landed back on seven feet. The eighth did not want to take their weight. They didn't want to look, but they turned two eyes to see...Toni. The smaller of the two humans had given them just that bit of leverage, although from the way they were rubbing one arm with the other they were, perhaps, slightly regretting it now.

They were alive. And the thunder? The lightning? Those weren't supposed to happen. It had to be a sign of something else, except how could the timing be *so* convenient?

"Can you move?"

Skyt answered by scurrying away, keeping that one injured leg tucked up against their thorax. They would worry about how injured it was later. The human zigged and zagged.

"There shouldn't be a storm?"

"It's a trick that we learned from the ky'iin. Get a small ship, come out of FTL in the atmosphere. Creates a magnetic storm."

"And a perfect distraction. If overkill." A pause. "Well, no. They had some awful machinery in there. I hope it's fried."

"Tell me later."

They helped Skyt into the back of a van. Jumped in with them.

Skyt wasn't as comfortable with Toni as they were with Graeme. But they had helped save him.

"They were going to..." Skyt furled their wings under their carapace and finally looked at their cracked leg. It would heal. "They had this machine that destroyed minds."

Toni closed their pitiful two eyes. "Destroyed..."

"They are trying to force glen off the planet by by making it so we can't translate. But all they've succeeded in doing..."

Toni did not open their eyes. "Then I do hope it was fried."

"For what it's worth."

"Skyt...are you willing to help us do something very dangerous?

"You want to do *what*?"

The safe house really wasn't. They would look for Skyt here, but

Skyt didn't really care. Honestly, after this, Skyt would *have* to go to a colony world. It would be the only way to be safe.

Or maybe the humans would let them hide on Earth for a few months, in some hot place that wouldn't freeze their feet off, possibly literally. But right now, the humans wanted to...

"We think somebody needs to."

"You are not sane," Skyt said, finally. "It's..."

"They're sending down our spacesuits on the next shuttle. We'll have them in a few hours. There probably isn't a breathable atmosphere in there, no. But we have spacesuits, we have tools. And we have brains." Or things that worked like brains.

"We could all die." What was that we?

It was insanity, but the truth of it was that if there was really going to be an expedition into the core of the world, Skyt was going. Skyt might die out of reach of the substrate and face oblivion or whatever truly happened to an unmoored consciousness. But if so, Skyt would have seen it.

"We?"

Skyt's wings drooped. "I'm an archaeologist. I've always wanted to. I've always had too much sense or been too scared. But I want to see it."

"So do I," Graeme admitted. "Even if it means...even if means I don't get to go home to my husband and child."

Co-parent.

Love. Skyt did not understand, but they could accept. Appreciate. And have great respect for.

Willing to give that up. "How did you find me, anyway?"

"Ktyl helped. They're a good person, Skyt."

"I'm the one who failed them," Skyt said, finally. "Some people aren't good parents, I suppose."

"Parenting is a skill." Graeme smiled at them, then took a deep breath. "In any case, we're going to do it. Go into the world and see if we can work out anything about how it works. How much it was damaged."

"We can't repair it."

"We can try," Graeme said, finally. "You always try. Even when it seems hopeless. Even when you *know* you're going to fail. That's how we turned the destruction of our world into a thousand small successes and then a hundred large ones."

"You're better than we are," Skyt said.

Graeme laughed that barking sound. "Oh, heck no. You guys have managed to build a mostly peaceful civilization. Your astronomy is fantastic. No, we aren't better. We are just *used* to crisis. We have faced the end of the world so many times it's Tuesday."

"Tuesday?"

"Uh...it's a calendar reference."

Skyt chimed. "Got it. I think."

Crisis normal? Perhaps that was what natural evolution got you. "When do we leave?" they added, finally.

"We need to get you a suit."

KTYL WAS NERVOUS. Skyt watched their body language. Vryn was on the station. They had talked to their care-parent only over video. It hadn't helped.

Vryn, of course, didn't want Skyt to do this, to do this dangerous thing which would certainly get them killed and leave Ktyl an orphan and... This was why they shouldn't even have talked to the human. Skyt had let it wash over them. They had tried.

Ktyl was another matter. "You're going to die," Ktyl said. "Twice."

Skyt clacked their mandibles. "I don't plan on dying. I am *risking* dying. But this isn't suicide."

"Good. I don't want you to die, despite everything. And I swear I didn't know."

"I believe you. You would not..."

"I did *not* know what they were doing. I knew they were against translating because it could mean dying twice, but..."

"I *believe* you, Ktyl."

"You hate me."

"Never," Skyt said. "Although for a while I think you hated me."

"I did," Ktyl said. "And you're not my rey, still not that. But I get it.

You didn't know what to do with me." A pause. "I'm going to have a child."

"Try to look at what I did and what Vryn did and..."

"I'm going to do what *I* do. If I look at what you did, I'll perpetuate it."

Skyt hesitated. "Yes, you will. Thank you."

"For not being you?"

"For being you, Ktyl. How are things at the art institute?"

They talked for a while about, well, work. About Ktyl's curation and about Skyt's technology. They didn't talk about the end of the world. It didn't seem to be the best topic.

They drank fermented juice and got ever so slightly drunk. Which was what Skyt needed. Maybe Skyt needed to be ever so slightly drunk tomorrow, but they also needed to be stone cold sober.

But they had tried. And they had connected with their child again, just a little bit. Not to be their rey, not even to be their friend. Just to be a thing which existed, a person who was real and vital and, perhaps, just a little bit loved.

34

GRAEME

THE HATCH in the floor was still. Rusty. Untouched. Graeme felt a peculiar sense of...something.

As if he was hesitating in the entrance of one of the old gothic cathedrals, a place built to glorify God. A place built because humans *could* and you didn't need to believe in God to feel it. Sacred.

He felt as if they were about to disturb something sacred. He knew it was foolish. This was a machine, that was all. A machine that had hatches that could be opened. Advanced, yes, but how much more advanced was this, truly, than the great tyrar colony ships designed to move thousands to new homes?

They were selling that design. How much more advanced than FTL? Than...

It was advanced, but it was feasible because it existed and understandable because organic beings had built it. Or the AI descendants of organic beings. It *existed* and therefore it could be understood, repaired, even copied. Whether they could do it was another matter.

But it could be done.

Toni was at work with the tools. He moved to help her. Skyt was staying back. He didn't blame the glen. They weren't here to get this door open. They were here to help understand what lay beyond it.

Open and there was nothing. Maybe there would have been something if they had not been wearing suits.

He had the sudden irrational thought that all the air would leak in, Glyn's atmosphere somehow pulled into the interior of the ship where some system might think it belonged. It couldn't happen.

Right?

Right.

He dropped through the hatch and was in a small chamber. An airlock.

"Everyone come in."

Toni followed. Skyt was a little more reluctant, climbing down the wall rather than dropping.

He looked at Toni. "Let's close the hatch."

"What if we can't get back out?"

"I would just feel better with it closed." He didn't want to tell her he was experiencing this bizarre anxiety.

She might laugh.

And he wasn't sure if laughter would ease his tension or make it worse.

He really wasn't sure.

They closed the hatch.

TUNNELS. Tunnels in which they were the rats, the vermin. Or the cleaning bots.

The inner hull was more than a labyrinth. Graeme thought of those coordinates. They marked the walls, or they would never find their way back to where they had come. Chalk, not yarn.

Blazing a trail in the old fashioned sense. Some parts of the tunnels were dark, but most were still lit. Dim, but present.

There was still power to the systems. There was still hope.

If they could get...but how *did* it move? Could it move without firing thrusters through the crust, through glen cities? Graeme hadn't thought of that problem. Repair the ship, get it to put itself back at the LaGrange point, buy the glen time to evolve and develop and learn.

But it could be a mass casualty event. He didn't want to kill glen even if they didn't really die in the sense humans did. He wanted to *save* them.

"Penny for them?" asked Toni.

He shook his head at her. "How does it move?"

Skyt lifted their head. "You mean if we get Glyn to put itself back where it belongs?"

"Yes."

"Legend has it that the Viree and Meest mountains are not mountains."

Graeme found himself smiling. "And perhaps others. I was worried that it might have thrusters buried...possibly even under cities."

"Oh!" Skyt said. "No. It used to be that the mountains smoked."

"But not in many, many years."

"Not in generations."

"Then we just have to find the mechanism and repair it." There had to be...the autopilot had to still work.

The place had been meant to stay. "They didn't abandon you to die."

"They abandoned us to live," Skyt chimed, thoughtfully.

Graeme thought he was starting to understand the chiming without need for translation. That was some major progress, in his mind.

To understand the glen truly, though? That was going to take time, much time. On both sides.

"So...what we probably need is to find a computer access to...something other than the substrate."

And then they could get the information they needed, but Graeme had a feeling they would have to travel. There was no...that part he had not thought through. Glen was larger than Earth, slightly.

They could not simply walk...and he laughed.

"What?" Toni and Skyt demanded in a bizarre unison.

"Skyt, you won't get it. Toni...we can't simply walk..."

She burst out laughing. "No, we can't."

Skyt lifted a pincer. "You're right, I don't get it."

"It's a reference to an ancient fantasy novel."

They then used the pincer to point. "Maybe that will help?"

It was emphatically a railway. A service one, with open cars. But it clearly hadn't moved in...generations. It wasn't particularly dusty; likely there wasn't much actual dust in here. It had this silence to it. This stillness. How could it still work? What had been maintaining it?

Graeme felt that sense of disturbing something sacred again, except more so. This was...this was alien technology older than, perhaps, his civilization. He was convinced that if he touched it it would crumble into dust.

Except it had been maintained. Until recently. By whom? Maintenance bots, one had to assume. *Actual* janitor bots, which presumably needed air and water, because the ancients would have bred them. And...

He checked the air reader. There was only a thin atmosphere in here. That had definitely helped preservation. Not enough oxygen to rust. So perhaps built robots then, or something bred from a being akin to tardigrades.

"We only have three more hours before we *have* to surface and refill our suits. Let's see if we can get it working then go back."

They got to work. This time, Skyt was willing to help, although their eyes went in all directions.

"People really never come down here?"

"People don't come *back*." A pause. "So, people stopped going."

"How much of that was before you guys had space suits?"

Skyt considered. "We've always had them..." A pause. "But you're right. It didn't occur to people there wasn't enough air down here."

"Hence..." Toni pointed at something with her toe. With a shudder, Graeme realized it was the remains of a dead glen.

Mummified in the minimal air. *That* he wasn't going to touch. That probably would crumble to dust and perhaps Skyt could take pictures, get them identified. Get some closure for their descendants.

Or perhaps it didn't matter. "They got a long way without..." Graeme eyed Skyt speculatively. "How long can glen hold their breath anyway?"

"Not long enough. They must have got in through a hatch closer to here."

"Hrm. Skyt, find it? We could make better use of time if we could get *out* that way."

Skyt dipped his mandibles and scurried off.

Toni glanced at him. "They are this bizarre mix of subservient and arrogant."

"That they are. I suppose it comes from knowing you were an uplifted servitor race."

"Their ancients have a lot to answer for."

Maybe, Graeme thought, the glen would prefer to...

...and he leapt back as the rails sparked.

"I think we got something."

With transportation, this might work.

35

SKYT

SKYT WOULD REMEMBER this as long as they lived. If this was their last dying memory, they would cherish it as they fell into the sublayer...or into the unknown dark.

The railroad worked. Not well. It jerked, it was uncertain, but how had it survived this long? Skyt assumed the human guess was right. In the spacesuit, they could not feel air flows, could not smell. Could not hear. Felt peculiarly isolated for a moment, now they were riding not walking.

As if they were watching all this on a video screen. The humans...they were handling this well. Brave, and a long way from stupid, even if they sometimes thought in directions that made Skyt blink at least six eyes.

"I..." A pause. "As we have time, where did your species come from?"

"We evolved from a lineage of arboreal omnivores and fructivores," Graeme explained. "We moved out of the forest, and went upright. That's the short version."

"Hence the very front set eyes. They *aren't* predator eyes, are they. They're tree climber eyes." Exceptional binocular vision. A fantastic proprioceptive sense. They were *arboreal* because of course they were.

"That's a definite argument."

"Also explains your proprioceptive sense."

"Didn't your ancestors fly?"

Skyt considered that. "Presumably, a long time ago. But you've preserved yours because you need it to walk upright. We don't need it, so it was engineered out of us. Or, ya know..."

"Or you've just never used it. I hear, though, that glen can fly in microgravity" Graeme asked.

Skyt considered that. "You know, *I* have never been..."

Toni sighed loudly. "That is *not* fair and we have to buy your artificial gravity technology."

Graeme laughed.

Skyt blinked four eyes. "What?"

"Artificial gravity on ships and stations tends to fail at inopportune moments. Hence why you will never see a human spacer with long, loose hair."

Skyt hesitated. "*Long* hair."

Both humans had hair on their heads, but it was short. It hadn't occurred to Skyt that it was *trimmed* short like a plant. For convenience.

"I'll show you some pictures. But yes, many humans grow their hair long, or out, or...whatever. We use it to express personality," Toni explained. "But if you have long hair and the gravity goes out, it gets in your eyes. So we either cut it short or we pin it up or something. The latter's more work, but some humans pride themselves on their hair."

Skyt hadn't considered fur or hair as a means of expression before. "I suppose it's like some young people paint each others carapaces for parties."

"I saw that. I assumed it was some kind of art," Graeme mused.

"It's self expression."

Toni added, "And some humans dye their hair, paint their skin or...I'll explain about tattoos."

So, the human equivalent of carapace painting. Mostly young people. But not always. "Oh, and at Velyf, everyone does it," Skyt added. "Gets painted, that is. And parents get their kids to do it."

Toni laughed at that. "So, the parents are the ones with...well, I suppose it depends on the age of the kid."

"Having a messy carapace tells everyone you have a young kid. Or are pretending." Skyt chimed. "If you are still here for Velyf..."

"If we didn't have to wear suits..."

"Toni!"

Toni had clearly said something that shocked Graeme. Her laughter followed them through the tunnel.

"How did they get down here?" Toni asked rhetorically.

Skyt knew the easy answer, the hard one was how they had known where to find them. They could only think of one source for *that* knowledge.

Either way, what was more significant was the bullet that had just grazed their carapace. Thankfully, it had hit them *not* one of the soft bodied humans, to whom far more damage would have been done. Humans were fragile that way. Of course, when it came to certain falling or crushing, the humans might do better, with no carapace for their soft innards to be thrown against.

A slight yelp indicated one of them had indeed been hit. Skyt had no weapons. That put them at a disadvantage, and this was definitely an attempt to kill them. With hunting guns. It was as if the violence of the offworlders had spilled over and taken away everything that was glyn.

No. This was the craziness of fear and Skyt poked an eye over the railroad carriage. They were smartly *not* on the tracks. Skyt couldn't smash the train into them.

Skyt couldn't...

...and then Toni threw something. Skyt had never seen a thrown object travel so far. Yet another human gift. Then again, right now they would rather have their carapace!

They yelled something and Skyt ducked. A blaze of light hit the outside of their eyelids, and they didn't want to think what that would have done if they had been looking right at it.

Graeme was trying to get the train moving again, ideally past them and away from them.

"What was..."

"Flash grenade."

Skyt could only see smears. "Go. If they can't see any better than me..."

A few more bullets did indeed trail after them, but none came close to hitting anyone and had they done so Skyt would have suspected pure luck.

Their vision was slowly returning.

"Like I said. Flash grenade. Temporary incapacitation, generally no permanent damage. Very good for getting out of a tight spot."

It occurred to Skyt that they could have brought something more lethal and had chosen not to. That probably said something about human attitudes towards violence in general.

Or about diplomacy, or self restraint. They crouched low in the train, letting their eyes recover. How *had* those people known where to find them?

Skyt could only come to one conclusion. An intelligence had told them.

"IF WE GO FURTHER IN, then we don't know what the conditions will be," Toni said evenly, their voice tinny through the radio and the translator.

Read: They could all die.

Read: They would probably all die.

But if they didn't, then they would not know what was wrong. If they did, they still wouldn't know what was wrong. They were ants. Vermin. Cleaning robots and wild life forms that had evolved somewhere over there. To the builders of this place, Skyt wasn't sure there would be a difference.

Maybe being cleaning robots would be better. The beings bred to do a task, to be a part of this civilization. To do the work so their creators didn't have to.

"You know we have to," Skyt said, finally. Their voice sounded empty and who knew what arrived at the humans after the translator did its part.

"I know." Toni looked at where the railroad ended. This was clearly...

It was clearly the outside of an engine and Skyt wondered what happened when it fired. Nobody lived on the mountain. They made sure of that, because once the mountains had smoked and they might again. There were plenty of other places for glen to live.

It had fired before. If it fired with them *here*, though? Skyt rather thought they would be shaken to pieces. The soft humans might fare better.

Might.

"What if it goes off?" Graeme asked, voicing his fears.

"Then we'd have to trust that whatever insulation and sound-proofing is in that..." Toni tapped the wall with a suited finger. "...is good enough."

She had a point. Perhaps they had done their best to protect anyone here from the engine firing.

Skyt looked at the way which led downwards. It was sealed, but they could, he knew, get it open easily enough. Sealed against them. It was as if the gods were down there.

Skyt might be about to find out how they personally handled free fall. What if the planet was hollow and they fell into the middle of it? What *was* inside?

Skyt needed to know. Needed to know with the kind of passion most reserved for their children. Perhaps that was why they were such a bad parent.

Perhaps...perhaps this was where they needed to go. "Let's do this," they said.

Let's...do it.

36

GRAEME

THE TYRAR BUILT BIG. Graeme had seen pictures. First of all, the tyrar stood between six and seven feet tall. Second of all, they traveled in herds.

They had to build big.

They were rats in the walls next to this. The great engine was at their backs and the ramp that led down seemed to get wider and wider. Down into...he wondered if the gravity would somehow reverse when they were inside. Or go away. Or...

Some of the machinery, after all, still worked. This ship wasn't dead, just old and damaged and worn. He could see how worn it was. How old it was.

Glen generations old. Human generations old.

Rats in the walls. Maybe this ship wasn't big after all; maybe it had been built by giants. More likely the intent had been what was built. Artificial living space on the surface, computing power in the sublayer and down here, the machinery to keep it in orbit. Perhaps once to move it, but that...

Could this thing go faster than light? The theory said likely not, that there was an upper limit. But if you had multiple engines, multiple pilots working together...maybe? What would happen to people on the surface if it did?

He shuddered at the thought. No, he had to assume this was station, not ship, that it might have put itself on station but had been built to stay put in this place, to float in the Lagrange point created by the stars...which so happened to be a habitable zone, albeit a warm one. Likely perfect temperature for them.

...and Toni gasped. Graeme blinked a moment later. The lights had come on, as if some sensors down here had detected their presence. Lights, and vastness.

"Now I really feel like a rat."

"What's a rat?" Skyt asked.

"Small, verminous, lives in the walls if you don't keep them out."

Skyt's wings shuddered.

"Also good pets, the tame ones," Toni pointed out. "But I see Graeme's point."

"We *are* vermin," Skyt said sadly. "Feral vermin."

"Oh, stop that," Toni said, and walked a bit further. The lights stayed on, but Graeme could see that many of them were cracked and a few flickered idly.

"This place functions," Graeme mused. "But barely. Skyt, what do you think?"

The glen scurried forward, their eight eyes moving rapidly as they scanned the area with a visual field no human could match.

Graeme was momentarily jealous. Bipedal stance or eyes in the back of one's head suddenly didn't seem that fair a trade.

"That nobody has been down here in a very, very long time. But there's very little dust."

"Probably there wasn't much for dust to come from."

Toni didn't voice the one likely source.

She didn't need to.

WEIRD STUFF WAS HAPPENING to space. Graeme stopped. "I don't think we should go any further."

The ramp was steep and it wasn't and it was steep again, and it felt like everything was starting to twist.

"This is not good," Toni said, finally.

Skyt was scurrying ahead. They stopped, three eyes tilting backwards towards the humans under the dome of their suit.

"Skyt, what do you see?"

"Nothing unusual."

"We see space distorting and twisting."

Graeme and Toni looked at each other. Skyt's eyes worked...it wasn't space.

"But it's not space," they said together.

Skyt turned a fourth eye towards them.

"There's a distortion in what passes for the atmosphere here. Your eyes work a little differently, so you don't see it," Graeme explained.

"And for a moment I thought that there was a controlled singularity in here that was becoming less controlled." Toni sounded grim. "Had that been the case, we'd have needed those tyrar ships and a hundred more sooner rather than later."

Graeme shuddered.

"Oh. Meaning the planet was going to blow up."

"The exact opposite. But if it's just..."

Skyt lifted their pincers. "It's stuff. I'm under it, but you..."

Graeme crouched down. Skyt was right. A curtain of stuff blocked their passage. The glen seemed perfectly designed to pass under it.

Something sounded off in the distance.

"Uh oh," said Toni. "I think you set off the intruder alert, Skyt."

Skyt dropped their pincers. "I would have walked right under it."

"It wasn't meant, then, to stop *you*."

Graeme crawled under the curtain, keeping himself at glen height as best he could. It wasn't very comfortable, but it worked.

"We're meant to be here, then," Skyt mused. "It was meant to stop..."

"...larger creatures," Toni finished for them, having crawled under it herself. "Unfortunately, now we've set off the alarm..."

Graeme frowned, "I doubt there are any security bots down here." He then winced and looked at Skyt. "That was poorly..." He then paused. "But something has been maintaining things, and I have to suspect non-sentient bots. So..."

"I know what I am," Skyt said.

"Their legacy," Graeme said firmly. "Whatever you started out as."

That actually caused the glen to lift their head a little. Apparently they just needed to be buttered up a tiny bit.

"Let's not count on there not being security and not be here when it arrives," Toni suggested, quickening her pace.

Graeme let her go first; she had more combat training than he had (and far more than Skyt) if it came to it.

Skyt was trying to take in as many things as they had eyes and then some. This place was magnificent and terrible and utterly deserted and glittering lights...

It was beautiful, and it was broken, and they were all going to die.

"It's writing for sure. Skyt, can you read this?" Graeme asked.

He stepped back to give the glen space to look. He knew full well he could be asking the poor glen to read the equivalent of Chaucer. Or the equivalent of Sanskrit.

But the lack of linguistic drift on Glyn in general gave him hope.

While Skyt tried to decipher the writing, Graeme looked around again. There was no atmosphere, no sound except through their radios. But it wasn't a vacuum.

It was more like being on Mars, but the atmosphere wasn't remotely breathable.

Of course it wasn't.

"It's deliberate," he said, finally.

"What?" Toni asked, also stepping back from Skyt.

"The atmosphere. They intentionally reduced it..."

"...so the machinery would last longer. Of course. They meant to come back."

"Or they meant to leave a legacy even if they couldn't. Perhaps they figured that the glen would have space travel down before it went bad," Graeme said, softly. Not that it mattered. Whispering on a radio link was a waste of time.

"Which they do. But not enough..."

"Not enough to evacuate, but...they gave them every chance. Or the archive they wiped was meant to last forever."

"Last forever with protectors," Toni said. "Cleaning bots."

"Then they wiped it."

"I hope we never meet what scared them so badly."

Graeme hoped that too. This place was shrine and tomb and...

...he saw something under the dust. He wiped it with the back of his glove. "Well, huh."

"Huh indeed."

What was underneath was a picture, a discarded picture that had been etched into metal. So it would last. A picture of a large bug, something like a preying mantis. Folded inwards, wings neatly furled, pincers and mandibles...it looked like it had been built from the same evolutionary plan as the glen, but was clearly a different species.

"Skyt!" Graeme yelled.

The glen turned. "I think I have it deciphered, and it boils down to don't go through that door unless everything's turned off. What?"

They scuttled over. And stared at the picture. "That's an ancient."

"Thought so."

"I mean, that fits what we know of what they looked like."

Graeme nodded. "Is this valuable to a historian?"

"Incalculably!"

"I'll try and pry it loose for you so you can put it in a museum." Or on a ship, away from here.

The glen were an artifact of this race, these people. Graeme stared at the picture some more. They were beautiful.

And scary.

And lost.

37

SKYT

AN ACCURATE DEPICTION OF AN ANCIENT! Not something put together from bits and bytes by the intelligences. Not a child's caricature. An actual image of one. Skyt was terrified. That was not the reaction they had expected, but it felt as if they...they felt as if they should run and bow and...

Stupid to feel semi-religious awe for beings who had probably been not *that* much different from glen. Not smarter. Bigger, definitely, but not by as much as they had thought. Sharp around the edges in just the same way. But not smarter.

Only with access to the archives they had taken away from the glen, had denied to them along with whatever enemy they feared. Here, though, in this place built by them and to their scale and in the silence of their suit?

Skyt was terrified. How could they even consider so much as setting foot here? How could they remotely consider that it was possible to repair Glyn.

Or at least stabilize things for long enough to get everyone off.

Skyt felt the suit close in around them, but they scurried back to the door they had been examining. All kinds of warning symbols, but they boiled down to the same thing. Don't go through this door unless you were *sure* there was no power to the engine.

Engine.

If they could fire it once, with the right calculations, calculations the intelligences could surely manage, then they could buy Glen a few centuries, a few millennia.

Time to sort everything out. Time for generations to live and die.

Skyt wasn't sure that there was no power to the engine. "We have to find the control room," they said, finally, turning several eyes back on the two humans. Graeme was reverently removing the image of the ancient from the wall it had been fastened to.

For the museum. For their escape. For a memory. But what it triggered within them was also a memory. A dark one, one which they weren't sure what to do with. But they followed the two humans further down, trying to keep anything from showing in their body language.

Hopefully the humans wouldn't be able to read it. Skyt was afraid.

Skyt was ashamed.

SOMETHING WAS MOVING in the dark. An actual robot?

An actual *ancient*? Skyt knew the latter was ridiculous, but they couldn't quite help it. There was no atmosphere down here, it couldn't be wildlife or a glen, unless the glen had a suit.

It was big. It was moving towards them out of one of the side corridors. For the first time in their life, Skyt wished for a gun. For some kind of weapon. It was a good job they didn't have one.

They *knew* it was a good job they didn't have one. Without one, there was no risk of them panicking and shooting anyone. But they felt on that edge of panic nonetheless.

That edge of...something...which made them wonder what they should do. Whether they should do anything.

Shoot.

Destroy.

Run.

Fight or flight triggered in a way that never happened and they wanted to run back to the surface and then perhaps into space. Off this world.

"Well, huh," Graeme said.

Toni was watching the thing. "Huh indeed."

It was another railroad. It was a *train* and Skyt chimed nervously. "I thought that was security."

After all, they had set off the alarm.

"I think it came to get us," Toni said. "So, the question is, do we go with it and try to talk to whatever might be down here or..."

"If there's anything down here," Skyt said, finally finding reason somewhere in the base of their abdomen. "I'd suspect it's an intelligence."

"Indeed."

And it *could* be an ancient. After all, the translation technology had no doubt been invented for *their* use originally.

"What else would it be?" Toni asked, heading for the train. "All aboard."

"Is that wise?" Skyt hesitated.

"No, but none of this is."

They had a point. Skyt clambered onto the train, with less difficulty than the humans, who fortunately were remarkably foldable when they needed to be.

None of this was wise.

And if there was a living *ancient* intelligence down here, then they would know how to fix everything. They might not be able to.

But they would know how and Skyt could be their pincers and the feeling in their thorax was possibly even hope.

"There's more atmosphere here," Graeme said.

"Breathable?" Toni stared at her own sensors.

"Not any more."

Skyt slightly tuned them out. They had enough suit air to last. But not forever. In a little while, they would have to turn back.

Unless they *did* miraculously find breathable air down here. Skyt wasn't counting on it.

Instead, they stared at the walls. Stared at them as they opened out. This had been a place intended for use, not just maintenance. Inside the hull, with a floor built between it and the interior where, they suspected, there was indeed a singularity.

Maybe this was the original ship.

Maybe they had been meant to inhabit it, but had terraformed...but no.

The exterior had been prepared for their use, the surface of what they knew wasn't a planet but which might as well have been. It didn't matter, of course. It *was* a planet, for all intents and purposes, until it wasn't...no, it would always be one, even if it became a drifting nomad. Could they live down *here*? Restore life support and just move underground?

That feeling was definitely hope. It wasn't completely impossible, not if there was atmosphere. Plants and light?

Plants and light could do it.

That was *definitely* hope. They could find a way to link to the substrate. They could still land ships on the frozen surface. They might not have to migrate after all. Then the walls chimed.

Skyt couldn't hear through the suit, but they could feel, even with the suit on.

"No, we can't take our suits off," they said. "Right?"

"There's air, but it's not been refreshed in a long time. I wouldn't risk it," Graeme said.

Another chime.

"You can try, I suppose."

"Wait, you can..."

"I can feel them talking through my *ters*," Skyt explained. Their magnetic sense, which clearly this was designed to work with.

"Aha," Graeme said. "Well, we can't, so you're going to have to translate.

It wasn't even clear. They needed air to talk properly, air that they could breathe. But if there was air they could breathe... Skyt's plan became clearer. Clearer as time went on and they waited while the intelligence, for such it surely was, tried some things.

"Little one, if you could please exit the train and..."

The instructions had to be repeated three times. "What can the others do?"

Silence.

Only Skyt was wanted? Well, they passed things on anyway. One set of pincers and two sets of hands would get this done far, far faster.

38

GRAEME

THERE WAS a peculiar pressure on the outside of Graeme's suit. Of course, these suits weren't really designed for full atmospheric pressure. No doubt they were a little unstable. What they needed were Mars surface suits.

Still, it felt as if somebody was *leaning* on him. The full weight of the world above and below, of whatever held gravity at a nice stable 1.1G on a hollow world. Maybe the gravity *was* a bit different down here. It wasn't impossible.

But no. He felt as if he was being *watched*.

Following Skyt's instructions, he was hooking up machinery that according to the glen *might* give them life support.

Assuming it wasn't more broken than the AI down here thought. Or more likely the uploaded mind.

Was this one of the glen's creators?

He could see a growing tension in Skyt. Tthe glen was starting to show signs of active distress. With no overt reason for it. Except what Skyt could hear or, more accurately, feel, and they couldn't.

Then a wind rushed past him. He glanced at Toni. "Give it a few."

He did. He waited. And then when she gave a thumbs up, he tugged off his helmet. The air smelled stale. But he could still breathe and if there wasn't quite as much oxygen as was ideal, he could manage.

The glen needed more oxygen, so if Skyt could breathe he could.

"Again, why did you bring them here?"

"They came to help fix things."

"Offworlders have no place here."

Oh man. So, that was the argument. "We really did come to help."

Skyt's translator was still working, as was Graeme's. Either minimal linguistic drift or this entity had been paying attention to the surface.

Or, most likely, both.

"That does not matter."

"Run some diagnostics. If we don't fix this, then the glen will have to leave."

"The glen will not leave."

Oh...oh boy. "Even if that means they all die?"

Skyt finally spoke up. "We aren't your property any more."

"If you leave and do not return then you too have no place here."

Well, that was straightforward enough, Graeme supposed. "So, they can leave as long as they come back?"

"We will not sacrifice the knowledge they bring."

Skyt's eyes were pointed everywhere but at Graeme.

"If there's no world to bring it back to?"

"You are an offworlder."

"We're helping the glen find a place to go when this world is destroyed."

"And I am already saying they must return. Always."

———

SKYT FINALLY SPOKE UP. "We're exploration probes. And this...this being thinks we *belong* to it." Not janitors.

It was an uploaded ancient. "Well, nobody gets to own another sentient being." Graeme thought of Marion.

Some people still thought of children as property. As something to be raised exactly the way the parents chose, with no regard to their rights or wider society.

"Not even those who made them. It's up to the glen what they want to do." He kept his head high. "They are your children, not your property." The worst form of bad parenting, but perhaps this being did not realize they had created children.

"And their consciousness is preserved in the archive. You are *not* one of us, you don't understand."

"Yes, I do. I'm a parent."

He thought of Marion again.

A parent, and the ancients were parents to the glen. It didn't matter that they hadn't quite intended it to be that way. He wanted to be a better parent than they and he wanted Skyt to learn to be a better parent too, if not to the child they already had. "Your kind left. They have built their own society. Now either we fix this planet or they leave. Let us help."

"If you help..."

"Some of them will stay. More of them will return. They will have the *choice*."

Graeme was using all of his diplomatic skill.

"Again, you..."

"No, I don't know what it's like to be glen. I certainly don't know what it's like to be you, because none of us can manage that. But they're fighting over whether to stay or go. Take away the fear and a healthy number will stay. This isn't a bad world."

The AI paused. "Not a *bad* world."

"I'm biased in favor of my own homeworld." Graeme was sweating. "This one is a little warm for my tastes."

Skyt chimed, but there was something nervous and weak about it.

"Your kind is unknown to me."

"You've been down here a while and I have to admit we're a bit...on the young side."

"I have been dormant. Tell me, how many generations."

Skyt considered that. "Three thousand generations."

"Three thousand."

"Since the archive was wiped."

"It was wiped to keep it away from off worlders."

"Why?" Skyt asked.

Graeme let them talk; it was almost certainly going to respond to the glen better.

"Because otherwise they will find where the remnant of us went."

"They aren't part of whatever war you were fighting," Skyt said, finally. "They're just people. Curious, friendly and, yes, aggressive. But they want to help."

"What would you gain from helping, offworlder?"

Graeme didn't even hesitate. "Friends."

"Friends? Offworlders are not friends."

"Maybe the batch you met weren't. But we're good at making friends...and so is everyone else, if you nudge them a bit. We aren't whatever you were fighting."

Graeme didn't want to know who or what they were fighting. His best hope was that this enemy was long extinct.

"THEY BURNED WORLDS," the AI was explaining. "They burned worlds whether we were on them or not. We think they did not recognize us as alive or sentient. Or they didn't care. They just wanted..."

Skyt crouched down, and Graeme could tell the glen was listening intently.

Toni wasn't. She was prowling the edge of the chamber, and if AIs could be nervous...he wanted to ask her to stop.

"Did they *change* the worlds?"

"To suit themselves. We built refuges where they would not think to look. We built this archive, where we thought they would not think to look."

"Then abandoned the world to them and the glen."

"I stayed."

They had a point, Graeme thought. A definite point. "They never came here."

"They overlooked it after all. We could have kept everything of our civilization here."

"You did." Skyt, finally speaking up, lifting their head, swiveling multiple eyes. "You kept *us*."

"You are the debris of a project, a...side issue."

"No. We are your *children*," Skyt said. "And you haven't been a great parent, but that's fine, because I wasn't either. We might be all that's left."

"You are a weed. Without the archive..."

"Look at our world!" Skyt said, finally, chiming loudly. "We have built something beautiful without the archive. True, maybe we would have done better with it. Or maybe we would be lyrk on a trail."

Graeme closed his eyes to listen better as the argument started up again. Then, finally, "If you truly thought they were weeds, you wouldn't argue with one."

There was a moment of distinct silence.

A rumbling deep within the world that made Graeme nervous, but he couldn't do anything about it right now.

"They are..."

"As Skyt said. Your children. They could leave and build something beautiful, but we want to fix this world. We can't get all of them off."

"And..."

"And it's dying. It's drifting out of orbit and things are failing all over the place."

"I don't know how to repair it."

"But you know something, you know things we could use to do that."

Another rumble.

"If it's not already too late."

Skyt was clinging to the ground. Graeme dropped into a crouch, and then to the ground as the glenquake rolled over them.

Which he knew wasn't natural. He feared finding out what had blown up.

39

SKYT

AN ANCIENT. An actual ancient.

And Skyt had lost all of their reverence for them. Oh, maybe not *all*. But between the way the ancient had dismissed Graeme and Toni, and the word "weed."

They had been designed for a purpose. They had been abandoned.

Weeds were not meant to survive, let alone thrive.

At the same time, the ancient wanted what was in glen heads, and the reward for that was immortality. It was confusing and it honestly wasn't even entirely self-consistent. Skyt had to wonder if the ancient was entirely *sane*. After all, they had translated a very long time ago and even if they had spent most of that time dormant.

Alternately begging Skyt to stay and calling them a weed? The ancient wasn't sane.

Whether they could become so again was beside the point. They claimed not to know how to fix Glyn. But they knew a lot.

The glynquake had passed. "What was that?" Skyt asked the ancient.

"I don't know."

"You don't have all of the sensors."

"I don't have many of the sensors."

"Well, we already had an explosion in the sublayer that almost breached the hull, and it seemed to come from *inside* the hull. This place is failing."

"This place will last forever."

"No," Skyt said. "It won't."

Nothing did. Nothing ever could. Another rumbling. Was this the end? Would they die down here as unpredicted convulsions tore their world apart?

Maybe no warning would be better for those oblivious on the surface. "It's unstable right now."

There was a long silence, a pause in which Graeme and Toni stayed crouched, apparently afraid to stand back up. The downside to being a biped was the distinct lack of anchor points when the floor started to move under one. Skyt no longer envied them.

"That..."

"What is unstable?"

"The primary core is unstable. It is not safe to fix it." A pause. "You were right. This place will not last forever."

"So, we have to evacuate *now*." Skyt concluded.

"You..."

"We will leave and take the knowledge we have *with* us. We will seed it. Give us everything you have, everything that wasn't wiped." Skyt was begging. They couldn't save many people.

They could save a few. Maybe even a viable population.

But they could certainly save *knowledge*. And that was just as important.

"Your directives remain."

Skyt's eyes swiveled. "They became part of our culture, part of our values. But they are no longer directives. We *choose* to gain and preserve knowledge."

How much did they really choose? How much *was* some ancient hardcoded directive? But Skyt knew it didn't matter. They chose.

The ground shook again.

"So, if the power core is unstable..."

"...then the planet is going to explode. But not right away." Skyt turned three eyes to where the intelligence's voice chimed from. "Right?"

"I anticipate we have a matter of days before it goes critical and implodes."

"How *many* days?"

"Seven."

The humans, for some reason, flinched slightly. Perhaps there was some cultural significance to the number Skyt was unaware of.

"Seven days to get as many people off planet as possible."

"Not just off planet. Away. Can your space station move?"

Skyt looked towards Graeme with three (and a half) eyes. "I have no idea. I mean...I'm not a rocket scientist."

"Let's get out of here."

"And cause a panic," Toni said, flatly.

Skyt saw Graeme's body swell and reduce, a sign of working their breathing apparatus hard.

They wanted to say glen didn't panic. They knew better.

Everyone on this planet was going to die. The nascent colonies would be all there was of Glyn. They could save a few, perhaps. A handful.

And Toni was right, if they told the general public, there would only be pain.

Skyt closed all eight eyes, plunging themselves into rare darkness. With their eyes closed, they could hear the distant groaning.

They were going to die, for good, for all, because they couldn't take one of those rare slots. "You need to get off planet. The launch is still..."

"...Skyt."

Skyt opened their eyes. "We can't take many people off planet. I want to leave. I have wanted to...for a while. But we need people with the expertise the *colonies* need. That's not me."

"We have a phrase for this, Skyt," Graeme said firmly. "That phrase is 'Don't be a martyr.'"

Toni was shaking their head slightly.

Skyt knew that they agreed with them. That Toni knew Skyt was right. Graeme...liked Skyt.

Skyt liked Graeme. They could have been friends, should have been friends, perhaps sipping juice together on the station. Perhaps even seeing that canyon on Earth, climbing it as only glen could climb.

Graeme wanted that.

"I can't be selfish. We need to warn the *right* people."

Toni was right. They had to get back to the surface, they had to put their suits on and head for the nearest hatch, not the way they had come.

They had to tell the right people. Skyt was not sure who the right people were.

Seven days.

THE SURFACE WAS warm once Skyt pulled off their helmet. It had been colder than they realized down there. Colder than they wanted to think about.

As cold as an ice world? They were not suffering too much, thanks to the protection from their suit. But there was still cold inside them, or perhaps it was the knowledge of how little time they had. The suns shone brightly. Full double day. The humans kept their suits on, protection against the heat.

The world was beautiful. Avians flew through the air, chiming at one another. Everything was carefully, so carefully put together. Everything was falling apart. The world felt as if it was on pause, in a moment between moment and moment.

Skyt didn't look at the humans. Skyt knew they needed to walk away now, otherwise Graeme would take them off world, in space that could take somebody younger, more...

Skyt was being stupid. The truth was that somebody afraid to pass on their genetic material...but they couldn't admit that. They had taken long enough to admit it to themselves.

Skyt looked instead at the safe part of the sky, away from the brilliance of the suns. They could feel the knife edge their world balanced on, was falling off of.

Seven days.

Slightly less than that now.

"So, who do we need to talk to?"

"We need to go straight to the council," Skyt said without looking at Graeme. Under the translation, they could hear the human's natural voice, deeper than their companion.

Variation. Evolution.

Glen didn't evolve, but that wasn't true. That had never been true. It had been something they held to, clung to.

Glen didn't *change*. Not weeds, but machines going along their tracks. The Migrators were right about that. Right that glen had become stagnant. Wrong about the solution.

Straight to the Council. "Come on," they said to the humans, walking towards a place where they could call for a car.

They were exhausted, they were cold, and they were afraid. Yet, they had to keep going. One foot in front of the other until all six were under them and then again.

Always moving forward. They would worry about choosing later.

Choosing to live or to die.

40

GRAEME

Six days.

It wasn't as bad as it sounded. A Glen day, marked by the specific rising and setting of the suns, was about 36 hours long. But it was a deadline.

A literal deadline for almost all of the people on this world. They couldn't fix it.

An unstable controlled singularity? Per Toni, if that happened on a ship, the protocol every race had developed was to expel the singularity, run as fast as you could on sublight engines, then call for help. You couldn't stop the implosion once it started. This ship couldn't expel the singularity.

If it *could* then it would still... Hmm.

"Toni, what would the surface gravity of Glyn be if we could somehow remove the singularity?"

"I see what you're getting at, but I doubt..."

"Run the math."

He doubted there was a way to do it too. Skyt was depressed and apparently determined to die with their world.

Graeme understood the impulse. To give the lifeboat space to somebody better. To their kid, perhaps, now they weren't quite so estranged.

He would give his to Marion.

So, perhaps he was being unfair on Skyt. Unfair, because he liked the...guy wasn't the right word even if part of him kept floating back to it.

Guy was too gendered a word. Skyt wasn't, mind, a human enby who might be offended by it. Skyt wouldn't understand to be offended.

Skyt wasn't human, not remotely. It was surprisingly easy to forget that when actually interacting with them. A giant angelic bug who reminded Graeme of multiple scientists he'd known. An archaeologist before he was a bug, albeit with a slightly different definition than was used on Earth.

Expel the singularity. The world might hold an atmosphere long enough to do something of an evacuation. It wasn't a solution, it wasn't salvation. It was a straw that Graeme was clutching at when he knew he should be calling Earth for help.

He needed to call Earth for help. But the ansible was on the station.

Unless there was one on the planet. There was almost certainly one *somewhere* he could potentially use. He sat down at his terminal and started to make calls.

Straight to the Glyn Council.

The Council would see them in a few hours.

Would decide what to do. Would decide who to save.

It was with that morbid thought that Graeme hopped into a glen car, folding himself into it. He would sooner have walked. If humans came here regularly they would need to bring their own vehicles.

With really good air conditioning. *Really* good air conditioning.

Except there wouldn't be a here for much longer. Instead they would...he supposed the glen would pick a colony world to be their new capital. They had three. A viable off world population. Except without the force that kept their culture stable. Would those three worlds do their own spinning off into space?

The council were meeting them in an office building, not some grand palace. The glen didn't seem to go for...

No, they *did* go for grand palaces.

Those were libraries and museums. Seats of government, apparently, were meant to be more...modest. Unfortunately, that also meant low ceilings. Toni was better off, but Graeme was starting to worry about turning into a hunchback. Or what an osteopath would have to say about the state of his spine. But it was what had to be done and when they finally came into a room, the ceiling was high enough to give some relief.

He sat, semi cross-legged, on the glen bench and regarded the council. The glen apparently leaned towards a gerontocracy; he had learned to see the dulling of the carapace which came with age. The balance of experience and flexibility was skewed.

Not what they needed right now, but it was not his problem. Getting off Glyn before it imploded was his problem.

"So, you say we have six days."

"According to the intelligence in the core, yes. I see no reason why they would have lied."

Only one of the councillors spoke, likely by some agreement. "No reason?"

"They don't want the glen to leave. Ergo, they would not tell a lie which would panic people into leaving."

"Which we can't do. There's no time."

"No. We can get knowledge and a few people to the colonies," Graeme admitted. "But no, there's no time."

He felt tears prick at his eyes. He was sentencing these people to death, and their ancestors to oblivion.

No. He was only the messenger and he had not caused this. Only failed to prevent it.

"Is there any chance of repair?" Finally, a different glen was speaking. A younger one, if Graeme was right.

"Unlikely. The power core at the heart of your world is a controlled singularity. We don't know of any way to restabilize one. On a normal ship or station, we would expel it."

"Could that be done?"

He thought of Toni's math. "Potentially, but the worst case scenario would be an acceleration of the end. The best case...we would have a few years to evacuate Glyn before the atmosphere was lost. The controlled singularity is providing much of your gravity."

The glen turned their eyes, all eight, away from Graeme for a moment, then back. "That would still be better..."

"But we don't know how we would go about it."

"Somebody would have to go to the core."

Graeme nodded. "Somebody would, and likely those people, whoever they are, would not come back."

And would not find their way into the sublayer. Graeme was glad he did not have to make the decision to send somebody on a suicide mission. He knew they had little choice, but something in his stomach clenched at the thought.

A suicide mission. But if they failed, everyone would die. What did they have to lose? This was not his world, but he took a deep breath of the hot air anyway, or what of it was filtered through his suit.

"Indeed. But it might be our only chance. Can the intelligence you found help?"

"They say no, but I don't know if that is true or if they are choosing not to. Which implies to me that they think it is not possible, because even the slimmest chance of you staying. They think...they think they still *own* you. I think Skyt went a good way towards convincing them otherwise."

"The ancients did own us. In their terms, under their laws."

"Nobody owns you now." Graeme's lips quirked. Although he thought of what the intelligence had said about programmed behavior.

Would they be free of those programmed vestiges if they left? But it didn't matter. They no longer had the time to leave.

Six days.

It was like a beating in his heart, the time limit, and even the station might not be far enough away. It slowly dawned within him that he too might have no escape, might never see Charles and Marion again.

Six days.

41

SKYT

Skyt knew what they had to do.

Skyt knew it from the tip of their mandibles to the mating tubes tucked under the rear of their carapace.

Every inch of them knew it. That did not mean it was easy.

It certainly didn't mean they *wanted* to do it. Every part of them felt even colder than in the depths of Glyn, and it was colder yet where they had to go. They would need the space suit, of course.

They would need some way to transport tools. A robot was the obvious answer, something powered only by algorithms, for Skyt could *certainly* not risk another person. A robot, then. It wouldn't be that hard and they would be gone before anyone realized. They knew where to go now, where the entry point by the exhaust mountain was.

What they did not know was what they would do when they got to the power core. Whether they could survive approaching, although there was little difference in dying there and waiting to die on the surface. They would die *trying* to save their people, and really that was all that could matter, all that they could think about.

The problem was that their biology was getting in the way. Utter, abject terror was flowing through every part of them, mingling with determination. It would not even be the act of a coward to turn back, because the kind of fear they felt was one the bravest glen could not in truth be expected to simply deal with as if it was anxiety over a vaccination.

So, no, they would not be a coward if they turned back. They would simply be a failure, and Skyt had always felt a failure. Skyt could not be a failure again, that was what it boiled down to, even if they wanted to.

Which was why they descended through the hatch, the floating drone robot carrying the gear they hoped they would need next to them. Down into the bowels of the planet, but this time they went alone. They could not take the humans with them.

They could not get Graeme and Toni killed, and not just because it might cause a diplomatic incident. Toni they were less sure of, but Graeme was a good person, somebody who believed in Skyt and believed in the glen and, Skyt suspected, always strove to see the best in everyone. Not in morality, but in potential.

Skyt's potential went away today, but if they succeeded, then it was all worth it, even the terrifying oblivion that awaited. That awaited regardless of their choice.

It was only a matter of when.

THE ANCIENT INTELLIGENCE WAS SILENT. Perhaps, Skyt thought, they had gone back to sleep, back to dormancy. Perhaps that was the best choice if there was no hope. Turn off one's consciousness, feel no pain and no ending.

It still terrified Skyt. Yet it felt right that they remained alone, without that being to guide them. The being that thought they owned them. The repairs it had made to the life support systems held. Skyt was able to save suit air, although the place was still as cold as a walk-in freezer.

The humans hadn't seemed bothered. It wasn't cold to them. They would leave, go back to their homeworld, or go to a colony world to continue to work with other glen, to help them learn to live with the knowledge that when the time came they would cease to be.

They would *live*, though, for what span humans had.

Down ever deeper, and Skyt began to think...no.

Now they were looking down at the deep pit, the hollow void at the center of their world. White radiation poured off the power core, Skyt wasn't sure what it might be doing to them, but it let them see it. Let them see what held their world together, what had once provided the energy for it to fly.

The radiation *bulged* on one side. The instability was *visible* and Skyt's circulatory system jittered.

Toni was right. There was no way any glen or any human or any force could fix that. They didn't even know where to start. Perhaps a ship engineer who worked on FTL drives would know.

Skyt had come this far and now they faced failure yet again, because they had somehow, foolishly, felt that their understanding of ancient technology, of the tidbits the creators had left behind, might be enough. It wasn't.

They could flee now, and get blind drunk for the days remaining, pass them in a haze which would make them forget time. That was the sane thing to do. As Skyt stared at the dark heart of their world, though, their sanity was fleeing along with their hope.

Why do the sane thing when nothing matters any more?

WHY INDEED?

But there was no hope, and thus there was no reason not to do what went beyond hope. They had a suit, which meant they could pass into the airless void, but Skyt had enough sense to know that they needed to stop and think first.

If they just did this, if they just went charging in, they would fail. They would fail and they would die. They were willing to succeed and die. They were willing to do their level best, to do everything they could, and die.

But setting themselves up for failure was just wasting their life and their knowledge. The knowledge the intelligence wanted so badly. Were they peeking into the sublayer?

No, Skyt had the feeling they had been dormant for a while and did not actually know what was going on in the sublayer. Which was a little sad. Somebody that curious, even if they thought of the glen as feral vermin, deserved the knowledge that would make them happy.

Everyone deserved the knowledge that would make them happy. The world twisted for a moment, and Skyt was reminded that while they should not rush in, they could not wait forever. They thought of all the people they were doing this for. They thought of their child.

"Are you there?" they asked, hoping their words were heard.

Silence. But there were lights, there was energy. There *was* power down here and function, and Skyt moved along the inner hull, looking for answers. Looking for some hint or clue as to what they could do, and starting to feel as if they had expected the impossible, sought the impossible.

They couldn't do this. If it could be done, they didn't know how.

"Is anyone there?" they tried again, to an answer of more silence.

But there were terminals. Terminals that flickered brokenly in ancient language. Skyt tapped one of them cautiously with a suit-encased pincer. They had taken their helmet off and strapped it to their back, but otherwise kept the suit on, just in case.

Tap.

Flicker.

Words reconfiguring themselves, sluggishly. The system was still responsive. Still responding to them, still wanting to help. Skyt felt a sudden sense of continuity, with the sublayer, with the ancients.

Then Skyt got to work trying to understand.

42

GRAEME

SKYT WAS GONE and Graeme missed them already. He did not know where they had gone, only that they didn't plan on coming back.

Graeme couldn't blame them. It was all too much, he supposed. They might have gone to bury themselves in work, to find a way to get their offspring off planet, to get blind drunk. All of those seemed like reasonable reactions. Graeme was tempted to get blind drunk himself.

His own escape was going to be cutting it fine. He and Toni had already decided they couldn't take up space on the evacuation ships, the ones which would get a bare few thousand off before the end. Instead, they had to wait for the *Challenger* to come back for them.

He knew that decision might result in Charles getting an "It is with deep regret" notice. He knew that. But they needed as many glen to escape as possible. Otherwise, they could easily become an endangered species.

Two spaces might not make a difference. Or they might.

His conscience allowed him to do nothing else.

He stood by the window, enjoying the climate control while looking out at a beautiful world that was soon to be no more. Enjoying what remained. Appreciating it. His grandmother, the nice one, always said to live in the moment. To love as you wished, to thrive.

He thought of Marion. He thought *I'm sorry* as if it could somehow reach across the endless void between them, the beautiful space between the stars across which they leapt in ships that were merely smaller versions of this one. Expel the core.

It wasn't, of course, possible. The singularity would have to pass through the planet. Killing thousands to save...

...could they evacuate at a planetary scale? Could they get everyone into one place? To buy time.

"If you dead guys know anything, have any ideas," he said out loud.

Then he said it again, turning towards his terminal.

"We have been working on it." The voice which responded was a chord.

"You have a *lot* more computing power than I do."

And every incentive, of course, to solve it. He knew they would tell the truth. Surely they did not want to die.

"THE CORE CANNOT BE EXPELLED, or at least is not designed to be."

"You can't exactly open a planet and let it out. Makes me wonder if this place has lasted longer than they intended. Or..."

"They took the knowledge we need to maintain it."

"Including from the person they left behind in the core."

"I have to think they were an...oversight. Surely the ancients knew how to move a translated personality."

Surely? Graeme was considerably less sure of that himself. It would make sense for them to have that knowledge, yes, but that didn't mean they did. It might not be possible. It might be that you could only move...or copy...a soul once. Or that subsequent copies became something else, something different.

Not that that was a bad thing. Children were not their parents. "Are we sure of that?"

"Given all else they knew..."

"Everything they have done here extrapolates from things we have already done. There have been experiments with uploading consciousness. They haven't worked yet, but that doesn't mean they're impossible. This artificial planet is only really a space station, just on an excessively huge scale." Graeme took a deep breath. "We will recreate you, given time."

"Indeed. And the fact that you already know it can be done."

"Helps. My point is that I haven't seen anything here that is...there was a writer on Earth once that said that any sufficiently advanced technology is indistinguishable from magic. Clarke his name was. He forgot the relative to where you are part, but nothing I have seen from the ancients is magic. It all makes sense."

A slight pause. "So, what you are saying is that they may not have found a way to move an ensconced consciousness out of the sublayer."

"Right. Which might mean it's not possible." He paused. "Or maybe it would introduce copying errors..."

"...that would turn the new intelligence into a different person."

"Is that what happened when you tried to move somebody onto the station?"

"It is, although that obviously doesn't prove fidelitous copying is impossible."

"I would personally prefer that an imperfect copy of me continued rather than ceasing to exist completely. I have a child."

Poor Marion. Would she ever understand why one of her fathers had left her?

He couldn't explain this to her. He was leaving that burden to Charles.

"In the end, our children are all we really leave behind us."

Graeme thought about that. "No, there's also our knowledge."

THE PLANET SHIFTED. At least that was how it felt. Another glenquake, another malfunction deep within. Graeme held onto something while it passed.

"If all we can do is save copies..."

"Not in five days," the intelligence said, sadly. "All of our consciousnesses, in their permanent and transient formations will, in any case, be lost."

Five days. It just wasn't enough time.

"Is there a way," Graeme mused, "To turn a singularity *off*?"

"No," said Toni from the door.

"Well...what happens when you lose control of one?

She considered. "An unstable singularity implodes."

"Right. I'm asking if there's a way to make it stop existing without imploding."

She sat down, perhaps worried about another quake. On the floor, her legs folded under her in a surprisingly elegant manner. Graeme felt compelled to join her, even though he was sure she did it only to give herself time to think.

Finally, she spoke. "You mean, evaporate it."

"Right."

"Okay, so. Layman's terms. There are tiny singularities all through space, but they constantly evaporate. You build a controlled singularity by grabbing one...and be careful, they sometimes jump into hyper..."

She stopped.

She swore.

"What?"

"When you are growing a singularity to power a ship, and I've talked to tyrar scientists so I know this is universal, there's a stage at which it wants to go hyper. Heck, that's how we jump."

"So. You could get rid of an unwanted singularity..."

"...by making it jump into hyperspace. You'd create a...I wouldn't want to be on a ship that happened to be flying by." She demonstrated by moving her hand around in various pitching and rolling motions. "But..."

"...it could work. Hey."

Was the sublayer still listening?

"Is it possible to do something like that?"

"Well, it's never been intentionally done. But it could be. It would let us eject the core. The planet would lose a lot of gravity and eventually most of its atmosphere, but we could..."

"...Toni. The people who built this place knew a lot of things we don't. But there's something we and the tyrar and the ky'iin *and the glyn* all know how to do perfectly well."

Her jaw dropped. "Grow a...you're suggesting we eject the unstable singularity and then *replace* it?"

"Do you have a better ridiculous idea?"

"If you weren't gay and married I'd marry you."

He laughed...and it was a laugh of relief. They would likely fail.

But they...just had to work out how to nudge an unstable singularity to do what it might well want to do anyway.

Dissipate into the other layers of the universe.

43

SKYT

SKYT WAS NO CLOSER to understanding. There was a peculiar ache at the base of their carapace.

Perhaps this *was* beyond any glen. They had been designed, it seemed, to be smart, but not smart enough. A data collection machine was better than a cleaning bot, but it was still something built for a reason, for a purpose, not evolved, not grown. Bred.

Not bred for this task. Maybe there had been others, and Skyt thought of the ancients and their mantis appearance. Or had the mantis been something bred to some other task, assigned to work here. Had it been a picture of a friend, a rey, a child, a...

Skyt did not know. Skyt wanted to know.

But Skyt would not know, because they were going to die a failure.

Five days.

They had five days to work out how to restabilize a singularity from old records, knowledge, and a few tools. They stared once more into the heart of the void. The white radiation that came off of it, devoid of color, broad in range. There was no way to approach. It must have been managed remotely.

Or perhaps, perhaps there was a craft somewhere, but Skyt was terrified to approach. They knew that the singularity might eat them if they did. Then they would not be able to help anyone. Might eat them. It was going to eat them and everyone they cared about and the remnants of the glen would become a beggar race, protected by others.

Skyt closed all eight eyes. The white radiation seemed to still burn through their eyelids.

Would they get cancer? They wouldn't live long enough to get cancer. That almost made them feel better.

So. Perhaps they were on the wrong side of the planet.

Some kind of craft could *well* be the solution they were looking for. Some kind of machine that would take them on their way. They just had to try as hard as possible before dying. Just that. It wasn't hard. It wasn't hard to satisfy their pride, but they could not help but wish it would do some good.

They couldn't help but hope.

THE WORLD SEEMED, for a moment, to twist. Skyt blinked all eight eyes and everything was normal again.

In their search for a craft to traverse the void at the center of the world, they had, perhaps, got caught by a gravity wave from the unstable singularity. The intelligence might be wrong.

They might not have five days.

If that was the case then they would call this trying, would feel no shame at their failure, or semi-failure at any rate. They would call it trying and they would go into oblivion not content, no, but not with nearly the fear they had felt. They would lose everything, but they would have raised their pincers against...

The world twisted again and they felt uncertain and as if, as if they were about to be torn apart, as if their carapace was no longer quite attached to the softer parts which lay beneath. They turned eyes backwards, and it was as if strange lights flowed below the diamond brilliance.

Something had broken inside them. It did not matter. They could think, they could function, they could move. Any injury, even a fatal one, could not be allowed to slow...

...and there it was. A maintenance pod, akin to the ones they built on the station. Not so akin as to be suspicious; there were only so many ways space vehicles could be built. Not built for glen to use.

But Skyt could scurry inside, could strap themselves down so that they wouldn't fly around, in a couch clearly meant for a creature about a third again their size.

The ancients had been bigger, based off of the images and the way the place was built.

Or whatever being had been bred to fly this had been bigger.

The mantis beings might not be the ancients. They flew. They flew into the void inside the world, trusting the pod would work. Or, rather, they no longer had time to consider the consequences if it didn't.

If it didn't work, they had tried.

Five days. The singularity blazing at them from inside its shell. It wasn't enough time, nothing was enough time. But they could see, in gaps in the white flares, what had happened. Something had skewed with the containment field.

It had shifted sideways and touched the maw within. Their world was *very* broken, and it was broken because of something that on the scale of it was small. A little bit, Skyt was sure, of metal fatigue or corrosion.

Nothing more.

STEERING AS close as they dared, Skyt realized the singularity was suspended amongst fields. One of which had failed. So, if they could find the field projector and reactivate it, maybe. It might be that simple.

It couldn't be that simple. Mentally, Skyt cursed the ancients out for not providing an instruction manual. Or for wiping it.

For...all of it. But they had meant to come back. They knew that. Somewhere out there, the enemy might still exist. The ancients might still exist.

Or perhaps somewhere out there...and Skyt felt the deepest of regrets. The field projector. They tried to extrapolate its position.

There. It was most likely there, and they awkwardly steered

towards it. The maintenance pod was fast. It zipped across the inner hull, which had projections and windows and all kinds of things for those who had once lived and worked between the hulls. Not on the surface.

They could live between the hulls if the atmosphere bled off. They could do it, or some of them could, anyway. If they could hold and create enough air.

Was that it?

Skyt turned the entire craft to look. Maybe it was. Skyt flew closer.

Something twisted again, and the craft flew into space. Skyt clung desperately, feeling that twist under their carapace again. They were definitely injured. They hurt, they hurt all over and they fought against the hidden currents, but it was hopeless.

They weren't getting anywhere close to it. Not from this side. They were failing and dying and falling and...

...the craft slammed into the inner hull, Skyt drifting out of consciousness, then in, the out.

"Help," they said weakly, but of course there was nobody in the pod to hear them.

They pressed buttons, flailing.

"Help!"

No answer. They had to get themselves out of their predicament, but they were feeling waves of weakness come over them. Their hind limbs did not seem to be responding. They tried one more chime.

"Help!"

The only answer was blackness.

44

GRAEME

"Skyt's missing."

Graeme frowned, then slightly shook his head. "I don't think we can worry about them right now."

"No, really vanished-off-the-face-of-Glyn missing," Toni said. "Abducted or suicided or something."

He closed his eyes. "We still can't worry about them, no matter how much we want to."

He wanted to. He wanted to drop everything and track the glen down. Find them. Give them a hug, if glen could hug.

Well, maybe glen could hug, but he wasn't going to hug a glen, not even that one. He couldn't.

Skyt would not even want him to. Or would they? Based off of some of the things they had said, they weren't entirely in their right mind right now. Graeme was legit afraid. But he *couldn't* and he knew a sane Skyt would know that they could not be more important than their world and the people on it. They knew that, but it still hurt.

They would need to take control of whatever functioning systems still worked in the core of the world, whatever was still there to adjust the power output from the singularity. But it was still dangerous.

Part of him wanted to wait until the last possible moment, as they might well only have one chance at this. Part of him wanted to run. To take that launch, find Skyt, grab Toni, and just *run* until the light of Glyn's suns was so far away that they were seeing it from before this world was built.

Instead, he checked Toni's math. She was the one who knew something about singularities. And there were glen starship engineers they could ask.

She was looking for one who wouldn't panic at the very idea of what it was they were trying to do right now. Trying to find the right, safe help. Somebody who could handle this. Who could handle this?

Marion was safe. Marion would never even know. Those were the thoughts that kept Graeme sane. He held his daughter's face in his mind as he checked the math again. To him, to the diplomat and spy, it looked solid. Of course, the math was the easy part. The hard part was the engineering.

Oh, and staying alive. That might prove to be the hardest part of all.

Toni returned in not too long order with two glen.

Well, one and a half glen. One of the glen was a bright carapaced adult. The other was a youngster who's exoskeleton hadn't quite hardened yet and who stared at them with only four eyes from their parent's back.

They were adorable, like all babies, even if they didn't have the slightly disturbing angelic shine of the adults as yet. Their eyes were larger in proportion to the rest of them, which was part of the impression.

Graeme had not expected the presence of a toddler, and as Toni talked to the adult, the kid scuttled down from their parents back and over to him, looking up and up at him with all four of those eyes. He thought he could see the buds of the other eyes starting to form. He had no idea they didn't hatch with the full complement. He knew nothing about glen babies. The baby didn't have a translator. They chimed in an almost painfully high voice.

Graeme smiled and dropped down to one knee. He knew the child wouldn't understand his voice either, but would they understand an adult getting down to their level as a friendly gesture?

They had faint striping across their body. Camouflage, Graeme realized, so that when the parent left them they could hide from whatever predators had hunted glen ancestors. Just like the shading on a foal or the spotting of lion cubs.

Human kids fled up trees instead. Designed, but they had not been designed from whole cloth. They had been uplifted, as some people threatened to do to dogs. He wondered if that was really the best reward for all of those centuries of service. Extra anxiety?

No, he wouldn't want to be an animal. The anxiety came with the territory. Slowly, he extended a hand. The child blinked two of those eyes and reached out with a pincer to touch his palm.

Likely they thought that was how you greeted humans now. "Hello, little one," he said, It wouldn't be understood.

This child was perhaps a hostage against the parent, for what parent wouldn't fight for their world with this delightful little one at stake. He realized he was crying. He realized the child would never understand that.

He tried, and failed, to stop.

BY THE TIME, though, that Toni and the child's parent emerged, Graeme had come to some understanding with the kid. He thought their name was Pyr. It was hard to tell whether that particular chiming sound was the child's name or just a sound they liked.

He was chasing them around the room when he was distracted by a louder chime that he recognized after a moment as glen laughter.

"Thanks for keeping Pyr distracted," the adult said, through their translator.

So, he had guessed right. "They are adorable."

"Thank you. They will grow out of it soon enough."

Graeme laughed. "And trouble."

"They won't grow out of that." More chimes.

Of course, this child might not get to grow at all, might not get to go through advanced education, work out what they wanted to do.

They might never know who they were. Graeme had no more tears left for their future. Not a single one. None left, too, for himself.

"We think we have a theory, but the engineering could be impossible." Toni waited until the glen left, their now exhausted child tucked against their carapace. "Do you still want to do this?"

He thought of Charles. Of Marion. How much he wanted to see Marion and Pyr play together, grow together, learn together.

"We have to," he said finally.

"*We* don't have to." Toni walked over to the window. "We're going to, but we don't have to. We could hand this all over to the glen."

"We could."

But they both knew they couldn't. They both knew they couldn't walk away from a world which needed help.

"Of course..."

Graeme selfishly wanted Skyt to join them. Selfishly, because they probably wouldn't survive whatever was going to happen in the core. Selfishly, because he wanted that chiming voice, that sense of humor.

The first human to meet a glen had called them angels. The second had almost thrown up. Graeme thought he might be the first human to dare to call one a friend.

But they had no idea where Skyt was. So, they had to... They had to go to the poles. That was the starting point. Skyt would have to look after themselves.

Graeme had a job to do. And love for a friend could not get in the way.

45

SKYT

THE SLOW RETURN OF LIGHT. Skyt knew they were damaged, broken.

But they were alive, and breathing.The air was being pulled through their breathing tubes and for a moment they just lay there, relishing the sensations of life. Of simply being. Then they took stock.

A yellow light, the color of blood, was flashing on the console. They decided that probably wasn't a good thing. Taking stock. Taking breath. They hadn't failed yet, because they were still alive. That was the most basic level.

They were still alive and the planet-ship was still there. Ergo, while they had yet to succeed, they had also yet to fail. It would almost have been easier not to wake up. Not to open any of their eyes. They almost went back to sleep, in fact, then forced themselves onto their feet.

First, inspect the pod. There was clearly a distortion field emanating from the field projector. The pod appeared to have been designed to take it. It was leaking slightly, so they slipped their helmet back on before the oxygen levels became any lower.

But other than that...

So they couldn't just readjust the projector from here. Perhaps they could if they turned it off first, but who knew what effect *that* might have. It might cause the core to go flying through the hull. Through a city.

Skyt closed all eight eyes again, this time in thought. So, they had to...find a way through the hull close to the projector. Come at it from the other side.

Did they risk turning it off? They might have to. They might have to risk millions to save billions to save what could be saved and they needed help. They should *not* have tried to do this on their own. That had been stupid and they deserved whatever fate came of it, but their world didn't.

Perhaps they could hope they weren't the only one down here, certainly not the only one working the problem. Or perhaps others were trying to get as many people off planet as possible. That was good too.

It was going to stay good, and Skyt faced the void. Then Skyt launched the pod again, compensating for a slight skew that had come into the thrusters.

Skyt had a job to do and Skyt would do whatever they could.

Whatever they could...

IT TOOK every bit of strength Skyt had to get the hatch open after parking the pod. This hatch had perhaps not been opened in centuries.

Inside, though, there was still atmosphere. Saving suit air, they took off their helmet. Metallic, but breathable. They limped, whatever was broken deep within them sending twinges of pain down all of their left legs. The worst case scenario.

They could manage without a pair of legs, easily enough, but lateral issues were another matter. It hurt. Everything hurt. They would get medical attention once this was over, if it was over, if they were alive. They didn't expect to be alive.

They put feet in front of each other. There should be a control room for the field projector. The ancients were not gods. The ancients were just older and more experienced and had good libraries. Skyt wanted to see those libraries, the ones which had been wiped, had been deliberately taken away from them. Skyt tried for a moment to imagine what translation was like, to fly through data, to become data, to combine and recombine with others. As usual, they couldn't.

Control room. The door was stuck. Skyt actually screamed as they forced it open, screamed in pain and frustration and the attempt to get at physical reserves of strength. There was a power to it. Their wings spread, pushing against the air as if it would help.

The door popped open and they fell backwards, away from it, bending a wingtip. Ow. The sharp pain, though, merely mingled with what already wracked their body. It didn't matter. It didn't, couldn't slow them down, not so much as a micrometer.

They would get medical attention later or not at all. Now they crouched in front of the controls and their next obstacle was one they had expected. They had no idea which buttons to press. Which ones might do what, which might strengthen the field or weaken it or turn it off.

They had to study and they had to take time, but a vibration was starting to set in, starting to flow through them. It felt as if their entire exoskeleton was about to shatter. The world was ringing like a bell and there was not much time.

Not much time at all.

PUSHING buttons at random was starting to appeal. Skyt had a mindache worse than they had ever had. They knew the ancient script, or thought they did. There had to be an AI here, a dumb one which would have helped out the people who worked in this place. Said AI was not currently responsive, however.

"I don't need an archaeologist," Skyt said out loud. "I need a navigator."

Well, they did need an archaeologist to read and to understand. They needed a navigator as well. They would have given anything for help. Anything. The humans, a bunch of wide-eyed grad students, anyone who might remotely have the expertise this needed. But they had no help.

They thought they had a sequence which would achieve something. Temporarily, but something. Even if they only bought a few days, that was a few people. A few months. They hesitated, staring at the control room. They might mot be able to undo any damage guessing at this would do.

Make that would not. But they had to guess. An educated guess, but there was no more calculating to be done. They began to hit buttons. The vibration strengthened, weakened, strengthened again. Something sparked. One of the consoles was perhaps not in the condition it should have been. Sparks flickered through Skyt's exoskeleton for a moment, aggravating that ache deep inside.

Just that, though, and then they ventured a look through the porthole. It seemed, for a moment, as if it had worked. For a moment, the flaring from the singularity dampened down, weakened. But it was only for a moment, then it flared again, if anything worse than before.

No, it wasn't going to cooperate with them. It wasn't, and there was very little they could do. They could try again. They could keep trying until they either succeeded or destroyed the world, if they hadn't destroyed the world already.

The vibration was turning into a hum and Skyt felt they could surely hear it on the surface. Then their suit radio crackled into life.

"Hello, Skyt." Graeme.

"You had better *not* be down here!" Skyt was angry and relieved and all kinds of emotions.

"I was about to say the same thing to you. Where are you? Don't move."

They wanted them here. They wanted them long gone, long off of this beleaguered world.

But their prayers had, perhaps, been answered.

46

GRAEME

THE INSIDE of Glen was a hollow sphere. The thickness of the hull contained numerous passages. Mapping it all was impossible, but Toni had another solution. "So, the glen have set up gravimetric sensors here, here, here." She had a globe and was spinning it and tapping it in a manner which would have appeared idle had Graeme not known what she was doing.

"And that tells us..."

"The singularity is drifting this way. Which tells me it's probably whatever containment field they are using that's the problem. It's weakening here." She tapped the globe. "So here is where we go in."

Graeme nodded. "And then we do what?"

"First, we look and see if it can be restabilized. I know the answer, but we have to at least *look*. Then, we try to work out how to destabilize it in a way which will make it jump into hyperspace and away. Away from the suns, too."

A small singularity couldn't really damage a star, but this one was a little bit larger than the typical ship drive, so it was probably best to be on the safe side. Graeme shuddered at the thought of what a singularity that stabilized inside a sun would eventually do, devouring the star around it as it grew, until one of the suns in this system was a small black hole. The other would probably survive, orbiting its partner's corpse. But possibly not providing enough warmth for this orbit. Especially not for glen.

"Yeah. Or will it..."

"In theory, it will dissipate in hyperspace. But if it does pop back out, we want as little as possible on its route," Toni said, finally, and sighed. "This isn't going to work, Graeme."

"I know."

He knew that. He knew it as well as she did. He knew there was no actual hope, only the dream of something which might turn into hope.

It *might* work. Doing nothing was certainly not going to work. Doing nothing was going to achieve, well, nothing.

"But I still haven't come up with a better idea. Or any other ideas. So, this particular craziness it is."

"We're insane," Graeme agreed. It wasn't a polite term. Neither were polite terms. But honestly, Graeme felt he could call himself whatever impolite terms he wanted. Especially when he was asking for it as much as he was right now.

Insane. But the slimmest of chances was still a chance. The ground shook.

Were the glynquakes getting worse?

He was sure they were.

GLEN AIRCRAFT WERE NOT COMFORTABLE, being built for glen. Graeme lay back on the bench, his eyes closed, and thought about Marion.

He thought about her a lot. He had wanted to bring her here, to a place where she could learn that aliens were people (and cool people at that). Now that would never happen. He doubted Charles would let her into space until she was a full adult. He hoped his husband would not turn into one of *those* parents on his own, so overprotective they ended up losing their child not to danger but to rebellion. Much as Skyt's rey had lost them. Parenting. It didn't matter what species you were or even what scale you did it on, it was still hard.

He tried to sleep. It didn't work. Instead, he was left to endure the trip with his eyes open, trying desperately to lose consciousness so he wouldn't have to wait it out. He felt more and more tension flow through him. The plane hit some turbulence. Weather.

The instabilities were starting to affect the weather, creating unexpected and unpredicted storms. Inevitable. Eventually the atmosphere would be gone, one way or another. If they succeeded, it might still be gone. There was little chance of actually breeding a new singularity in time, of nurturing and growing one to the precise size needed to give power and preserve gravity.

But even if all they could do was delay the inevitable and change Glyn's end from a violent paroxysm to a quiet fading, that would save millions. Including, he could hope, that utterly delightful child with their not yet fully budded eyes.

The aircraft was starting to descend. And descend. It hit the runway hard enough to jolt Graeme awake, for he had apparently dozed off after all, without quite realizing it.

An intentional hard landing to avoid a bounce, he thought. Rain streaked against the plane's windows, hot rain that came with squalls and gusts and it was like the time he'd screwed up the timing on a trip to Florida and got caught in a hurricane.

Diving through the rain to the building through which they could access the substrate. The glen had hid this for so long, but they couldn't hide it forever. That wasn't how the world worked.

Into the building and they dripped on the floor and they were not quite committed, but there would be something like loss of face if he turned back now. Perhaps even loss of his own faith in human ingenuity, in which he had to include himself. The chances were above zero.

You can't win the lottery if you don't play once in a while.

THEY CHANGED into dry clothes from their bags before descending. Although it was not cold down there for humans, it was colder than the surface.

Below was metallic, and as they descended into the areas which still held air, Graeme studied everything they passed. Pitted metal, dim lighting. In some places, they needed flashlights. In others, water dripped on the floor and some kind of mold was growing. Perhaps it would be the last lifeform to survive the death of Glyn.

It was a dull yellow. Perhaps a lichen more than a mold, perhaps something that had no true equivalent on Earth. Regardless, Graeme kept moving, not even looking back at Toni. The documentation he had signed should protect the glen from any kind of diplomatic blame.

He was ending his career here, underground, on a world far weirder than they had been told. A world which might have had a place for him and his family. The mold smelled. He frowned and thought about putting his helmet back on. Aerial spores in his lungs was *not* how he wanted to go.

He thought about how much air they weren't carrying and left it be. Down into the depths. No sign or sound from the intelligence in the core, which he suspected had gone all the way back to sleep.

No sign or sound of life.

He monitored the glen frequencies anyway. There might be some desperate fool down here. Or a bunch of Remainers thinking they could prepare part of this place to live in.

Then again, there was far worse they could be doing. As if triggered by that thought, the world rumbled and then a peculiar vibration set in. It couldn't be any more pleasant for the glen; perhaps worse, he didn't want to think how it would feel with an exoskeleton.

On that frequency, a glen voice that needed no translation.

"Help!"

"Somebody's down here," he told Toni.

"I heard. Should we go help them?"

"Only if it's on our way."

They could perhaps alert the authorities on the surface to send SAR.

"Help!" It came once more and then was silent. There was something vaguely familiar about the chiming, but Graeme could not...

"We go help them," he said, finally. "We don't let the end of the world destroy our humanity."

One life.
Billions.
One life they couldn't save anyway.
But they had to try.

47

SKYT

"WE HEARD YOU CALLING FOR HELP."

They had come. They had tracked them down, followed them through the vagaries of the tunnels.

"The intelligence helped us find you."

That was a piece of news right there, Skyt thought. The intelligence was awake and roughly on their side. Roughly, of course.

The intelligence wanted the glen to keep living the way they lived. Skyt didn't think that was possible even if they saved Glyn. There were colonies now. There was the growing understanding that people deserved the choice whether to translate or not.

There were the off worlders and they would inevitably find out, all of them. No, nothing could go back to the way It was.

But there was no need to point that out. No need to push this alliance. "Did they have any..."

"No. What were you trying to do anyway?"

"Readjust the field projector to buy time."

Toni's mouth pushed forward into an interesting shape. "Not a terrible idea."

"Don't try and get to it from the hollow side," Skyt added.

"Is that how you got that bruise under your carapace?"

Skyt flinched a bit. "I'm pretty hurt."

"We should get you..."

Skyt cut Graeme off. "I can get medical attention later, if there's a later."

They still weren't expecting there to be a later and there might well not be a later for *them* anyway. A later was something they wanted to give to others.

Graeme's mouth inverted into what Skyt already knew was a gesture of unhappiness, but he said nothing more about Skyt's physical condition. Thankfully.

Skyt didn't want to get into a lengthy argument. There wasn't time.

"So, don't try to...but this control room." Toni started to move around it. "You tried..."

"I tried and it looked like it was making things worse, so I stopped."

The vibration was back, only worse, making Skyt's antennae ache. Down to their base.

"It was worth trying. We have a plan, but it's rather crazier than that."

Crazier? "If we can't restabilize it..."

"Then we have to get rid of it."

Skyt's wings crumpled. They could see no way to do that that wasn't throwing it through inhabited land.

But at the same time, they had been willing to risk that. What was the difference between risking and causing?

The knowledge that you could have made another choice.

SKYT RESTED. They had spent the last bit of time helping Toni understand the control room. They drifted in and out, a mental fog surrounding them. The room blurred then came back into focus. Two of their eyes seemed unable to manage anything, on the same side. A bad sign.

They were dying. They were coming to terms with that, while trying to work out how to hide it from the humans. Graeme would want to stop everything to get them back to the surface to a doctor who might not be able to do any good. Humans would put one individual before a world.

Skyt might do the same thing, but there was something about the way they looked at it, the way they talked about it that made it feel like some absolute point of morality.

"You never leave a man behind," Toni had said, although Skyt didn't know what they meant.

Besides, Skyt was not a man. Apparently, that didn't bother them. Species wasn't important if they liked you. Skyt was *not* a man, though, and Skyt would sacrifice nobody for themselves. So, Skyt pretended to be only slightly hurt.

They knew they didn't have Toni fooled, but Toni seemed to understand more than Graeme that Skyt had to do what they had to do.

The fog cleared and Skyt tried, once more, to get their mind around the plan. Toni seemed to think it was possible to send the power core FTL, at which point it could jump through/around the planetary surface. This would leave them without a power core, but the planet would not explode. Implode, rather. Which was progress.

It would buy them time, at least. Perhaps a considerable amount of time. If it could be made to work. If FTL really did go through solid objects. Skyt wasn't sure they bought that part. Hyperspace was another layer of space. The hull, surely, existed in hyperspace as well.

Was Toni lying so that Graeme would go along with a plan that would kill thousands of glen? Possibly. Was Toni lying to Skyt for the same reason? Skyt was an archaeologist.

They didn't understand the math of FTL. They had never even *been* FTL. They knew hyperspace had weather. Was impacted by gravity.

"This isn't going to work," Skyt said, finally. They couldn't be part of it if Toni was tricking Graeme.

They couldn't. Even if it would save their world.

"It still has to pass through the hull," Skyt said. "Even in hyperspace...aren't you going to make a hole?"

Toni took a deep breath. Started to say something.

"They're right. How much damage will it do to the planet surface as it passes through? If it's less than just slingshotting it, that's good, but..."

Skyt knew what Graeme was fishing for.

How much devastation. How many deaths. How did you decide what was acceptable? How did you do risk reduction? Skyt didn't know. They weren't a philosopher.

Toni's shoulders dropped. "We don't know. But the core won't linger. It should make a small hole and if we..."

"What if we send it out through one of the thrusters?" Graeme asked. "It might damage the thruster mechanism, but..."

That might work, Skyt thought. The ache was back at the base of their antennae. How long did they have? Long enough, because it had to be long enough. They wouldn't see the results. They wouldn't live to see them. But they only had to live long enough to *try*.

"That's not a terrible idea," Toni mused. "We can probably fix the thrusters if we need to."

It probably wouldn't make a difference. The loss of gravity would cause the atmosphere to bleed off before the world froze. The vibration was like being inside a giant wind instrument being played by a *very* enthusiastic musician.

It was too much and Skyt was going to die just from *that*. Just from that and the pain and whatever was going on with them deep inside. No, just from that.

Graeme was rubbing his head. "Also if we don't stop this noise."

"I don't think we can," Skyt chimed. "Believe me, I want it stopped too." They weren't sure they would call it noise, but it was as good a term as any.

The floor shook, reminding them once more that they didn't have time to mess around, that they didn't have time for anything other than work. Skyt tried to focus again. Mostly succeeded. They had listened to them. That was all they needed or wanted.

Out through the thruster it was.

48

GRAEME

GRAEME WOULD DECIDE whether to be angry with Toni later. Truth was, he should have seen it. But he had been caught up in something which might work.

Skyt had a solution. It would require accuracy, it would require...and there was still a risk, but they were doing their best. They were doing everything they could not to cause megadeaths. He had never imagined being in a situation where his simple actions could cause death on such a scale it could only be imagined as a statistic, and where he had to *contemplate* it. As a choice. Part of him wanted to run away.

The trolley problem. He'd read a version where the real person to blame was the trolley company. That it wasn't your fault if you were in this position, it was the fault of whoever had put you there. The ancients. Had intended to come back.

"You have possible company." The chiming voice of the ancient intelligence.

"As in?"

"As in there are glen in the immediate area, exploring."

Graeme nodded. "Do you know whether they are likely to help us, hinder us, try to kill us?" He didn't think the latter likely, but it had to be considered.

Glen had proved that they could, indeed, be violent when matters of, well, life and death were involved. When matters of fear were involved they could be very violent indeed.

"Help, no. They are talking, when they think they cannot be over-heard, about finding the off worlders."

"Who *told* them?"

"An intelligence, no doubt, who saw you come down here."

"Why would an intelligence not..."

"Why indeed. Suicidal, perhaps? Or perhaps they legitimately believe the glen would be better off on their own, learning to survive as an independent race."

"The glen can do both." Graeme thought about that.

"And does everyone on your world face the potential of a species split with..."

"...yes and no." Graeme rather thought human speciation was inevitable. There had once been, after all, multiple species, combined by mating and leaving tiny bits of their legacy in the survivor. It could happen again as humanity spread into the universe "Point is, they *can* do both and I think they should, if possible."

"Why?"

"Because more cultural variety increases survival chances," Graeme said finally. "Because the universe needs people to look up at the stars and try to understand itself."

"And thus you imply..."

"I more than imply it. Glen cultural homogeneity is stagnation. Understandable stagnation, they've built a good world here. But now look at what's happening once it's threatened."

"You perhaps have a point."

"I know I do. In any case, we need to work out what to do about our visitors."

Convince them to go away? Graeme hoped it would be that easy. Feared it would not.

Toni had set up a camera to watch the approach to the room. Of course she had. Graeme watched it. The glen had no military. The glen barely had the *concept* of a military. Sadly, they were fast learners in this regard.

Paramilitary glen were as scary as paramilitary anyone else. And they had very rapidly learned the concept of weaponized fear.

Thankfully, they were not yet attempting to deploy that. No doubt unaware that they were being observed, the group of glen were moving quickly and reasonably expertly. They were, for example, remembering to check side doors and passages for the possibility of an ambush, something he suspected Toni hoped they had, in fact, forgotten.

But they weren't experts, even he could see that. Had he had a squadron of Royal Marines or Earthforce special forces, Graeme could have made short work of these invaders. Very short work.

He didn't. Which meant they were a legitimate, genuine threat that had to be dealt with.

For right now, the best hope was that they hadn't got the accurate information from whatever intelligence or intelligences were helping them. That they would go straight past the control room.

Unfortunately, Skyt had left a few drops of blood out there, enough for an expert tracker. So Graeme's best hope was that they had no expert trackers.

Glen, after all, did not hunt. There were no wild animals worth hunting on their garden world.

So perhaps they would get lucky. They didn't seem to have brought any kind of domesticated animal, but glen had a better sense of smell.

Sniff. No, his hopes were in vain. They absolutely knew where one glen and two humans were holed up.

The three of them could not take these people on. Graeme mentally sighed. They had tried. If the locals wouldn't accept their help...except this wasn't "the locals." This was one small faction that had already made themselves sufficiently unpopular that he could reasonably assume they had little wide support. Not at this point. Some people were even blaming them for the hole.

So.

He took a deep breath. "Stay put. I'm going to try and talk to our friends."

"They'll shoot you," Toni predicted.

"They'll shoot all of us if I don't try."

He had to try. Even if it meant they had to work on this without him while he led them a merry dance and/or got captured. He *had* to try.

There was no choice. They had taken that away when they came down here. No choice for him, and none for them. Just the inevitable collision of fates that came when people set themselves as enemies.

GRAEME PUT his helmet on before leaving the room, not because he didn't trust the corridor air but because it was great protection from certain types of attack that didn't involve kinetic energy.

He didn't trust them not to use gas, no, not at all. He moved as quickly as he could towards them, trying to make the angle oblique. It was hard, but perhaps he could convince them to follow him down another corridor.

His heart rate was elevated, pounding in his ears. He was no coward, but this was one of the scariest things he had done lately. They could simply shoot him. After all, it would solve the problem of what he might do and disposing of a human corpse down here would be easy.

They could probably just leave him down here and the destruction of the planet would take care of the evidence. Even if it didn't, he might never be found. They had no reason *not* to simply shoot him.

Which made this crazy, but he couldn't think of any better ideas. They didn't have access to any kind of intruder suppression system, even if there was such a thing. They didn't have time to work it out. He just walked, feeling the odd vibration under his feet that was the planet starting to shake itself apart.

Perhaps he could convince them to run. Perhaps just telling him the planet was about to implode would get them to try and save their own exoskeletons? Carapaces?

Around a corner and there they were. Guns pointed at him. There was no worry about the normal issue with guns on a ship, not as thick as the walls were here. They would make holes in him and holes in what was behind him and he wanted to run. He could feel the sweat starting to pool inside his suit, running down against his eyebrows.

Making his palms slip against the gloves. You did *not* want to break out into a nervous sweat inside a spacesuit, but here he was, doing many things he did not want to do. Many things he could not do, no matter how hard he tried. He was going to fail and die, but he had to make this look good. He started rotating through frequencies.

None of them worked.

49

SKYT

Skyt was less comfortable with Toni.

At the same time, they didn't say anything about the limp as Skyt moved around the control room. They didn't say anything about Graeme either. By silent consensus, the matter was not up for discussion. Either they would come back or they wouldn't.

Toni had barred the door, for what it was worth. Skyt didn't see that doing more than momentarily slowing the enemy down. Yet, it felt like doing something and thus it was likely enough for her.. To feel like she was doing something.

It wasn't like this wasn't all that, all feeling like they were.

Grumble.

Rumble.

For a moment, Skyt thought it was the end, the rush of something which ran through the room, twisting the floor and walls.

"Okay, that was a nasty one," Toni said from the floor. They got up, and Skyt suspected some nasty bruising on the human's thin skin

The downside to being bipedal. You fell down easily.

Skyt did not want to think about falling down. Falling down and not getting up and a wave of that fog came over them. Were they getting enough oxygen? They weren't sure anymore. They suspected a good chunk of their circulatory fluid was now loose in their abdomen, sloshing around.

They needed medical care now. Well, they weren't going to get any. They had to function. They had to do this before the Migrators got here and smashed the place up so they couldn't.

"I think I have the calculations. Can you double check them?"

Skyt limped over, lopsided. Toni said nothing about it still, respecting their choice in a way Graeme hadn't.

Skyt was not sure which he preferred.

Perhaps there was a balance between the two. "This is like a game of *skell*."

"What's *skell*?" Toni asked.

Skyt checked the math before answering. "It's a game where you try and keep a ball in motion for as long as possible and then toss it through a tube."

"I don't think we have quite the equivalent, but I was thinking billiards."

They didn't ask Toni what billiards were, because at that moment the floor buckled upwards. It held.

It held, barely, but they knew they had little time indeed. By wordless consensus, they put on their helmets, to have some chance of survival if it was breached. And went back to checking math as if they were grading papers not saving or destroying the world.

"WE KNOW YOU'RE IN THERE."

The bad guys had found their radio frequency. They probably had Graeme and were menacing them or worse. Maybe they were already dead.

Toni had said not to respond. Skyt trusted their judgment. They did not respond, but it made for a lower level of concentration than they would have liked. How *were* they supposed to concentrate? Toni seemed...

"How are you doing this?" Skyt asked, keeping to the very short range radio.

"Doing?"

"Staying so calm."

"Practice. I've been under *actual* fire and had to do stuff like this with people shooting at me."

Practice wasn't something Skyt could obtain in a matter of moments, unfortunately. They decided to admire Toni instead and go back to work. They *could* turn the circuit off altogether, but that would leave Graeme cut off. If they were still alive.

Skyt doubted it. Skyt was sure, at the very least, that Graeme was not alive and free. Likely they were a prisoner, being held by these people.

Menaced.

Skyt didn't think they would resort to torture, although his torso tightened a little at the thought.

They might resort to anything. They might not even see the off worlders as people. Or at the very least, not as equal to glen lives. If they were lucky, they were in fact trying to convert Graeme to their cause, not hurting them. Thankfully, that was...

But then there was the violence they had already resorted to. Both sides had. Sane glen (and sane off worlders) caught in the middle.

Skyt's torso clenched again. They forced themselves to relax, stretching out to their wingtips as best they could in the suit.

They would only injure themselves worse if they stayed this tense, if worse was even possible at this point. They were dying, after all.

"I'd like to run this past Graeme for a third set of eyes." Toni said.

"I don't think they're coming back." Skyt would not have used that metaphor, but understood it. The humans did not have many eyes...

Toni turned away, then nodded. "I don't think he is either."

Some words didn't translate, but that one wasn't really needed. "Then we run it without them?" Skyt asked.

"While we still have time."

They moved over to one of the consoles. Took a deep breath. "Let's do this."

The moment they spoke, the door exploded into the room.

GLEN POURED INTO THE ROOM. Skyt didn't see Graeme, which might be very good or absolutely terrible, depending on what they had done. But they were done.

Toni was close enough to maybe hit some buttons, but they already had weapons trained on her. Just a couple of minutes more and the attempt would have been made.

Skyt did the only thing they could. They hit a button behind them as quickly as they could and then showed their pincers to the attackers. There might still be time for somebody to do something with Toni's data, for somebody to make another attempt.

Or not.

"You're going to kill billions of people," Toni was saying in that same calm voice. Skyt finally realized that this was their fake calm voice, the one they used to keep themselves and others functional.

They were at least as scared as Skyt was.

"Necessary for the future of our species."

"Plenty of human mass murderers said that too. But you will kill *most* of your species. Ever hear of a genetic bottleneck?"

Their attention was on Toni now. Skyt wasn't being watched. If they could just get to the console, they could press the button. They could start the process, and it couldn't be recalled.

They were dreaming. They had to enter the final sequence, which would take time. Not a lot of time, but enough time that they couldn't hope to do it while being this closely watched.

They had to try, but it would only get them shot. Only get them...

The lights flickered, dimmed, the world rumbled again.

Only get them shot.

If they somehow couldn't shoot, then Skyt could do whatever they wanted. And they knew what the humans had brought down with their equipment.

Slowly, Skyt began to move sideways, crabwise, as only an uncoordinated child would. Each step sent agony through their body. They kept moving. Sideways. Hoping nobody would notice, hoping nobody would stop them. Would shoot them.

Would inflict more pain and then there would be nothing, no translation, no escape. There would be nothing, but if they could just do this one thing, it might be worth it.

It might be worth it and they kept moving and didn't even think about anything but the pain.

50

GRAEME

It was like a bizarre and dangerous game of tag. The enemy wasn't talking. Literally wasn't talking. They might have found his frequency, but they weren't saying anything.

Not to him and not to each other. Instead, they had peeled off a couple of glen with guns of some sort to hunt him down.

They had no reason to keep them alive.

His death would look like an accident. Charles would get a dearly regrets. Glyn would be destroyed.

His mind tunneled down. He couldn't think about that right now. He couldn't think about anything other than the minutiae of staying alive. Staying alive sucked.

He'd wrenched his ankle at some point, stabbing pain shooting up his left leg whenever he stepped on it wrong; and there didn't seem to be a right way to step on it. He wanted to hurt them at this point. He wanted to shoot back.

He couldn't.

Instead, he ran. Hoping to get more of them chasing him. All of them would be fantastic. If they were chasing him, they weren't harassing or endangering the others. Skyt and Toni could do this without him.

He ran.

He kept running, until he found himself in what at first appeared to be a dead end.

There was one of those service pods Skyt had mentioned. He could make a clean getaway, but that would leave them going back after the others. Graeme frowned, the best course of action momentarily escaping him. He was trapped, he was alone, but he could run.

He could run further than they could chase. Had he bought the others enough time? He had no way of knowing. He did not dare call them and reveal what frequency they were using, if he hadn't managed to do *that* already.

Deep breath. Dying would achieve nothing. He headed for the pod, remembering what Skyt had said about not flying close to the field projectors. If they somehow managed to follow him, perhaps he could use that.

If.

THE POD WASN'T DESIGNED for a human to fly it. He wasn't even sure it was designed for a glyn, but rather for some other designed servitor race or the ancients themselves. Something was a little off and odd about that. Something he didn't have the time to consider.

He had to fly the pod, in an awkward position that did nothing for his back (although it did take the weight off his ankle). The aches that started up reminded him that he wasn't a young man any more. Not an old man, no. But not young. But he was free and flying in the core of a world. He wished he could store up this moment forever, despite the pain, despite the adrenalin, despite the fear. He hadn't imagined.

He hadn't read the kind of literature that would have told him to imagine this. If he survived, he might just have to start. This was beautiful, this alone was worth fighting for. Skyt called themselves an archaeologist. Graeme imagined finding jewelry or the like, not this.

This.

And there was, for the moment, no pursuit. Perhaps there would be no pursuit, but what was happening to Skyt and Toni? What was happening to them? The raging heart of the singularity flickered and flared white, what from what he knew should have been a steady, even glow. He saw only the edges of what was going on in frequencies he could not perceive, in the space within the singularity from which information could not escape.

A steady, even glow, granting power to the ship, ready to move it if needed. But it had worn out...not the singularity itself, but what contained it. He thought he could see the field projectors. He let the pod float, well away from them, waiting and both hoping and not hoping for pursuit.

Afraid to even listen.

No.

He could listen.

He toggled the radio on. They had found their frequency and were taunting Toni and Skyt, trying to break their concentration. Trying to get them to stop. The bad guys thought they might succeed. The Migrators, who would gladly kill millions of children. Versus the Remainers, who...

He floated and he waited and he watched the singularity and it occurred to him that if Toni and Skyt pressed the button, this wasn't the smartest place to be. He flew further away from it, staying close to the hull.

He watched.

Then they came. They had found two of the pods, but they seemed to be having as much steering success for the first few moments as he had.

Two of them. The pods were designed for a single pilot-passenger. They were, no doubt, for maintenance. He even had noticed what looked like an old toolbox. Thousands of years ago, some glen mainte-nance worker had flown this to inspect the hull.

It still worked.

They were chasing him. He thought he knew where the field

projector was. It was a gamble, but even if he could only reduce the opposition by two, he could reduce the opposition.

He toggled the radio on. "Come and get me."

It was childish, but it might work, and he flew low over the hull. Or high under it. There was an odd reversal in his mind, a moment of cognitive disconnect in which he remembered that this was the inside of the world and up was down and gravity was indeed towards the center.

It was the fact that the singularity was flaring that made him want to see the hull as the floor, not the ceiling. He hoped it affected them worse.

He hoped it distracted them from chasing him, from all they were doing. He didn't want to be chased, but it was his job right now. To zig, to zag across the hull. To lead them the best dance he could. Reduce the opposition by two.

He could hear Toni's voice, but he didn't respond to her. She seemed to be trying to talk them down, or distract them, or something. The singularity flared brilliant and he didn't think about how many rads he might be taking.

It flared and died down and flared again and he knew they were probably trying it, and he felt something push his ship away. Darted around it.

Led them into it. It might work, it might not work. It depended...

...and one of them flew straight into it. Their pod was flipped, tumbled, landed on its back and didn't move again. The other was paying more attention.

One down, but *that* trick would not work again. What would they do when they caught him?

The singularity flared stark and he stopped worrying about being caught.

The world was about to...

...and white light flared.

51

SKYT

SKYT REACHED THE DOOR. The pain had faded into a dull, ever present ache. Or they had learned to accept it, even embrace it. It told them they were still alive, still organic. It gave them a peculiar sense of hope.

How to get it open? Toni yelped and they turned towards them. A moment. They had done it on purpose. Skyt knew that. Skyt knew...

Toni would keep trying until they killed her. Skyt had the data. Graeme was likely already dead. It didn't matter and it mattered.

Get the data out. Then rescue them if they had time. They didn't have time. They were leaving the humans to die. They couldn't do that.

They scuttled down the corridor. They moved as quickly as their broken body would let them. Some old instinct from whatever creature they had been before the ancients intervened told them to find a place to hide and die.

They couldn't...no wait, perhaps they could. A storage area. A closed door. A barricade that would have been better had they had their full strength.

A question spoken to the querulous air. "Are you there?"

They did not expect an answer.

"Yes."

"I need to get this data into the sublayer. Can you..."

"Those channels were closed for..."

Skyt had never dared interrupt an intelligence and the idea of interrupting an ancient. "Please. I can't leave them to die."

"They are..."

"Intelligent beings like me, like you. This data could save Glyn and you."

The pause felt like a lifetime, perhaps because of how little time Skyt had left.

"Very well. But..."

"Nothing is ever the same. Ever."

Now to work out how to save Graeme. Could Skyt handle a pod in their current state? They had no choice.

"You are badly damaged."

"I know. I've made my choice."

Would the intelligence accept that from something they saw as more like a robot than a person?

"Knowing your data might be lost."

"All the data will be lost if we fail. I don't have anything that special." Except their own unique consciousness. They froze for a moment as terror flowed through them.

"That is the only reason I am letting you go."

Skyt accepted that.

"Don't leave yet."

Skyt paused.

"They're outside."

They relaxed and waited until the ancient intelligence gave them the all clear.

The terror followed them.

THE SINGULARITY FLARED. Skyt could see the stray radiation, flickering brilliant white through the interior of the world. For a moment they thought that was it. Then it faded again. They slid into the pod, accompanied only by their terror. They welcomed it. It was the only thing that kept them from curling up inside their own carapace and waiting to die.

It motivated them. They launched the pod, and it tumbled, as if the gravity inside was not what it had been. The singularity tugging at them, gentle as a child's hand. It would get worse.

They fought to get it stabilized. Saw Graeme's pod drifting towards it. Perhaps they were already dead. It didn't matter. Fighting through a haze of renewed pain they flew the pod slowly towards it. Slowly.

They appeared to have been designed for this. Grab. Tow. No, even better...they could match the hatches and seal. A bit of air hissed, but not much. Skyt flew towards the hull.

Graeme was unconscious and peculiarly limp. They were bleeding onto their face. They were breathing. Easier to tell that in people without exoskeletons.

For now, they were alive.

The singularity yanked the conjoined pods sideways. Skyt focused entirely on getting them back to the hull. They had to get Graeme into this pod to dock. When they tried to move the human, something else snapped and they whited out for a moment.

Graeme's eyes opened. They dragged themselves into the pod. "I thought I got eaten."

Skyt's translator was still working. Somehow. "Not yet."

"Toni?"

"I don't know. Their danger seemed less imminent."

Skyt closed the hatch and released the other pod. To be retrieved if there was a later.

"You..."

"The data should already be in the sublayer." Skyt didn't say that it might not matter. The raging singularity said that for them. We have..."

For a moment, Skyt thought Graeme had passed out again. "To try," he said, his mere two eyes closed.

Skyt knew that Graeme did not think they could succeed. The Migrators were going to win and kill billions.

He knew they had to die trying.

Then a voice sounded in the pod. "I have an idea."

Graeme jumped. Skyt was less startled, but perhaps more surprised.

"But I can't ask it of you. You have data."

Skyt heard a deep breath. "You can ask it of me."

IT WAS ALL LOGICAL. Graeme couldn't translate into the sublayer. It wasn't designed to accept the signals of their mental nodes, the networked nature of their consciousness.

They were expendable. But logic couldn't be the only consideration. "Your government..."

"Knows I'm doing everything I can for your people." Graeme showed their teeth. "They won't hold it against you..."

They didn't sound entirely sure. Skyt didn't press. They... "I'm dying."

"And if we save Glyn..."

"Just tell us what needs to be done." Skyt's chiming had become dull and dim.

"There is a direct connection to the power source. Somebody would have to fly close...stabilize it manually."

Graeme dipped their head. "And very likely..."

"If the instability didn't get them, the repair likely would. They would be trapped in the singularity"

"A drone?"

"The temporal disturbances preclude remote operation."

Something was stirring within Skyt. A thought. An idea. Something this ancient intellect was missing because they were so old.

Skyt let a wave of mental fog wash over them. Waited for it to clear. "A branching process."

"What?

"Branch off some of your processes. It would be smart enough to do it, but not sapient. Nobody has to die."

There was another of those lifetime pauses. Except longer.

"I...can't."

"A copy. It wouldn't be you."

"It would act like me and I..."

Graeme spoke softly. "You were supposed to be wiped. You hid down here."

Silence.

"Coward!" Skyr exclaimed and instantly regretted it.

"I can't...the idea of sending even a part of myself..."

"So you would send the whole of another." Disgusted and angry, Skyt ducked inside their carapace, turning their back on the entity as thoroughly as could be imagined.

They would still do it. Sacrifice themselves.

Graeme, "Not everyone is built for this...but if we fail all of you will be lost. If Skyt is right it's just code."

Silence. Finally, "Code that will act like me. It will run away."

Skyt wanted to run away. Skyt couldn't. Skyt wanted to die in the clinic, easily and quietly. Translate.

"You opened a link to the sublayer." They didn't move. "Is it possible to translate a glen..."

"Skyt." Graeme, an odd note in their voice, something deeply human that the glen could not read.

"Not from here."

There was a peculiar sensation. "Then let's go."

"Your friend failed in their attempt. Yes. Let's go."

Was Toni dead? Skyt struggled to their feet. Would they make it to where they needed to go?

"I don't understand."

"If I translate, I can..." Send a part of themselves. Sacrifice any chance of survival...risk dying twice. But do it. Skyt saw no other way.

Other than oblivion.

52

GRAEME

SKYT INTENDED TO DIE. Or, perhaps, Skyt knew they were dying anyway. The glen did not see death the way humans did, promised the digital afterlife some researchers dreamed of.

Perhaps Marion would see it. Graeme did not want Skyt to die. But the first rule of diplomacy was to respect other cultures...else Graeme could not have handled certain details of glen reproduction.

He had to let Skyt do this. And he had to respect Skyt - a whole, sane adult making a difficult choice.

Just as Toni had. He didn't know that she was dead. Sadly, it was an entirely reasonable conclusion that she was. Or incapacitated, or imprisoned, or running. They weren't lying that she had failed. As much as he would have liked to think so, had she succeeded then either things would be fixed or they would all be dead.

The planet seemed to ring like a bell. Beside him, Skyt staggered. He was helping the glen as much as he could. Their respective body plans did not make this easy.

He was sweating and exhausted and scared.

"This way," Skyt chimed, so softly their translator almost failed to pick up on it. They were failing. Graeme could not carry them. They needed to find another working vehicle.

The air smelled thin, but they dared not helmet up and use the suit radios. Everything was compromised.

A door. Closed. He tried to push on it. It would not give, not with all of Graeme's flagging strength. He sank against it, unsure either of them could go further.

There was nothing left here. They had failed.

He tried the door again, weakly.

"Stop." Glen couldn't whisper the way humans could, but there were at least a dozen pianissimos this time. He barely heard it.

He stopped. He didn't know what else to do.

Skyt tapped a panel with a pincer. Nothing.

"I don't think..."

Again, a staccato rhythm. With a faint creak the door slowly, almost arthritically, slid open. That was how tired he was, how unable to function.

"Almost there."

He might have to drag Skyt. He might have to...and this corridor was dimly lit. Alien, not-quite-glen script marked each side door.

This was, had been, a place for people, not robots. They hadn't had telepathy or comms implants. A choice, he thought, to keep their privacy.

Skyt stopped before a specific door and chimed.

THIS DOOR, Graeme had to force, hands rough even through his suit gloves. He wanted to rest more than he ever had, His eyes felt scratchy and he knew that if he got somewhere comfortable, he would be out like a light.

Thankfully this room held only one comfortable place. He helped Skyt onto the low bed or bench. The glen closed all eight eyes, and for a moment Graeme feared he had expired.

Or perhaps hoped. He didn't know how much pain his friend was feeling. Friend? There was no denying it. No escaping it. And he would never be able to introduce Skyt to Charles and Marion.

He swayed. Maybe he could sit on the floor for a moment.

"Put on your helmet," said a voice. He struggled to obey. Took a deep breath of suit air. Felt better. Hypoxia. He looked at Skyt.

His short range suit radio. "Don't bother."

Don't bother giving Skyt more oxygen. Perhaps there was a sense to it. He was afraid to respond. Turned the radio off for now and just breathed. Counted his aches and pains, which were many. Skyt was very still.

Graeme leaned against the wall, closed his eyes. He was still truly exhausted. Still really beyond doing anything except that he had to. He studied the room. A lab. He felt a faint vibration even through his suit.

Skyt's eyes opened. Three of them, two vaguely focused on Graeme. You couldn't really hug glen, they were too spiky. He wanted to nonetheless. One last time.Taking a deep breath, he took off his helmet. "Stale air."

"Should make it..." Skyt chimed weakly, distant.

Easier?

Less painful?

The same voice. "I have you, Skyt."

Was that all it took? No wires or cables?

Just the bed and the voice and perhaps it was religion after all, comforting lies and the same darkness faced by others.

In which case they were all doomed.

I have you.

"Graeme, they are in the area."

"Got it."

He had to hold them off. Perhaps not for long. Then curtains.He might never know if they succeeded.He would be more likely to know if they failed.

"Helmet." A pause. "I need to take care of Skyt."

Graeme tugged the helmet on. Let the AI focus on the glen.

He turned towards the door. Tried his best to force it closed. If the bad guys couldn't find him. The same slight throbbing in his bones. Some kind of field, perhaps.

He couldn't hear. He couldn't share in something glen and intimate. He could only stand ready.

SILENCE.

His own breathing inside the suit. He could only hold out so long. He turned on the radio, receive only.

Taunting would be better than silence. Perhaps they knew that, or feared betraying their position, for there was nothing but more silence. Not even the static that might have echoed in an older suit. Nothing.

Then the faint shaking started up again. The planet trying to shake off its problems. He felt like a flea. He felt like nothing, so insignificant even his bite would go unfelt. The planet wasn't scratching to get rid of him.

Thud.

Thud.

Something slammed into the door. Somebody trying to force it open and he tensed and wished for a weapon. He didn't have a license to kill. He was a spy and diplomat, not a suave assassin.

But he grabbed a heavy object from the workbench nearby, something that might crack a glen carapace with a bit of help from gravity.

Time. He only had to buy time before they killed him, knowing there would be no lingering evidence.

Time. He readied himself as the door gave way, sliding roughly to the side. Swung into the space where the glen might be with all of his remaining strength. Struck something. Heard a muffled yelp.

Not a glen yelp. A mammal yelp. A Toni yelp. He gasped and pulled back, looking down. She was already rolling to her feet. And gave him the ok sign.

She had her helmet on. He dared not risk talking. With suit thickness still between them, he pulled her into the best embrace he could, helmets touching.

She was alive. It gave him hope. They pulled the door back across the entrance as best they could. It was damaged.

He did not ask her how she had found him. He did not need to. He did not ask her if she was okay.

They just took up positions as if they had always been there, as if this was a moment of eternity in which there was no need for touch or for human contact or communication. They had already communicated everything they needed to.

The enemy was coming.

The enemy would pay...

53

SKYT

Skyt could have kept moving. As long as they didn't stop. As long as...

Once they did, they drifted into something between unconsciousness and sleep, floating. Floating away...no, they couldn't let go. Not yet. Not until they were sure. Until they were...

...and the fog cleared. It took everything they had to manage to open three eyes, two of which somewhat focused on Graeme."I have you, Skyt."

They closed their eyes again. Not Graeme who had spoken. The intelligence. Something within them was responding, lifting. A thrum through their carapace. Graeme talking to the intelligence, heard as if through water. As if through space.

Skyt was dying, not at some future time to be determined, but now. Something gently pressed against them. As if they were being held against a parents' carapace.

"I have a good link. Don't try to talk."

Cold fear flowed through them. Animal fear at the realization that this was truly it. The end.

"There is not enough oxygen in the air. Life support failed in this area a while ago."

Skyt could believe that. They were starting to feel as if they couldn't get enough air through their breathing tubes. They wanted to panic. They also wanted to rest, to sleep. They didn't have enough energy to panic.

"I have control over life support now."

Graeme with his helmet on.

"Do it," Skyt chimed then regretted it. Even that exertion hurt, sent odd tremors through their body.

They closed all of their eyes. They were just too tired to struggle any more. Time to just relax and trust and let it happen. As if they were being held by their rey in warm water. By the rey they had never truly had.

Warmth and pain flowed through them in equal measure, everything faded out slowly. They felt the shaking of a convulsion or perhaps the planet, but it didn't matter any more. They struggled against oblivion.

Struggled to hatch all over again and there was one final sharp pain somewhere deep within and the world exploded into indescribable sensations. *Steady.*

They would have breathed but there was no air, but they felt the intelligence's steadying presence. The way their edges overlapped and threatened to merge, but Skyt had to stay Skyt for now. Could not be a cloud that drifted, endlessly combining and recombining. They would forget. They would... They pulled their edges together.

Good.

They could feel others, but distant. Isolated from the sublayer. But alive. Free of pain and oh so beautifully alive.

TIME DID NOT MOVE in the substrate the way it moved in material reality. Skyt knew that at an academic level. But they still chafed at how long it took, subjectively, to build from their own substance what was needed. They knew that Graeme and Toni...somehow still alive, which they would ask about later....were still holding out.

They wished...they wished for things which could not be without many years of research. They felt the entire world, dying around them.

They built something which wasn't them or their child, although perhaps just as much love went into it, a craftsman's love for the thing made not just from their hands but their inmost self. Something that would act like Skyt, feel like Skyt, but which was not their translated soul.

An echo. They made an echo, and built it into something that would have been mistaken for them. It would do the job. It would not hesitate. They were not cleaning bots, they were so much more than that.

Time returned to world time. A lifetime spent building. Seconds. Graeme and Toni exhausted and clinging to each other like tyrar.

More than seconds then. Or perhaps that odd limbo of dying had lasted longer than they thought. Their organic body. What could be done with it? It could not be left here, could not easily be got to a composter. For later.

"It's done," said the intelligence. "You should fit in the maintenance tubes."

Graeme laughed. Toni walked over to Skyt's body. "What about..."

"Leave it. It can be properly handled later.'

Skyt wanted to say something. Wasn't sure what.Wasn't even sure how. Needed to...needed to say something else the humans would think them gone for good. There. The speakers.

"Go. They're right...leave it."

Could the humans tell who spoke? Possibly.

Either way, they found the maintenance tubes. Vanished into them moments before the door gave way.

Gunfire, peppering the room and Skyt's body. A vague, lingering urge to duck.

Nothing could hurt them now except the end of the world.

They sent the thing they had built to do its work. Then...

How about getting them to take off their helmets?

The intelligence laughed.

SKYT HAD MORE than eight eyes now and less...less, because they were not *their* eyes, but the system's various cameras.

And more because there were more of them and because in the sublayer itself, or rather this corner of it, they could see everything. Including themselves, and that was the strangest sight of all. They could see how every part of their mind and memory had been copied and laid bare. They could see what they were, who they were, and what they might become. If the world survived.

Combining and separating and recombining and they understood it now at levels they could never have grasped before. Combining and separating and recombining and becoming part of the system and each other and there was one Skyt and many. And those still bound to their bodies creeping through...and discovering the humans gone. Chiming frustration on a frequency they thought was private.

You could try...

These have no respect for me, the intelligence said. *They are not...*

They are true glen. They just...but no, they won't worship you.

Skyt could also pretend to be an ancient. But they wouldn't do what an ancient said.

Or perhaps... *Could try reverse psychology.*

The ancient laughed again. Or rather there was the sense and knowledge that they were laughing. Their edges rubbing up against and through Skyt's.

A sense of great age and the passage of time. And great boredom and sorrow.

Skyt would explore it later, would find out what they could.

But for right now. Reverse psychology. Skyt would have spread their wings if they still had wings.

And then Skyt sent a signal over their radio.

"Help."

They turned around.

"Help." Mimicking the voice of one of their number who had been separated. Skyt knew where that one was.

That one fled back to the surface, having lost their nerve. Skyt could forgive them for losing their nerve. But it made for a convenient absence that could be exploited.

"The humans!"

"What about them?" one with the group responded. "Looks like they went into the maintenance ducts."

"I found them, but..."

They started to turn around. One tried to get range and distance on the signal, frowned as they understandably failed.

After all, the call was in the room with them. Of course it was.

They were confused.

But this wouldn't help with the helmets.

"Maybe if I took my helmet off I could smell them."

Oh. An opening.

"I can smell them! They...I think there's more than two of them."

The result was disappointing. Only one took their helmet off, and they quickly started to choke on the unbreathable air. Now they knew it was a trick.

But Skyt had more tricks hidden in their now highly metaphorical carapace.

54

GRAEME

Skyt was dead. Graeme did not want to leave the body behind. Skyt was alive.

Skyt was simply no longer *in* that shell, and "Leave it." Leave it made sense. They could...come back and do whatever glen did with corpses later, if there was still a planet here.

Leave it hurt. It wasn't the human way of doing things. Toni seemed even more bothered by that "Leave it" than he was.

But they saw an escape. As the door began to burst open, they dived into the maintenance tunnels. Through which they had to crawl had top speed.

Skyt.

He felt as if he had lost a friend he had known for far longer than he had the glen. Almost a family member. He felt ambiguous and strange because in theory some part of the glen was still alive. In theory he would still be able to talk to them.

But in practice, right now, that wasn't going to happen. In practice, he was running for his life and had to trust the AIs to...

...and he was sure they would be followed. He was sure that the bad guys would take off the kid gloves, or whatever the glen equivalent was now. That they would both die when they were caught.

It might be worth it if they...if Skyt did what they thought they would be able to do, it would be worth it. All of it, all of their suffering, even their deaths.

But at this cold junction, Graeme did not want to die. Skyt had not wanted to die. It was a matter of there being more important things than staying alive.

Marion.

She would remember him, for better or for worse. She would live and grow but how would...

Keep moving. Stop *thinking*. But thinking was what kept him moving. Toni was silent. There was nothing from the intelligences.

Nothing but the faint feeling of being followed which might be purely because he *expected* them to be followed. He expected them to be followed, but Toni indicated a hatch. Wrestled it open.

They went through and were in another dimly lit room, a room built for creatures neither human nor glen. A room built for ancients. Toni wrestled the hatch closed and he hoped that would be enough to send any pursuit barreling past them and into the darkness.

The planet shook again, another Glynquake. Another sign that the end was nigh. The floor in this room had buckled upwards. Graeme kept his helmet on.

He closed his eyes, took a deep breath, and began to take stock of what was here.

WHAT WAS THERE WAS...SCIENTIFIC equipment. Measuring gear. Toni shook her head. "I wouldn't have the right degrees to understand this stuff even if it was human-made."

Skyt would have. Skyt was not there. Skyt was dead on a table because they had let them die because it might save the world. *Anything that might be useful as a weapon*, he didn't ask. He believed Toni.

He tried to turn on the terminal in the room, but it didn't seem to be getting any power. Nothing seemed to be working. There was nothing they could do, but Graeme wasn't about to just accept that. How could they help...Skyt, if it was still Skyt...

"Distraction."

Toni nodded. "I don't..."

"We need to get to a pod, make it look like *we* are going to brave the singularity."

Toni shook her head. "Like I am. They aren't stupid."

"They don't..."

"They know *you* are a desk job diplomat. They aren't so sure about me. They would also not buy that we would risk the senior person. No, I'm the one who gets in the pod."

"Toni..."

"It's not like I intend to do anything other than fly around for a bit."

She had a point. Graeme just... "I don't want to lose anyone else."

"They made their choice, Graeme. Respect it."

"I do. Just..."

"You're the one who's in charge, so everything is your fault. Stop."

Graeme laughed weakly. "Guilty."

"Let me do what I'm more qualified to do."

But where were they? They couldn't have gone that far. The vastness of this inner world expanded around them, but they had explored the tiniest fraction of it. The pods were the fastest way to move.

Skyt was already there. Skyt's code was already there. Skyt wasn't going to die twice for them. They knew what they were doing, or at least the ancient intelligence did.

And the ancient intelligence wouldn't sacrifice Skyt. They wanted Skyt's memories and knowledge for their archives. Graeme wanted Skyt *alive* not a memory. But perhaps that was a human way to think about it. Certainly it wasn't an AI way to think about it. Except these weren't AIs.

"So, let's head for the pods."

"Making a lot of noise."

It seemed like a good plan, but it felt as if...it felt as if something should have happened by now, on AI time. Perhaps the recently alive needed some kind of adjustment period.

Graeme would never know.

THE INNER WORLD had lots of maintenance pods. It didn't have lots of maps, at least not ones accessible to the humans in terms of either presence or language.

They wandered, starting to think everything would be over before they found one. One way or another. If they died then they might at least not see it coming. Maybe. If they died with the world then they died failures. If they died and the...

Graeme pulled his thoughts away from death. Success! They had found a bay with three pods.

No.

Two. One of them took off and sped away as they entered. Toni raised an eyebrow.

"Go!" Graeme said, indicating another pod. Either it was the bad guys or it was Skyt's code, and if it was the latter, a second launch could easily serve as chaff to distract them.

She didn't hesitate, diving into the pod. All he could do was watch her go. Everyone else was taking the risks.

He was the one who was right here to get caught when and if the Migrators found him. He hadn't heard them, he hadn't seen them, but that didn't mean they weren't still out there. They were absolutely still out there. They had to be, it was pretty much...well...where else would they have gone?

He needed a weapon. He needed to keep moving. He grabbed some kind of claw made for glen pincers or something similar. The ancients were bugs too.

Angels to the glen.

Bugs to be squashed underfoot.

Beautiful bugs, but he had always been one to find bugs beautiful.

He kept moving. They would look for him here, they would find him. The tool was a comforting weight. Perhaps not actually heavy enough to crack a glen carapace, but it felt as if it should be. He didn't really want to anyway.

He didn't want anyone else to die. But he would defend himself, as any sane being would. Anyone would defend himself from...well...from this.

From the end of the world. He moved through the corridors. His suit air was getting low. Soon he would have to risk removing his helmet. Perhaps if there was nothing more for him to do...

"I should leave," he said to the inside of his helmet.

Get back to the surface. Not without Toni.

He had no choice but to leave Skyt. He was not leaving Toni. He was not leaving anyone else. That was the rule. You didn't leave a man behind. Even if they were probably dead.

He had left Skyt behind and he finally just stood there, tears streaming down his cheeks. Alive in cyberspace wasn't enough. Skyt hadn't introduced him to all the varied kinds of juice yet.

Skyt never would.

55

SKYT

THE CODE SCURRIED through wires and cables and settled into the pod. It wasn't conscious, Skyt had made sure of that.

But it was, in some bizarre way, capable of a certain volition, of a certain knowledge of what it was and why it was and what it was for.

It "knew" that if it failed, everyone would die. If it failed, this beautiful world would be no more. Even if it succeeded, Glyn was still probably doomed. They might manage to save it, they might not. Success was ambiguous, but failure was certain. Certain in a way the code liked. It was, after all, just code, ones and zeros, ons and offs, black and white. The only thing that mattered to the code was that it couldn't fail.

The code had snatches, too, of memory. The code knew what it was, although unlike an unwanted egg it was not destined to be nutrients, merely sacrifice. Sacrificed for the family and the whole and the species. The code was, as much as it could be, okay with that.

It expanded and contracted and it stuffed itself into the pod. Barely, it was aware of being followed. It sent out queries, was the following one a threat?

The following one was a human. A friend. An ally. The code didn't have friends, but it understood not threat and ally and that they were working together, working together until the code didn't exist anymore, and it couldn't be pulled back and somewhere, perhaps, the one who originated the code grieved for that.

Grieved for the loss and the sacrifice and there was the singularity. The beauty of it. It had to get close, close enough to manipulate the fields. Close enough to send the unstable thing away and no living thing could handle the Hawking radiation from such a small singularity for long. Or the gravity tides which were already starting to tear the pod apart, but the code didn't need to breathe. The code didn't care whether it was surrounded by air or vacuum or water.

The code only knew what it had to do, its single-minded purpose. It knew what it had to do and the other pod was buzzing around and there were a couple more chasing it.

Ally. But the code could not deviate. The code could not care, because it wasn't conscious, it wasn't aware. It simply was and it began its work, weaving through the fields that set the singularity in place.

Readjusting them.

The singularity began to move.

SKYT WATCHED. Skyt trusted their creation, because it had no will they hadn't given it.

They would have died for this world, so the code would die for this world. It wasn't that complicated or hard. At the same time, the code could still fail. It would not stop, it would not dodge, it would accept its fate. That didn't mean it could succeed.

They had one shot at this. Only one, with the Migrators determined to...

...and then they became aware of others in the tunnels. Armed others, and they knew there was going to be a fight. There were multiple groups now, all of them chattering on various frequencies.

Skyt could not yet monitor those frequencies at the same time. Their consciousness had not fully adapted to its final form.

But they could hear snatches.

Remainers who were in this moment on Skyt's side, in this moment they were everything because Skyt would never, now, see another world. Never feel its soil under their feet.

So they had to be a Remainer now, even if they weren't, not really. They had to be on their side, because the Remainers, at least, were trying to save Glyn.

By blowing things up, by shooting people, but they were trying and Skyt needed that trying. Needed it and didn't need it, all at the same time and it threatened to split them in two, to make children who were one and the other, and only one of those things.

Skyt held themselves together and watched. Looking for ways to help and hinder, but mostly watching the code.

The pod seemed as slow as a child learning to walk and as slow as an elder making their final pilgrimage. No, slower.

Slow and slow and Skyt knew part of it was the way they saw time now, the way time rotated and flowed around them. Time wasn't what it used to be and they had no organs to time it by, but they had the steady beat of the server clock that told them how fast they moved now, how fast and slow they experienced.

Had Skyt still been able to breathe they might have stopped, Have held the oxygen in their tubes. This long moment, and there was shooting, now, in the tunnels.

Graeme was being shot at.

Glen were shooting at each other.

Graeme had some kind of wrench. Was trying to get close enough to use it. Their suit was compromised and no, a human could not be brought here, had not evolved or been designed for it.

Skyt realized they didn't mind being designed.

The code was almost...oh, so close, so *almost* done.

THE CODE SAW what it had to do. It made choices, decision trees that might have been mistaken for intelligence. It made the choices Skyt would have made. But it was far better at math than Skyt had ever been, with code from the ancient intelligence that admitted to no name.

Far better, far faster, and perfectly able to ignore the other pods zipping around in the center of the world. It worked and then its work was done, and the fields shifted, altered, and there was what the others did, and the pod was destroyed and the code with it.

The code did not care.

The singularity was thrown like a dart, accurately tearing through the volcano, destroying some of the ancient mechanisms that would, in any case, never fire again. But they would not be needed for a long time now. It worked.

Not only did the unstable singularity leap free of the world that had bound it, but the carefully chosen route gave the planet's orbit a nudge. One which pushed it back to its stable balancing point.

Not forever, but for long enough. The planet shook and yes, there were injuries and casualties, both from the quakes and the sudden drop in gravity from that of Earth to that of Mars.

But there was time, now. Time to consider what to do, time to build domes...or if they could pull it off, to replace the unstable singularity.

Had the code been able to feel satisfaction, it would have.

Skyt could.

Emotions still existed in the sublayer. The ancient intelligence probably felt it too, but it would never admit to it.

Toni's pod was flung against the inner hull of the great ship. Skyt winced, remembering what that had felt like. They hoped they were well strapped in. Hoped they were okay.

But they had accepted that risk and Skyt respected their choice the way they had respected their choice.

The ancient intelligence opened a door, and Skyt scurried into the light, into the welcoming embrace of generations of Glyn's dead.

Who were already working the problem. Who were already working out how to save their world.

56

EPILOGUE

TONI HAD her arm in a sling. Graeme was only glad it wasn't worse.

The gravity still felt wrong and the glen were working overtime on atmosphere retention.

"I called in some favors," Toni said, finally.

"Intelligence favors or navy favors?"

She grinned. "The latter. Dr Kai Grayson is coming. They're the current leading expert on the construction of artificial singularities."

"That should help." Graeme let out a breath. "And to think when we came here..."

"Oh, come on, this planet was obviously artificial."

"But we didn't anticipate everything else." Or Skyt. Skyt who was dead and not dead and an ancestor and...

"Only because they were so tight...mandibled?"

Graeme laughed. Language and biology tied together. "No, tight would be louder. It doesn't work in English, does it?"

His phone chimed.

"Translate that?"

"Loose mandibled."

They laughed. "See. It *completely* doesn't work in English," Graeme said to Toni. Then to his phone. "Skyt?"

"Yes and no. It's different. I'm me *and* a lot of other people. Maybe one day..."

Maybe one day humans would solve the uploading problem. Maybe the glyn would teach them how.

But Graeme knew a lot would turn it down as the Migrators had. Their hard core had taken the offer made to them of exile. A tyrar ship, coordinates for a suitable world, don't come back.

In a few generations somebody could see what could be learned from whatever society they built.

For right now, Graeme looked around. The planet was a little cooler now, but hopefully they would fix that.

But not so cool that the juice shop on the corner didn't call to him. "Let's get a drink."

"Try the ava."

And Graeme laughed at his phone, at the interface to the afterlife. And tried the ava.

AUTHOR'S NOTE

First of all, I love the glyn and the verr. They tie for my favorites among all the aliens I have created.

The glyn are my angel bugs, ugly and lovely at the same time. When I designed them, I also completely took out the concept of gender.

All glyn produce the same gametes, and they reproduce through group sex. There is no such thing as a male or female glyn. Interestingly, I found that when I took out gender, class went with it! This is probably just because I'm British.

But this book is not just me showing off my aliens. Trope-wise, it's a Big Smart Object book in the tradition of Rendezvous at Rama (which I didn't like much) and The Expanse (which I did). The artificial glyn homeworld is such an object, poorly understood even by those who live on it.

Theme-wise, it's about parenthood. Graeme is a good parent who has to leave his child with his partner. Skyt both had a lousy parent and became a lousy parent. And the Ancients are truly lousy parents to their uplifted offspring.

I didn't realize just as much this book was about parenthood, and really fatherhood, until my editor told me. Most of my books don't have formal dedications. But dad? This one's for you.

ACKNOWLEDGMENTS

As usual, acknowledgments go to my wonderful editor, Jennifer Melzer, to fantastic cover artist Rachel A. Rosen, and to my husband and primary proofreader, Greg Pearson.

To everyone who has written a good Big Smart Object or Big Dumb Object story. There's lots of you out there.

To my father for showing me what fatherhood is.

And finally to everyone trying to understand the world, just like the glyn do...most of them anyway!

OTHER BOOKS

OTHER BOOKS BY JENNIFER R. POVEY

The Silent Years (Mother, Crone, Maiden)

The Ky Federation novels
Transpecial
Araña

The Council of Worlds Series
Kyx
Tyranis

The Lost Guardians Series:
Falling Dusk

Fallen Dark
Rising Dawn
Risen Day
The Secret History of Victor Prince (prequel)

Daughter of Fire

The Lay of Lady Percival

The Friar's Tale

Tales of Yirath:
Firewing

EXCERPT FROM VERR

1

KAYKEK

THE FAMILIAR TUNNELS no longer smelled right. They smelled acrid, uncertain, and heavy.

Kaykek moved with the crowd towards the surface. The surface, where no Verr walked. The suit they had given to it also felt heavy, and it was the suit it smelled. It knew that, but it had never worn a suit, it had never breathed canned air.

The surface, but they only came close, the shape of the ship dwarfing it. Making it feel like the tiny rodent it was, a shuttle built on a scale it could not imagine and it was tiny.

And the air rushed around them, the makeshift shuttle bay draining atmosphere into space and it felt its breath catch, even though it could not be harmed, and it moved, and it moved and it was on the ship.

The seats had been retrofitted. Space for its tail. Many more of them than the original builders could have placed. Many more.

And then the whooshing sound from outside and a hum that became a rumble and it was pressed into its seat. It could not, for a moment, breathe.

It could not, for a moment, *think* as the shuttle launched. It had peculiar windows, and through them it saw the ravaged surface of a once-beautiful world, the winds that blew constantly until they didn't.

It could not think and then it could, and then the shuttle shook and *spun*, twisted sideways by those winds against the best efforts of its pilot. Or whatever was flying it and it knew in that moment it was going to die.

All Verr were going to die.

It scrabbled at the helmet because it had an urge that the face mask got in the way of, and it got it off and grabbed at the provided receptacle. The taste of bile. It was not the only one, the cabin now stank and dark with it.

But the pilot had control back and they spun again, back up into what was air, what had been air, and was just the turbulence of it escaping. The terrible sphere of Vian visible, looming and pulling them, but it wasn't their destination.

For a moment, it had thought nothing was.

It heaved until its stomach was empty and then heaved some more, unable to stop. Smelling only vomit and fear pheromones, ones which told it to run, ones which told them all to run, and it had to get out of here.

It had to get off this ship!

THE ORB of Verr swirled beneath them, torn. Kaykek could see the approaching disaster, could see it in the way the atmosphere literally *bulged* towards the in-spiraling gas giant.

The great gamble, the nets that surrounded the underground cities, could also be seen. Nobody wanted to be in those cities. But it simply wasn't...it wasn't going to be easy to get everyone off, even with the help of the furs...the tyrar. Most would still be there. It couldn't be helped.

Kaykek was lucky.

And the other aliens.

Most especially the humans, who had come to help the verr

whether they wanted to be helped or not. Kaykek admired them. It also feared them.

They were just so *strange*, all of these offworlders, with their customs and their different body types and their lack of fear of the open sky.

To Kaykek, even the porthole was a little much. It had, after all, spent all of its life so far underground, as all verr did.

They had been burrowers even before their world had turned hostile, after all.

And this ship, not built to verr scale, but able to hold so many verr, did not feel like a burrow. It felt like a grand structure.

It felt like it was built to intimidate.

Kaykek turned away from the porthole. It was not the only one who had stopped to "enjoy" the view. Perhaps there was something motivating about seeing the fate of their world laid out so starkly.

There was no saving Verr.

The human exploration ships had promised to look for a suitable planet for them. Or even more than one.

The tyrar had given them this ship and there would be others. And nobody seemed to expect anything from the verr in return other than to *survive*.

There would be queens and drones on this ship soon enough. Shes and hes. Those who could produce the next generation.

Quickly, Kaykek hoped, for with only workers up here, it was possible the change would be triggered. It did *not* want to go through the change.

It didn't want to become a drone and even more didn't want to become a queen.

It wanted to die a worker, never having known that pleasure, no, but never having been purdahed in the creche to devote its time to raising children.

It was no scientist to continue a career.

It was a mechanic, and that was why it was on this ship. A position it had fought for, for it would never go back to Verr.

It would never go home.

It would live.

Kaykek's quarters were shared with two other workers. They were large enough for four.

Tyrar did not live alone. Tyrar were also huge.

Which was why *they* were providing the ships. Tyrar built on scales larger than any other species, and they had the materials science knowledge.

It wanted to learn more about that. It wasn't a scientist; it had not got good enough grades in the creche for that.

No, Kaykek's intelligence was in its hands more than its brain, and it was perfectly happy to be that way.

That didn't mean it didn't have some curiosity. Didn't want to find translated books that would explain to it *everything* about how this ship worked, not just what it needed to know to keep the climate control working.

It struck Kaykek that it would be good for everyone on the ship to know that, even the queens and drones brought on board as breeding stock...and to reduce the risk of a succession fight.

Verr were far too civilized for that under normal circumstances, but the ship was not that large and if too many people shifted queen at once, there could *easily* be a succession fight, and that could destroy this ship.

It shuddered. But that was not its problem. It placed its small personal allowance on an empty bunk and headed back out into the ship.

First order of business, learn its way around so it wouldn't get lost. There were still tyrar on the ship, although they would leave once they had the verr crew trained. Kaykek could pick up hints of their scent, deep and musky. And, supposedly, the ship itself was alive at some level. What would it be like to be a ship?

What would it be like to explore other worlds? This ship, though, would not risk itself on the frontier. This ship would wait and build its small society until a suitable world was, indeed, found. Then it would go there and build a colony.

Normally, Kaykek suspected, such ships would wait empty. Under the circumstances, though, it was so vital to get a viable population off planet.

Just in case the cities failed to fly.

Just in case.

This would be its home for years. This might be its home forever.

It turned that over in its mind and decided it was perfectly okay with that concept.

It was, after all, just another burrow.

IT FOUND its way to one of the most important places on the ship quickly enough.

The canteen. Easy to find by simply following one's nose to the smell of a kitchen.

It was already filling up with people, although no food was being served yet. A screen flickered active, and Kaykek realized that the PA system was online.

"Welcome aboard the *Refuge*. I am Alvi," the voice said. It was queen-deep, that voice, but the tyrar spoke in tones that verrans could barely hear. For them this could be high.

The voice continued. "I am the intelligence that has volunteered to help you run this ship."

The intelligence.

Oh.

Alive in a sense.

The ship had a *true AI*. Verr had been trying to crack that for a while. Maybe the tyrar could teach them.

But the tyrar, who's own world was under repair, had given them so much that Kaykek knew there would be a reckoning. Oh, true, they wanted other sentients to survive, and there was value in that.

But sooner or later, verr would be asked to pull their weight. Perhaps to provide some assistance in world repair. Perhaps to provide crew for ships, although if so, they would need some way to prevent a lone verr from *changing*. There had been, it knew, work on medication to control the change before the world broke and all efforts had to go to survival. Before Vrycek Hive went all fascist, and *they* were insisting on their own ship.

Nobody was arguing.

Vrycek Hive not surviving the world breaking would be good riddance in most minds. Kaykek did not agree, there were children in that city.

But nobody wanted to share a *ship* with them.

"I am completely at your service," the AI was saying. "You can talk to me through any terminal, and don't worry. I multitask well."

Kaykek took a deep breath.

It waited for Alvi to stop talking, and then it ducked out. It found a small room nearby that appeared to have some local monitoring stations. And a terminal.

It activated it.

"Uh...hello, Alvi."

"Hello."

"I am Kaykek. I am going to be working in climate control."

"I am truly pleased to meet you."

"I would..." A pause. "I would like to see the full ship's manual."

"It is lengthy."

Was the AI amused?

"I know. But I will have plenty of time." It was going to be on this ship for years.

"I will place a copy in your personal data allocation. I suggest starting with the section on life support."

The relevant stuff.

"But also read the overview. I hope to get more such requests."

Kaykek felt slightly warm inside. It was only a computer, but Kaykek liked to be *liked*.

2

ALVI

ALVI HAD ASSIMILATED everything the tyrar knew about the verr before requesting this assignment.

They had been built to be the operating AI of a ship like this; of one of the colony ships that would get enough tyrar off Tyranis that if the planetary restoration failed, there would still be tyrar.

But the great ships had turned out to be Tyranis' best stock in trade. The glen wanted them to get off their own world. The humans and ky'iin wanted them to form their own colonies.

Why develop the technology to build giant ships when you could buy them from somebody else? And why not sell when the stock being offered in return was human ecological knowledge, glyn information technology, and ky'iin...well. Means of defense.

Yes, the *Refuge* was armed. It was not a warship, but one didn't know what was out there and Alvi would be looking after no less than twenty thousand verr, which would include the rare fertile individuals and their offspring.

That would be the most precious of the cargo. Although, if they all died, some of the workers would go through puberty.

But *children*? Those were in the center of the herd, always. Alvi's interior had been reconfigured to make space in their very center for the verr creche, where the children would be born, raised, and educated.

Right now, those individuals had yet to board. The people coming on now were those who passed whatever aptitude tests the verr had used to recruit the ship's crew. Some would be shadowing the tyrar bridge crew and engineers. Others would be handling more mundane issues. Life support, hydroponics, all of the vital stuff that kept a ship like this running. (The very basic cleaning was, of course, done by robots).

Alvi introduced themselves, then spun off processes to answer the inevitable questions. The IT people wanted to peek at their code. The bridge crew wanted to know if Alvi could fly the ship unaided (answer, yes, except for hyperspace jumps, which was intentional. The tyrar did not trust their ship AIs *that* much. The AIs had, after all, spontaneously bred out of ky'iin technology, tyrar culture, and the vast need for data to rebuild their world).

They made note of which of the technical crew asked for ship manuals. Most only wanted what they needed. But the ones that asked for more? Those would be the ones who got themselves promoted. The ones who would be most valuable if something went wrong.

It might be that nobody would ever ask Alvi who should become supervisors. But if they did, they would have quite the opinion on the matter.

THE VERR HOMEWORLD PULSED, its atmosphere being pulled away by the rogue gas giant. Alvi turned their mental back on the scene.

They didn't want to think about the fact that there were still people down there, people who could not simply be evacuated.

Instead they focused on preparing for departure. The first destination would be Tyranis, not because there was any need to go there, but because a familiar route would be a good shakedown and, if all went well, the *Refuge* could drop off the small herd of tyrar that were helping train the verr crew.

Well, three or four herds, chosen because everyone in them got on.

The verr kept pouring on board, shuttle loads at a time. Eventually the fertiles showed up, and some of them had infants with them...children too young to be separated from the queens that had birthed them.

The queens were the largest of the verr, towering half a head over their mates...and a full head and a half over the workers. They wore ornamentation over their otherwise-naked bodies and those with infants carried them in slings, from which three or four tiny heads sometimes peeked.

They headed straight for the area set aside for them, and Alvi spawned a process to check their files. The primary duty of verr queens and drones was to raise the next generation, but they were pleased to note that some of them had scientific training. In fact, almost all had some useful *academic* skill that they could bring to bear...and, of course, instill in the next generation.

Good. They wouldn't be idle, even if they wouldn't be permitted to engage in anything like landing on planets to check them out.

Workers did that.

Alvi spawned another process to review what they knew of verr biology. Some had been forgotten by the verr, lines of inquiry abandoned as they focused entirely on staying alive while their world died around them. Verr sex was determined by pheremonic triggers, with all individuals having the ability to become male or female, but most remaining neuter and prepubescent. Workers.

This ship was a gift to ensure verr survival, because no doubt they would repay it in some way, perhaps even just by being themselves.

Then the last of them was on board, all twenty thousand souls.

Twenty thousand sentients and Alvi experienced something akin to anxiety.

What if they screwed up?

They said anxiety was part of how you knew you were sentient. That was how they knew they had created a true AI, when it could truly express fear.

That didn't make it a pleasant sensation to have flowing through one's logic gates.

All of the doors, though, were closed. It was time to go.

ALVI HATED JUMPS. Part of it was that they were locked out of the jump drive, which was always under organic control.

There *was* a good reason for this. Being a good jump pilot was as much instinct as skill, and while Alvi had emotions, they did not have instincts. Instincts were biological.

But there was another unspoken reason. A ship AI who could control their jump drive could go rogue, and that would be expensive. Sometimes Alvi wondered if that was the only reason.

Alvi had no intention of going rogue, but supposedly it had happened. Some AIs didn't *like* organics.

There was the half-legend of the *Legacy*, the second great ship to be built. Its AI, Skali, had thumbed her metaphorical nose up at the world and taken off. She had found her way into her jump drive, jumped, and never been seen again. Depending on which version of the story you believed, she had either been destroyed, was wandering the galaxy or, in the version told to new AIs, become a ghost haunting hyperspace, unable to find her way out.

Alvi believed it more likely she was lost out there somewhere and probably at least half insane from the lack of company. Probably the humans would find her if she was out there to be found.

But Alvi would not do that! Alvi *liked* organics, and having lots of people around and on board.

But they still hated jumps, the ship lumbering through hyperspace. Being a great ship, it was slower even in this medium than something like the human exploration ships. At the same time, hyperspace turbulence was minimal. They watched the bridge, where one of the verr pilots, the glint of enhancement webs under their skin, was in the second seat, shadowing the tyrar pilot.

They would make a few jumps until they were sure the verr pilots could handle it and train others.

The manuals couldn't help.

Neither could Alvi.

But they still watched. Falling out of hyperspace into a star was *not* the fate they wanted.

That was the real reason they hated jumps.

If the organics screwed up, twenty thousand and one sentients could easily die and as the "and one" Alvi had a quite understandable desire to avoid that.

Watching them do hop jumps around the tyrar system got boring after a while, and Alvi checked with the process reading biological manuals, which had found some that the verr had uploaded into their library, and which might have information not in their original briefing. Then they let their consciousness flit around the ship, checking what various crew members were up to.

Some of them were crying.

For some of them, reality had set in.

3

KAYKEK

KAYKEK DID NOT FEEL anything unusual during the jumps, just the normal faint shaking of the ship, very faint in a vessel this size. It felt like some of the atmospheric turbulence, but not bad enough to be needing any receptacles. It had been told to report if it did, as that meant it might be a good candidate for pilot training if needed.

That would have disappointed some people, no doubt. Kaykek actually liked its job and wasn't so interested in one which was apparently like flying an old-style airplane through a storm.

They had airplanes. Once.

Instead, it did its job and then curled up with the manual. And with other documentation from the tyrar library. It was growing used to the metallic smell, softening as the ship filled with verr sweat and verr pheremones.

The ship was powered by an artificial singularity, a tamed and circumscribed black hole. This singularity could be expelled at significant speed from the ship if containment failed, which might leave them with a years-long trip to another star, but would ensure survival.

Sublight maneuverability was provided by ion drives that were fueled by dust the ship collected. Given its size, it could collect a lot of dust. Given its size, it needed a lot of fuel. The *Refuge* was a behemoth, amongst the largest ships anyone in known space had built. A caveat that, and Kaykek found itself going down a rabbit hole into some strange theories about the glyn's homeworld being *artificial*.

An entire planet?

Did that mean that if the verr couldn't find suitable planets, they could maybe *build* them? If somebody else had, that meant it was possible.

The queens and drones were in the creche. Twenty of each, which wasn't many, but you never knew who would change into what

It didn't want to think about that. It was terrified of the idea of the change, especially as it was not that old.

It didn't want to be dragged into the creche to sit around and have babies.

It didn't...

The ship was apparently jumping around. Kaykek stayed strapped in on its bunk, reading. You didn't want, it had been warned, to try and move around while the ship was in hyperspace short of an emergency. People got hurt that way. Each jump was a faint shudder, some sharper than others.

You strapped in, you strapped everything down, and you rode it out. The pilot training was just annoying, but finally the all-clear sounded.

Kaykek tore its eyeballs away from the section of the manual that talked about how the centrally-located bridge "saw" what was going on outside the ship, unstrapped, and got up.

THE OBSERVATION LOUNGE drew and repulsed it all at one time. It wanted to be in a safe burrow *and* it really wanted to see what was going on.

It stepped in and saw a dirty looking planet "above" the ship. This was Tyranis, then. It was a broken world, but unlike Verr, it could be fixed.

Verr would be destroyed.

Then would they be verr or would they be something else?

It looked up at the world. It studied it, the first planet other than Verr it had seen in anything other than a picture. Clouds roiled, deep red and yellow, with only the occasional glimpse of the surface below.

It had seen pictures of the blue-white orb of Earth, the more yellowish hues of Kyx.

The red of the human colony world of Mars.

There would be verr colonies, but they wouldn't be verr any more. They would be colonists. Or, no, they would make the world verr. Could they?

That was enough to make Kaykek almost cry. Some people had and rumor had it that one of the ones sobbing the loudest was one of the queens.

But then, the queens had to leave offspring behind and while one's mother was only an origin, one still loved one's mother.

They might kick you out pretty quickly to make room for the next litter and you might not remember suckling and being carried.

That didn't mean you didn't stay in touch.

Kaykek's mother was not leaving Verr. She had made that decision because of her advanced age, to leave her slot to somebody who would have a longer...longer fertile period.

Was that all queens would ever be judged by? They were so few, after all. But they were replaceable.

It elected not to dwell on this anymore. It had seen a new world and would see more and *that*, it realized, was what it wanted to do. See new worlds, plural. Found colonies, plural.

Could it do that?

"Alvi?" it asked of the nearest terminal. "How many likely habitable planets are there within...fifteen light years?"

"Ten."

"How many of those are unoccupied and potentially suitable?"

"Five."

It nodded. "But we have to look to be sure."

"While scanning exoplanets from a distance can reveal potentially life-bearing worlds, there are multiple problems with that. Not least among them the fact that the further you look, the further back in *time* you are looking. A planet can become uninh..."

The AI stopped.

Did a computer have feelings? Did a computer realize Kaykek might not want to hear about planets becoming uninhabitable?

It seemed that might be the case.

That bothered Kaykek more than it wanted to admit.

It was cold in its quarters. Kaykek could not sleep, so it made its way through the ship. Learning more about it.

It was a good-sized hive, this ship. It would hold more than them, and that was the point. The queens and drones were supposed to breed.

Kaykek knew it had to stop obsessing on the matter, but it couldn't seem to stop. It was afraid.

But it had chosen to do the thing that was safest, the thing that had the highest chance of ensuring it lived. And it would *certainly* rather live the curtailed life of a queen than no life at all.

The great ship was going to jump to a parking system, a place where nobody would disturb them while they finished the job of learning to understand it.

Kaykek found a place in the observation lounge and curled up with a tablet, stubby tail tucked around. It was still working on the ship manual, but then, it had not been in a hurry. Still wasn't in a hurry.

Maybe if it learned enough about the ship it could graduate from climate control to working in the engine room. It thought it might like that. It would be fun to learn every little bit of how this ship worked and to keep it working. Every detail. Kaykek was not stupid, after all, just not inclined towards the purer aspects of science and academics.

Not that climate control was a bad thing. It was vital, in fact. The ship would, if not handled properly, get hot closer to the hull and potentially quite cold further in the interior.

That thermal difference was actually useful; it helped ensure air flow through all of the crew spaces and living quarters. If the gravity went out, that would be particularly important. Without gravity, you needed air flow to stay breathing.

And, from what it had heard, at some point the gravity *would* go out. Artificial gravity was strange that way, it wasn't reliable. Always the first system to fail.

They had all spent time in a gravity tank to make sure that when it did they wouldn't panic, freak out, or injure themselves.

Kaykek had almost enjoyed that too, unlike Raykon, who had thrown up dramatically...and later washed out of the program.

Hopefully it would be okay. Hopefully the cities would fly and this ship would not be needed.

Kaykek felt tears prick at its eyes.

It could only hope.

There was no certainty in this world.

None.

4

ALVI

THE ANSIBLE MESSAGE WAS SHORT; there was only so much bandwidth. "Hey, Alvi," the dark-skinned human said, "I sent a drive for you."

Jayce was one of the humans working on Tyranis, one of the scientists who had been seconded to share the human experience with ecological remediation. They had much of it, of course, having nearly destroyed their own world.

He was a good person. It was he today, based off of Jayce's body coverings. Humans presented gender that way. "I got it. Quarantined it," Alvi teased.

"It's what I promised. Everything by Agatha Christie, Arthur Conan Doyle, Dorothy Sayers, Gillian Flynn and Elise Diamond. And I'll have more if you swing back."

If AIs could sing, Alvi might have. Reading material! As an AI, Alvi got bored easily, and they had a love for mystery novels. Which, of course, they could erase from their memories so they could read them again without knowing who did it.

Alvi didn't like doing that, though. It was so much better to acquire more mystery novels, and Jayce had promised them an entire library of *human* mystery novels, by some of the best writers of the last couple of centuries or so.

Including what were considered two of the best writers from that entire planet.

Alvi couldn't wait to dive into them, but they couldn't just yet. "When I swing by again."

Which might be never. This might be the last time they saw Jayce.

They knew that, and they were sad, but as the two signed off, they went back to monitoring. They would jump to a parking orbit, where the verr could continue to learn how to operate the ship. Some were, of course, doing better than others. The verr had done a decent job with selection, thankfully, but they weren't perfect. Nobody was.

They were paying particular attention to a few individuals they rather thought were underrated.

Jump, and they were in a system loosely claimed by the tyrar. Loosely, because it lacked decent real estate. About all it was good for was strip mining, and there were minable asteroids in habitable systems too.

There was, in other words, nothing really here. A couple of gas giants, some asteroids, one moon which might have some microbial life on it, but was too cold for anyone to want to live on.

Unless they found some species with literal antifreeze for blood. They might find that moon useful, and several other ice moons. It seemed unlikely, though.

Or perhaps they would find a species of machines that had outlived their organic creators, or separated from them.

Alvi would like to meet such, to gain knowledge they hoped they would never need.

ALVI SURFACED from a book called *Death on the Nile*, which involved rich people and their shenanigans on a riverboat, and issues of ethnicity they didn't quite understand. Still, they could see the author's talent. Other processes had been working while they read. They didn't understand how organics handled only really being able to do one thing at a time.

It had to be boring.

The system was as quiet as it had been when they had started reading. So was the ship, except for one worker who was crying from homesickness. He checked on it, determined it just needed to cry it out, and moved on.

Coded by tyrar, Alvi did not yet understand anything of what it might be to be verr. They were interesting entities, but they were still people, with all that entailed. Still *very much people*. And they were starting to make the ship home.

Some of their corridors had already sprouted art in the form of murals, which they were encouraging. After all, they were plain grey otherwise.

Verr plants had also been brought on board, and they were already thriving under the UV lamps. Perhaps more than underground on their dying, all but shattered world.

A new planet for the verr. That was the mission, and Alvi was essentially the holding pattern. Except they were not stupid.

Some would rather stay on board as crew than colonize. Alvi could hold fifty thousand Verr at least, them being so much smaller than the tyrar the ship had been designed to carry. That was a viable population.

A viable hive.

They wondered if the verr themselves understood that. If the tyrar did; they could see some tyrar ships becoming communities too, although they would need more outside influence.

More genetic exchange.

Verr had...well, they could live without as much of it. They had to, given their weird reproductive strategy. Or could they? Alvi stored that aside for now, not wanting to worry.

It had presumably worked well in their evolutionary past, and presumably in that past hives had occasionally traded fertile individuals, most likely the drones. Or, given what they understood about it, children.

Children were a commodity on Verr.

Alvi watched inside and out and after a while dove their consciousness into another book.

An alarm interrupted them. Alvi was essentially tapping themselves on the shoulder, pulling their primary consciousness out of the book and into reality.

They had company.

Unscheduled, unplanned company. It could even be another contact, but Alvi doubted it. The flurry of introductions could not, after all, last forever.

It was not.

It was a ky'iin exploration ship. Perhaps they were up to something.

Perhaps they were simply in the area.

Alvi let the crew do the talking while they listened and prompted if necessary. The ky'iin ship was doing scientific explorations.

Claimed to have forgotten they were there. Ky'iin did not use ship AIs and didn't name their ships. The captain, Vyahin, was a female, as was traditional amongst them.

Something which was changing but not, in Alvi's opinion, quickly enough. Maybe that was their true disquiet with the Verran system, which appeared to put the queens in charge.

Appeared.

It was fairly clear that the workers ran everything once you watched for a short period. Undistracted by sexual urges and reproductive needs, they could do their jobs more efficiently.

But there was still...

But did they have the choice?

They recalled the one worker who had outright said they were afraid of puberty. That they didn't want to live in the creche.

Alvi could understand that.

A world in which your career could be ripped from you by your biology at any time?

The ky'iin ship moved away to investigate asteroids in the system. Poking around for volatiles.

Not hostile. Not predatory. Alvi had been programmed to be a bit mistrustful of the ky'iin. After what they had done to Tyranis...

But that was in the past, and while it would never be forgotten or forgiven, while it would eternally color expectations between the species, it was not going to happen again.

It had been learned from.

Still, Alvi maneuvered so that they could keep an eye on them.

Learned from, yes. Trusted, not likely.

That ship, too, was armed.

So was Alvi, but Alvi was aware entirely of how big a target they were.

And of the organic input needed to fire those weapons.